Retirement Man

Retirement Man

A Novel

David L. Brown

ISBN: 978-0-9966085-3-4

This is a work of fiction. All characters and events other than historical persons and events mentioned in passing are purely the creations of the author's imagination and bear no resemblance to any persons, living or dead. Any apparent similarities are purely coincidental.

Book design by David L. Brown. Cover image: iStockphoto.

This book was printed in the United States of America.

Moab BookWorks
375 S. Main Street, #322
Moab, UT 84532

www.moabbookworks.com

Chapter One

Luis Flores

The body is displayed on the desert sand like an offering to the gods. It lies on its back, head to the east, feet pointed west. It is the corpse of a man in executive suit, coat buttoned, hands crossed on chest, sightless eyes staring into the blue New Mexico sky.

Except for the neat little bullet hole low in the center of the forehead, Bernalillo County sheriff's detective Luis Flores can imagine the victim is taking a quick nap between meetings, that the man is about to stretch, yawn and tuck back a light blue French-cuffed sleeve to glance at the gold Rolex that glitters there.

But this is no longer a man, not a thing that walks and talks and breathes. This is mere meat, gristle and bone, the empty remnants of something that was once alive, the primary evidence in a most puzzling crime of murder.

Flores stands about 20 feet away watching the crime scene team at work. A forensic photographer is circling the body, taking advantage of the West-sinking sun to capture everything with stills and videos. His flashgun winks again and again to bring out details of each image.

Near the victim's head a female criminalist kneels on the ground, searching for clues. From time to time she uses a pair of tweezers to pick up something that might be evidence and placing each item carefully into numbered paper envelopes. As she works she dictates notes into a mike clipped to the collar of her uniform shirt.

Further away two more techs carefully walk within a 50-foot circle, studying each pebble or twig. About a hundred yards to the North a paramedic vehicle is parked on a slight rise. Its crew waits patiently for their turn on-stage in this impromptu drama, body bag and gurney ready. Two BCSD cruisers, Flores's unmarked, and the CSI van also are parked nearby and a pair of uniformed deputies are posted further up the sandy path to keep away any curious members of the public. The medical examiner is expected soon.

Flores turns to gaze toward the distant skyline of Albuquerque's Old Town, pasted in sharp contrast against the rugged backdrop of the Sandia Crest. The setting sun is beginning to transmute molten gold from the windows of the high-rise buildings. Far to the northeast a few colorful hot air balloons are settling toward the ground as the day draws to an end.

Flores fumbles for a Marlboro and turns to leave the crime scene, following a path marked with little yellow flags. Like the others his shoes are covered in plastic bags to avoid contaminating footprint evidence.

But there is no such evidence, at least not that they've found so far. The scene has been carefully sanitized, with only the faintest signs that the sand and dust around the corpse has been swept clean. The nearby dusty track bears the marks of at least a dozen vehicles but there is nothing to indicate which if any belonged to the killer.

Wandering toward a shallow arroyo about 50 yards away from the body Flores places a cigarette between his lips and flicks his battered Zippo. The lighter's chrome plating and Marine Corps emblem are nearly worn away by more than two decades of use. He sucks the acrid smoke into his lungs, holds it for a moment, then lets it stream out in a long, sighing wisp.

He's tall for a Hispanic man and looks to be in his late 30s but is in fact nearing 45. He wears an off-the-rack business suit in olive-gray Glen Plaid, white shirt, black socks. Beneath the plastic bags are well-worn but polished brogues. His collar is unbuttoned and secured with a silver-and-turquoise bola in simple Navajo design. Since advancing from uniformed duty fifteen years ago Flores has worn his hair stylishly long. Now dark curls peek from beneath the brim of a dove-gray Stetson.

Although as a plainclothes detective he tries to look like Mr. Ordinary, his black moustache is trimmed in a way that practically shouts "cop" to anyone who notices. And that isn't the only tell: His eyes are hidden behind stylish dark glasses that he hopes make him look like a Federal agent, and which his daughter describes as "way cool".

His weathered face has the olive cast of the Mediterranean, the heritage of a Spanish great-grandfather nine times removed who came to this new land a decade before the Pilgrims discovered Plymouth Rock. As evidence of that Castilian lineage his lips are thin, nose aquiline. He has the expressive hands of a guitarist, long-fingered and strong with just enough calluses to reveal a man of actions.

The senior detective is about six-one and weighs no more than 180, not beanpole lean but with muscle on his bones. He works out twice a week at the department's exercise room, generally goes to the range at least monthly to run a box of 9mm cartridges through his Glock, and often spends free days hiking in the nearby Jemez Mountains or on the trails that lead to the high peak of the Sandia Crest overlooking the city.

One of the forensic techs breaks away from the peri–

meter search and saunters over to join him. Wordlessly Flores holds out the red-and-white pack, shaking it to partially eject a filter tip. The tech takes the offering, grimacing as if in remorse at a habit he cannot break. Flores flicks the lighter and for a long moment they stand wreathed in sunlight and smoke. Standing with their backs to the puzzling crime scene they watch the shadow of the night rise out of the east to swallow the day. Neither man speaks.

After a moment the tech pinches the ember from the half-smoked butt, scatters the un-smoked shreds and rolls the paper and filter into a little ball that he places in his pocket. Introducing spurious elements into a crime scene is a serious no-no, but here in the arroyo a few flakes of tobacco will make no difference. Nodding to Flores, the man returns to the search for traces of the killer, now using a long black flashlight to probe the shadows as the sun nears the horizon.

The detective continues to puff for a moment then disposes of his own smoke and walks carefully back toward the heart of the crime scene. The photographer has finished his work there and moved to the nearby roadway to document tire tracks. Having completed her survey of the immediate area, the criminalist is beginning a careful examination of the body itself. She places plastic bags over the victim's hands to preserve for the postmortem examiner any evidence that might be caught beneath the nails. Using tools from her field kit she begins to take samples of body fluids, skin and hair and places them in labeled glass vials.

Flores steps closer to examine the corpse. It's carefully arranged, "displayed" as the experts at the FBI call it, a sure sign that a psychopath has been at work here and is sending a message. The legs are straight, shoes aligned side-by-side and clean, almost as if the killer has run over them with a polishing cloth. The back is straight, shoul–ders squared, nothing out of place. The tie is knotted in a proper Windsor, not too tight, just right.

By God, the fucker even combed his victim's hair, Flores realizes as the technician tweezes a loose strand for her collection of evidence. Except for the third eye in the forehead, centered precisely on a line with the nose, it's a job worthy of a master embalmer, ready for viewing by the bereaved. *Shit,* Flores thinks, *the victim should be clutching a bouquet of lilies!*

The criminalist looks up as Flores steps nearer, giving him a wan smile.

"This is different," she murmurs almost to herself, turning her attention back to her work. She thrusts the snout of an electronic thermometer into the ear of the corpse and notes the reading.

Flores stares for a moment, trying to take in the full implications of her statement.

"No," he says at last. "Different doesn't start to tell it. It's unique, an all-time first." She doesn't comment.

Flores watches as the sun makes its final descent, casting long shadows among the walking stick *cholla,* rabbit brush and creosote bushes. As the light fades the woman stands and shouts to the photographer, calling for him to bring a light bar to illuminate the scene. While waiting she steps away from the body and stretches to work the stiffness from her legs and hips.

"Yeah, lieutenant, you're right," she says at last. "Whoever did this wanted to tell us something — but what?"

Flores shrugs. He wants another cigarette but knows he can't light up so near the corpse. He turns to watch the photographer struggling to bring the lights and their heavy battery from the crime scene van.

"The vic looks like a department store mannequin,"

the woman remarks, shuffling one foot in the desert sand. "It's like part of a window display."

"Yeah," Flores responds without turning around. "A display. That's exactly what it is." His left hand begins to reach for the cigarette pack. Catching himself he scratches his chin instead. He slips off his sunglasses, hooks them over his breast pocket and gazes to the west where high clouds are turning to waves of orange and red.

"The killer went to a lot of trouble to show off his work," he observes at last, turning back to the technician. "It's his way of giving a big 'fuck you' to the world."

They stand silently as the photographer sets down the battery pack and begins unfolding a stand. In a moment he flips a switch and hot tungsten light floods over the scene. Saying no more the investigator returns to her careful examination. Flores watches and wonders.

Presently she stands again, pulling a pair of rubber gloves from her kit. She hands them to Flores.

"Help me turn him over," she says. Nodding he pulls on the gloves and bends beside her to lift the body, raising it onto one side. What had once been a man is still warm but rigor mortis has set in, indicating that death occurred at least three hours before and probably more. The body's shaded parts feel cooler to Flores' hand, confirming that at least some of the warmth resulted from the baking rays of the Sun rather than any sign of recent life.

There's no exit wound to match the third eye in the man's forehead, confirming Flores' guess that the weapon used was a .22. The tiny, low-velocity bullet would have ricocheted around inside the skull, mincing the brain. He knows the .22 is a popular choice among professional assassins, effective at close range and making much less noise than a bigger gun.

For a moment Flores ponders the possibility that

this is a contract killing, but discards it almost at once. No professional killer would create an elaborate display of the body. That's the mark of the psychopath.

"What's your guess?" he asks, and the tech knows what he means.

"Based on the body temperature I estimate he was killed sometime in late morning," she tells him. "I'm almost positive it took place somewhere else," she adds, pointing at the sand. "Everything's too neat. No blood. The face seems to have actually been washed."

Flores nods and continues to watch her work. After a few minutes he reaches down and gently pats the victim's back pocket where the bulge of a wallet can be seen. He gestures to the criminalist. Nodding she takes a pair of tongs from her kit and uses them to carefully withdraw the billfold, holding it by one edge. She pops open a paper evidence bag and prepares to insert the wallet. Flores watches dolefully.

"Gotta get it to the lab for trace," she tells him. He nods but she catches the hunger in his eyes. "Although," she continues as if in afterthought, "if I'm careful I could fan it open first to see if we can get an ID." Flores nods emphatically.

Carefully holding the wallet by one edge with the tongs she uses a probe to spread it open on top of the evidence bag. It's a handsome piece of leatherwork, apparently genuine crocodile. The right side bears the usual array of credit cards in slots. On the left side is a window pocket displaying a driver's license with a picture of the victim sans third eye.

"Ah," Flores breathes. He leans close, reaching for his notebook and pen.

Chapter Two

Rob Charlton. Six months later

I set the alarm for my tiny two-room office and step outside into a wall of late afternoon heat. The parking lot in front of the strip mall is nearly deserted, thanks to a seemingly endless recession that hits small businesses like hawks to baby rabbits. I glance next door to what was once Chan's Qwik-Chow, now boarded up and boasting a fading FOR RENT sign. Just down the way is another empty space where a beauty parlor once lived. Beyond that are a deceased clothing store and two other defunct shops, each one the husk of a failed dream.

My eyes travel across this depressing scene, ending on Marv's Liquor at the far end of the strip. It's the only place left that shows any hope of survival, and judging from Marv's gloomy demeanor these days, even he must not be doing so hot.

I wonder at my own chances of making a go of it. Five months ago, fed up with retirement after a year of bumming around the beaches in Central America, I returned to the Southwest where my 30 years with the FBI had ended thanks to mandatory retirement and my failure to advance beyond the rank of Special Agent in Charge. I chose Albuquerque for my new base and easily passed the exams for a private investigator's license.

I turn to examine the glass door with its simple lettering. In tasteful sans-serif type it reads: Rob Charlton, JD, Private Investigations. Plain and simple, no frills, no tacky images of magnifying glasses or deerstalker hats as suggested by the sign painter. My business card is Spartan, too, merely noting my previous FBI connection as a hint of my sleuthing skills and listing my cell phone number in boldface.

I wonder for probably the hundredth time if it was a mistake to mention my law degree. Lawyers have never been the most trusted or beloved members of society, sometimes ranked between used car salesmen and pedophiles. I don't practice the black arts of the law but the association might be a put-off to some. I'll have to think about that.

To my chagrin, five months of trying has failed to yield enough business to justify the rent and overhead on this pathetic little office. I've logged several assignments to spy on cheating spouses; a job researching an auto parts dealer's habit of pocketing money rightfully belonging to his partner; and the task of investigating a rancher's claim that a neighbor was stealing his cattle.

I sigh at the recollection of the ingrate cattleman. He tried to stiff me on my bill after I found the missing animals had merely wandered off and taken up housekeeping in a distant corner of his ranch. Now the unjustly accused neighbor is threatening to sue me for slander, even though all I did was falsify the claims of his suspicious neighbor. The bastard should be thanking me.

Some days it doesn't pay to get out of bed, and this is another in a long string of them.

I jingle my keys impatiently as I walk to my car. It's a well-maintained Ford Crown Vic that I bought used. It's just like the ones I used to drive for the government, but without the extra radio antennas and special lights hidden behind the grille. It isn't the traditional black or dark blue of the government cars—that would have been going too far—but otherwise my maroon baby is a reminder of my glory days.

I sit at the wheel for a moment, deciding whether to retreat to my lonely apartment or hang at the sports bar I sometimes frequent. I recall there's a Rangers game on tonight and somehow the macho ambience of a sports bar makes a ball game more exciting. I decide to watch it while enjoying a bacon cheeseburger and a cold beer. Maybe even two. Beers that is.

Just as I reach to put the key into the ignition my cell phone goes off. The ringtone is the theme from the old TV show *The Untouchables,* which I thought was clever at the time but now the joke's grown stale since so few seem to recognize it. Another sign that I'm getting old. Hell, even I was too young to watch that show except on late-night reruns as a kid, but I'm convinced it had a bearing on my career choice.

I sigh and glance in the rearview mirror as I fumble for the phone. Yep, just a few years the wrong side of 50 and there's that telltale gray in a hairline that's receding almost perceptively from day to day. I pull out the phone and punch it on.

"Hello, Rob Charlton Investigations," I say, putting an upbeat lilt in my voice. I've practiced with my tape recorder and think I've got it to sound almost sincere. "How may I help you?"

There's a moment of silence and I'm about to hang up when a woman's voice comes on the line.

"Is this Mr. Charlton?"

"Yep," I chirp. "That's me."

"The former FBI agent?" The speaker ends the sentence on an upward note to emphasize the question mark. "I saw your ad in the yellow pages."

"That is correct," I tell her, groaning inwardly. She probably needs someone to rescue her cat from a tree or catch her husband in some bed he's not supposed to be in. Why am I doing this? For crying out loud I'm an experienced professional, formerly lead investigator on several dozen murders and other major federal crimes.

"I'm Rob Charlton," I repeat. My happy demeanor is in danger of lapsing into grumpiness.

There's another pause. I wait patiently for a long beat, thinking of that cheeseburger and how I so very much don't care whether Fluffy ever gets out of the tree.

"Oh, Mr. Charlton, I hope you can help me," says the caller. "It's my husband."

Oh Lord, of course it's the husband. Not Fluffy after all, but the husband. He's probably shacked up with a trio of hot young babes, living his male menopause minute to the hilt, and this old bat not only wants me to help her spoil his fun but destroy him for good in divorce court.

But then she says something that grabs my attention like a bolt of lightning.

"He was murdered and the police won't do anything about it," she tells me, her voice breaking as if she's struggling to hold back tears.

Well, that word grabs me all right. The M word, that is. "Murder." It's like poetry to my ears. I know about murder. I've been there and done that, so to speak. Solving them, that is. It's the very thing I did so well. Many a killer languishing in federal pens across the nation is there due to my detecting skills. Rescuing Fluffy and betraying hubby is work for hacks. Murder, that's for the big boys, like I used to be. In the Bureau, murder was practically my middle name.

"Excuse me," I say, hoping I hadn't misheard. "You say murdered?"

"Yes," comes the answer. "Killed in cold blood. Shot.

And that man at the Sheriff's office hasn't done anything about it even though I keep asking him to. Now he's told me to stop calling him. He threatened to get a court order..."

Uh oh. Sounds like I'm on the phone with a crackpot. Law enforcement officers don't often ask for court protection from a victim's survivors. This lady must be a real hot pistol mama, maybe even a candidate for a rubber room with complimentary straitjacket.

"Um, what man is that?" I venture with a cautious note in my voice.

"Why, that lieutenant Flores," she answers. Her voice is angry now, filled with venom. "It's been six months and he hasn't arrested anyone. Now he's sent back all my husband's things and told me not to call him anymore. I'm sure he's given up on the case."

I let this soak into my head for a moment before hazarding a response.

"Well," I say, beginning to negotiate a careful retreat, "this sounds like something for the police, or in this case apparently the sheriff's office. As a private investigator I generally deal in civil crimes, not felony cases, and certainly not an open case in the hands of the authorities."

I hope this will slow her down and for an instant. I catch the clear glimmer of an escape from what could obviously turn into a nasty situation. As a newcomer to the business, the last thing I need is to be caught between official law and some batty victim's widow. It's bad enough being a former Fed, perceived as the natural enemy by all local police agencies. Sadly, independent investigators are ranked even below Feebies on the scale of the despised, well advised to keep their distance from the real business of crime fighting.

But my hope of wriggling out through the art of

logical refutation fails as the woman begins to lay down her trump cards.

"I understand that, Mr. Charlton," she asserts in an exasperated tone. She's actually lecturing me, I realize. "My attorney has explained it to me. I am certainly not asking you to interfere with the police."

"Um, okay," I murmur as she continues.

"I merely want some answers," she continues, "a review of the case through your experienced eyes. A professional consultation if you will. My husband's estate left me quite well off and I'm prepared to pay you a handsome retainer."

I stare through the windshield of my car, spattered with the tiny flattened corpses of countless bugs and coated with the thin brown dust of the desert. Consultation sounds okay, maybe. It could give me a legitimate role. Temptation and reason struggle in my mind and standing to the side, as it were, is the thought of my rent bill coming due in a few days. It seems to be waving to get my attention.

If I walk away from this challenge, do I deserve to succeed in my new endeavor? Hell, if I don't have the balls to jump at what might be a real case, I might as well go back to the Costa Rican beaches and all those piña coladas and tequila shots, to spend my remaining days watching my belly go to flab and my hairline recede over the horizon.

Still cautious, I decide to meet her halfway, suggesting that we meet before I decide whether there's anything I can do for her. She agrees and we set a date for the next morning, ten o'clock at her house in the Northeast Heights. I enter her name, Marsha Greenwald, in my iPhone appointment calendar.

I click off the phone and sit pondering for a moment before starting the engine. I decide to go home instead of to the sports bar. There's a frozen lasagna in my freezer, just begging to be popped in the microwave, and I can make do with my own company for the Rangers game.

I drive to the other end of the parking lot and go into the package liquor store intending to buy a six-pack. Hell, I change my mind and emerge clutching a bottle of 15-year-old Macallan Scotch single malt whiskey and a bottle of nice red wine from Italy. My wallet feels definitely lighter but I leave Marv with a smile on his face for once.

Chapter Three

Rob Charlton

I'm not surprised to find that Mrs. Greenwald lives in what can only be called a mansion, standing on a large lot with a view across the entire valley and city of Albuquerque. The Georgian style house seems a bit out of place here in the Southwest, but I'm no expert on architecture and I always say whatever floats your boat is fine with me. I park on the circle drive just at ten o'clock and shut off the motor.

A thin, well-dressed woman stands on the porch, obviously anxious for our meeting to begin. I get out of the car and approach with a business card in my hand. She takes it with her left and offers her right. We shake and I'm surprised at the strength in her slender arms.

"Mrs. Greenwald," I murmur. "Rob Charlton."

"Thank you for coming, Mr. Charlton," she replies, gazing steadily into my eyes as if seeking a sign. "You don't know how glad I am to be able to speak with you. Please come in. Would you like some tea?"

Ah, so it's tea, with crumpets no doubt. English bone china and clotted cream perhaps. I smile inwardly at the thought as she leads me into a vast foyer extending up two stories to a massive skylight. A life size statue of some ancient Greek-type dude is displayed in the center and paintings hang on the walls. Everything looks expensive. She opens double doors into a sitting room and gestures to a leather armchair.

"Please sit there. It was my husband's favorite chair." I sit and she takes her place across from me on a settee. She leans forward to pick up a silver bell from the little coffee table between us and rings it vigorously. In a moment a Hispanic woman appears from another door and takes an order for "tea and biscuits".

I know that in England biscuits are what we call cookies, not the things I like to eat with sausage gravy. I smile and look around the comfortable room. There are more paintings on the walls and a rich carpet on the floor. A marble fireplace forms a focal point, flanked by bookcases that line the walls on either side.

I draw my eyes back and see that she's still gazing at me expectantly. I get the feeling she's hoping I'm some miracle worker who can wave a wand to make all her troubles disappear.

I know more now than I did when she called the previous day, thanks to the wonders of Google and the worldwide web. Her husband had been Donald Green–wald, a successful architect and real estate developer who specialized in commercial properties such as hotels and office complexes. He was found dead in the desert some six months previously, shortly before I returned to Albuquerque, the apparent victim of an execution-style killing. News reports variously hinted it was the work of a serial killer, a psychopath, a disgruntled client or perhaps just some everyday maniac gone over the edge. The lead investigator, sheriff's detective Luis Flores, had made few statements and the story had quickly faded from the press and airwaves.

We make small talk as we await the tea service. When it arrives Mrs. Greenwald serves, offering the choice of lemon or cream. She holds up a plate of cookies dusted with powdered sugar, which I decline in the interests of my less-than-boyish waistline. Well, I would have made an exception for real biscuits, the ones with the gravy, but these I can do without.

I'm trying to project my upbeat, positive attitude and keep a little smile pasted on my face. I comment on the delicacy of the bone china and the taste of the tea. My eyes roam the room again, feeling out the character of its owner. Then we get down to business.

"Mrs. Greenwald," I begin, "I've read the news reports and have a general idea of how your husband died. Do you mind if I ask you to tell me exactly what's occurred since then and why you think there's something the sheriff's department is withholding from you?"

She sits back on the little sofa and crosses her arms under her breasts. A defensive sign, no doubt of it. I keep smiling and make a little gesture with my right hand to encourage her to begin speaking.

"Well, as I told you he was found in the desert. In the desert! He hated that desert and would never have gone there. He'd been shot in the forehead, according to the police report. And I saw it, I saw the wound in his forehead. I had to identify the body, you know..."

Setting my face in a serious expression I nod encouragingly as she hesitates. After a moment she resumes.

"That lieutenant Flores says he was, oh, what did he call it? Don's body was arranged in a special way, but just lying in the desert, on the sand."

"I believe the term is 'displayed,' that the killer displayed the body to make a statement."

"Yes, that's it, that's what Flores told me. He said it was a mark of a serial killer. But when I asked him what kind of 'statement' that was, he told me he didn't know.

Why, I would think it would be something he could figure out, being a detective and all."

She looks into my eyes questioningly before continuing in a beseeching tone. "I don't know why anyone would want to make a statement about my husband…"

"Mrs. Greenwald," I interject, "there's no way to understand the workings of a psychotic mind. Whatever his intention, no one can imagine except himself. I've seen many examples and there's no fixed pattern to it."

The woman relaxes and lowers her arms.

"Oh," she breathes. "I see. You know, that's what Flores told me, too, but I didn't really believe him. Now that I hear it from you, with your expertise as an FBI agent, I can see he may have been right."

I nod and sip the tea, rolling the musky liquid around my mouth. I wait for her to continue but she seems lost in thought.

"Why do you think someone would have done this to your husband?" I ask at last. "Did he have any enemies? Surely detective Flores must have asked you that."

"Oh, yes, of course he asked. But I don't know of anyone who could have done such an evil thing to my Don." A tear drips from her left eye and rolls down her cheek. "My poor, dear Donald," she adds, wiping the tear away with the corner of a napkin.

"Tell me about your husband. What kind of man was he?"

"Why, he was a wonderful man. My knight in shining armor, ever since we met at NMU. He was an architect you know. I met him when he was just about to finish up his graduate studies and I was a junior in the communications department. We were married just over a year later, right after we graduated."

"Did you and your husband have any troubles during your life together?"

"Oh, no." She pauses then adds, "Well only the usual things but nothing serious. He was always fair to me and did what he could to be a good husband. We never had a child..."

I wait, watching the regret of childlessness wash over her face. She dabs at her cheek again then folds the napkin carefully and places it on the table.

"Don made a lot of money, as you can see." She waves a hand vaguely around to indicate the house and its embarrassment of riches. "He was a success almost from the start, first with a leading firm where he became the chief executive, then with his own business. We never lacked."

"Was there anything going on in his life when it happened? Anything you can think of?"

"No." She's emphatic. "Everything was fine. We were very happy together. His business was doing well."

I sit back in the chair and sip my tea, pondering. This may be a mystery that will have no answer. I guess that Flores and his team have done a bang-up job and hit a solid brick wall. I saw many such cases in my years with the Bureau, cases where no evidence could be found, no motive determined, no suspect identified. Cold cases like those are the main cause of frustration for dedicated law enforcers.

"Tell me more about your relationship with Flores," I probe. "Why did he tell you to stop calling him?"

She looks down at her hands, folded in her lap.

"Well, I guess maybe I was a little too pushy with him. I just wanted him to do his job, to catch the person who killed my Don..."

"You say he actually suggested he'd get a court order against you?"

"Yes he did, and it made me damned mad." She glares at me. "He shouldn't have taken such an attitude. I just wanted to help him, really, to keep him from giving up on the case."

I ponder some more, take another sip of the tea then look her in the eye.

"So, how many times did you call him?" I inquire in a mild tone. She looks stricken and takes a moment to respond.

"Um, well, quite a lot I guess," she admits, her eyes returning to the hands in her lap.

"What's 'quite a lot'? Once a week? Once every day or two? How often did you call him?"

"Oh, my, you make me seem like a meddling fool. I guess I called him every day."

"Every day just once?"

"Well, maybe several times. Sometimes maybe five times…or six…" Her voice trailed off.

My goodness! No wonder Flores had cut her off. Pushy isn't the least of it. This was out-and-out harassment.

"Mrs. Greenwald, did you call him at work, or did you also make calls to him on his personal time?"

She looks up with a small, embarrassed smile.

"Oh, yes, I called him on his personal phone. He had the number changed but one of my friends got his new number, his cell phone you know, so I kept on calling him at night and on weekends when he was out of the office. I suppose it was wrong of me, wasn't it?"

I smile, filled with empathy for the poor besieged detective Flores, a man of limited patience who had finally drawn a line in the sand.

"What did you say when you called?"

"Well, of course I would ask him how he was doing on the case. Why hadn't he caught the killer, that kind of thing you know? And I made suggestions, like whether he could check with other police agencies or the government to see if they knew something that could help. I read something about DNA testing and told him about that. I was just trying to help."

Now my heart goes out to this woman. Her obsession with the mystery of her husband's death has torn her apart and led her to make a considerable nuisance of herself. I think of asking if she's sought professional grief counseling but decide not to go there.

"Mrs. Greenwald," I begin and she interrupts.

"Please, call me Marsha. I don't think of myself as a 'Mrs.' anymore. I'm a widow now. I've always been Marsha and that's what I want to be called."

"All right Marsha. I've seen a lot of cases like this one, and you should know that there's a rule-of-thumb in the law enforcement business. If a crime is not well on the way to being solved within 48 hours the chances become increasingly likely the perpetrator will never be found. When several weeks or even months go by without any definitive evidence coming to light, it becomes what's called a 'cold case,' which means there's little point in actively continuing to try to find a solution."

"Yes, that's what Flores said it was. A cold case. I thought that was a terrible thing to say."

"Why?"

"Because it just seemed, well, like he was just giving up on it. Do you know what I mean?"

I ruminate for a moment.

"It isn't what you think," I say at last. "It's just common sense. An investigator on a cold case is just butting his head against a wall. There's no benefit to keep doing it. He has better things to do, more productive cases to work. But you should know that even cold cases are not closed cases. Only when a crime is solved is a case closed. Meanwhile the investigators just have to patiently wait for some new lead to appear."

Marsha gazes at me with the eyes of a child. I shift in my seat and watch as she assimilates this. At last she speaks.

"Thank you for explaining that," she says. I begin to relax, but then her voice hardens. "Now, what can you do to break this case open again? To make it come out of the freezer, so to speak?"

Oh my goodness, here we are again. She wants me to step in and solve this case, a stone cold case that has obviously defied the authorities. As a private investigator I have no foundation on which to meddle in such things. How to explain it?

"Marsha," I begin, setting down my teacup and reaching out a comforting hand to her, which she takes. "You need to leave this to the proper authorities. I'm certain they've done all that can be done, and that they'll keep the case open so they can proceed if and when further evidence should appear." I realize I'm sounding like a dork but there's no help for it. I squeeze her hand gently then release it and sit back in my chair.

"As I told you yesterday, I can't deal in a felony crime investigation like this one. As a private investigator I'm not an authorized officer of the law. It's true I'm experienced in crime work, but that's no longer my role. You suggested yesterday that I could provide you with consultation. I'm doing so as a courtesy and at no cost. That's all that I can do and I'm happy to have been of service."

New tears appear and the napkin is once again applied. I watch as she absorbs the disappointment. Several uncomfortable minutes pass until she looks up again.

"All right, I think I understand. But I have one more question. Why did Flores return my husband's clothing and personal effects? Aren't they possible evidence? It was when he did that that I felt he had given up on the case for good."

"I'm sure that all of your husband's things were carefully examined for clues," I assure her. "Any trace evidence such as hairs, fingerprints and so forth would have been documented and made a part of the permanent case file. Any true evidence would have been kept. I think that by returning the effects he was trying to bring closure to you…and maybe, quite frankly, to get you off his back. He wouldn't actually close the case."

"Oh." Her eyes fall again and her hands are folded in her lap. "I thought… Well, I don't know what I thought. Would you like to see them?"

"What, his personal effects? Well, I don't see the point."

"Oh, who knows what the point is, I just want you to see them."

Good grief, I'm trying to back away and she keeps dragging me further into her spider's lair. Okay, I decide, I'll take a look at the possessions then make my excuses and depart. That won't hurt. Shouldn't take but a moment.

I nod and she jumps up and hurries out of the room, returning a moment later with a sealed evidence bag.

"You haven't opened it?"

"No," she admits. "I was afraid to."

Shrugging I break the seal on the bag and begin to remove the objects inside. First is a pair of black business shoes, size ten. I set them aside and reach to pull out a folded shirt, a belt, a pair of trousers, a tie, socks—all the requirements of the well-dressed man. In the bottom of the bag I find a smaller sealed pouch that holds a wallet, a wedding band and a gold watch.

"I presume Flores asked you to identify these items when the case was first opened," I say.

She nods. "Yes, I couldn't see anything that was missing.

I look at the wallet, lifting each credit cart and fingering the driver's license. There are six twenties, two tens and a five in the money compartment. I remove these and hand them to her, suggesting that money is, after all, money. She takes the bills in silence.

Next I examine the wedding band, a plain gold ring with no engraving. I set it aside and reach for the gold watch. A Rolex, worth a small fortune no doubt. I turn it in my hand and see the inscription on the back. It reads: "Happy Retirement. June 14, 1975."

"I take it this watch originally belonged to someone else," I say. A puzzled look crosses her face.

"No, of course not. I bought it for him myself for our tenth wedding anniversary."

"And that would have been when?"

"In 1988. We were married in 1978."

"Well, it seems rather odd that it's engraved with a date of 1975 and references a retirement. Was this some kind of private joke?"

This draws a blank expression. "What? What are you saying?"

Wordlessly I hold out the watch. She grabs it from my hand and holds it up to her eyes.

"My God," she breathes. "That isn't Don's watch. This doesn't make any sense at all. What's going on here? Did that Flores make a switch or something?"

"No," I reply after a moment's consideration. "But I think he may have missed an important clue."

Chapter Four

Rob Charlton

Well, I did it, stuck my foot in it up to my butt. I've committed to conducting a private investigation into the death of Donald Greenwald. May the gracious saints of criminal investigation, whoever they are, preserve me.

I make a heroic effort to wriggle out of it, but Marsha is adamant. I try to convince her to alert the sheriff's detective to the new evidence, but she makes the excellent point that we have no idea what the mysterious engraving with its precise date and reference to retirement actually means. I suspect it's a part of the displaying behavior of the killer, another element of his message. As such it may or may not constitute meaningful evidence. We can defer that to later.

And of course there's the fact that she's already poisoned the well with Flores.

Marsha makes another excellent point by writing a check for ten grand to yours truly. If I hold down the expenses it's enough to cover my overhead for several months, and hey, what harm could there be in doing a little private sleuthing into an unexplained killing?

I tell myself I can just poke around at the edges without getting into trouble, and if I come up with anything concrete I'll immediately bring Flores into the picture.

We shake on the deal and on the way back to my office I stop by the bank to deposit my retainer. Settling into my lair I fire up the computer and begin to build a case file.

In addition to the information Marsha volunteered I've grilled her for some general facts about her husband's activities around the time of the date inscribed on the back of the watch, June 14, 1975. At that time he was still an undergraduate in architectural school, had not yet met Marsha, and was struggling to work his way through university.

I begin to draw up a skeletal timeline that might help focus on that special date. The trouble is that Marsha couldn't provide very many facts about that phase of her husband's life.

I enter what data I can into an Excel spreadsheet, leaving many blanks and rows of question marks. I print out a copy on legal sized paper and tack it to my bulletin board. Then I lean back, put my feet on the desk and stare at the wall. If you're me, this is a very creative thing to do. I've done some of my best thinking just lounging in my chair or driving down an empty highway. Sometimes I get good ideas that way. In fact, it happens this time.

Sitting up I reach into my briefcase and pull out the Rolex watch that Marsha has entrusted to me. I study it carefully. It seems solid enough, heavy. The engraving is professional. But what does this mean?

Assuming that the killer had switched the real watch with this one leads to several likely conclusions. First, he had to have known the particular style of watch that Donald Greenwald wore. This implies a deep level of premeditation. Second, he had to engrave the watch or have it done professionally. Another thought occurs to me:

Could this actually be Greenwald's gold watch and the murderer merely added the engraving? Or, if it's in fact a substitute, would the killer have replaced a valuable Rolex watch with an equally expensive genuine one? I think not.

These thoughts give me the hint of a possible thread of evidence to pursue. Dropping the watch into my pocket I check the yellow pages for the name of the nearest Rolex dealer. Twenty minutes later I'm standing at a glass counter showing the watch to a certified watchmaker. He studies it briefly and chuckles.

"That's a pretty good fake," he says. "We see them from time to time, usually brought in by people who thought they were getting a steal. More like they were robbed. These are made in China and you can buy one for a couple hundred bucks."

That answers one of my questions, and also demonstrates the killer isn't stupid. So how would one obtain such a magnificently faux timepiece?

"You can buy these things on the internet from fronts in Asia," the jeweler tells me. He describes how sellers send them to U.S. addresses by ordinary mail with return receipt requested to an offshore address. The counterfeit watches are illegal so customs agents confiscate them if found. But since the watches are so cheap, the sellers simply guarantee delivery and mail a second watch if the first one fails to arrive.

Well, that knocks out one possible evidentiary lead. The watch could have been obtained without leaving any trace. Obviously the killer had kept the real watch, probably as a trophy. What about the engraving?

The jeweler screws a loupe into one eye and examines the letters and numbers closely.

"It was done with a laser engraving machine," he tells me. He leads me back to his workspace to show me just such a device. Linked to a computer, it allows the user to create professional work that would have made an old-time hand engraver green with envy.

I inquire whether such a job would have to be done in a jewelry shop like this one.

"Not necessarily," comes the answer. He explains that anyone can buy an engraving machine for a few thousand dollars and it takes only a couple of hours to become proficient with them.

So, that means the killer could have done the engraving himself, but that would have involved considerable expense. I ask whether it would make sense for me to check with other jewelers to see if anyone recognizes the work. The watchmaker shakes his head.

"No reputable dealer would engrave a counterfeit watch," he declares. "That would give legitimacy to the fakes and that's the last thing we want."

So that means either the killer used a disreputable jeweler, one who wouldn't be eager to admit it, or actually invested the money to get his own machine. I was coming up with nothing but dead ends in what is apparently a quite elaborate crime.

I thank the jeweler and walk back out to my car, wondering why a person would go to so much trouble to create a message to be sent through the medium of bloody murder. There has to be a reason, a serious motive for this strange killing.

I've run into a dead end with the question of the watch itself and its engraving. The only thread left to follow is the date, June 14, 1975. About all I know is that the victim was a student at the time, so my next stop will be the University of New Mexico campus.

Chapter Five

Rob Charlton

A bit of Googling informs me that the UNM School of Architecture and Planning is housed in Pearl Hall, a spectacular 110,000 square foot building that serves as an entry to the campus itself. Internationally known, the school is one of the university's five quasi-autonomous professional schools, along with law, medicine, engin–eering and nursing.

I park several blocks away on Central Avenue and secure my Glock in the glove compartment, thanks to the campus rules against concealed carry. Little do they know that by this policy they actually encourage violence since would-be mass killers are drawn to gun-free zones like flies to sugar. It always ticks me off that rule makers refuse to understand that making people defenseless only encourages violent crime.

I wander around inside Pearl Hall for a while gawking at the high ceilings with massive beams and broad skylights. It's an odd sort of building in my uninformed opinion, rather more like a factory than a university facility. But as I always say, whatever floats your boat.

After a while I discover the inner sanctum, the administrative offices. When I ask to see the dean, the receptionist responds with skepticism. I'm informed this isn't possible without an appointment. Then she turns on the heat to squeeze me for information. The lady missed her calling—she should be an interrogator at Guantanamo Bay. The poor terrorists wouldn't stand a chance.

I answer vaguely, realizing that because of my unofficial status in the investigation, the last thing I want to do is tell anyone my true mission. All during my career with the FBI I had merely to flip my badge case and almost every door would open before me like the one to Aladdin's cave at the utterance of 'Open sesame'. Alas, I no longer have that power.

I decide to wing it and pose as a freelance writer interested in learning more about the history of the school, and particularly the period around the 1970's. She asks me for a business card. I pat my pockets vaguely and grin sheepishly.

"Uh huh," she comments. She gazes at me for a moment with her gimlet eyes until at last a tiny smile peeks through her mask.

"Well, the 1970's were quite a long time ago," she remarks. "I hate to tell you this, but our dean was probably still in high school then."

I consider this for a moment before inquiring whether there might be someone among the senior staff who could fill me in on that era of the school's history. She thinks for a moment.

"Actually, Professor Humphrey would be a good choice. He's emeritus now, of course, so he doesn't keep regular hours."

"Emeritus?" I raise my eyebrows, wondering if this is some kind of new disease. She notices my confusion.

"Emeritus is like being retired but still with the privileges of the position. Doctor Humphrey must be about 80, but he still likes to hang around sometimes."

"Do you think he's here today?"

"No, I hardly think so. I haven't seen him in weeks, actually. He's moved up to a place near Taos and spends most of his time up there. He's been working with the Taos Pueblo on some renovation work. He's quite an expert on native architecture. You know, adobe construction and like that."

I nod knowingly and pull out a notebook and pen.

"He sounds like just the man I need to see," I tell her. "Can you tell me how to reach him?"

The skeptical look returns for a moment but I guess my honest face has won her over because she reaches into a drawer and pulls out a thin binder. Leafing through it she finds the right page and reads off his address and phone number.

"He's in the book anyway," she remarks, as if to assure me no violation of privacy is taking place. I write down the name Willard Humphrey and his address and phone number. It looks like a trip to Taos is in my future.

David L. Brown

Chapter Six

Jeremy Barth

The vast, echoing office literally hums with activity. Around the huge bullpen with its rows of tiny cubicles dozens of traders with rolled up sleeves stare impassively at arrays of monitors. Some talk excitedly into headset microphones, the apparent enthusiasm in contrast to the bored expressions on their empty faces. Others scurry from place to place, carrying file folders, printouts or cups of coffee. At their island desks busy assistants attack keyboards with fury. The hum goes on throughout the trading day and even into the night. It's the sound of money, the effect of billions of dollars flowing through this investment bank from every corner of the Earth in an endless and invisible flood of electronic signals.

In the relative calm of a glassed in box, one of several lined up along the outside wall of the bullpen, Barth closes a folder and glances at the clock. Four twenty-six. He sighs and leans back in his chair, clasping his hands behind his balding head to stare up at the ceiling.

Barth is a medium-sized man with medium-sized features, a quite ordinary looking man who never stands out in a crowd. He wears a three-piece Brooks Brothers suit, a few years old but in the timeless style that's always acceptable in the big money milieu of Wall Street.

Contemplating the pattern of holes in acoustic tiles he sits at ease in a dark brown leather swivel chair that has recently begun to list to one side and squeak in protest when he shifts his weight.

Barth's office is as plain and unremarkable as himself. The desk is of good, solid oak but bears the marks of many years of use. A matching bookcase to one side holds well-thumbed volumes on subjects related to tax accounting, financial regulations and investment models. The floor is covered with the same ugly, dirt-colored carpeting that has spread like kudzu throughout the vast office complex. A side chair squats next to the bookcase, an old-fashioned satchel-style leather briefcase resting on its seat. Two little-used visitor chairs stand at attention before the desk.

The tan vinyl walls are bare except for two framed diplomas from the University of New Mexico and several certificates including one naming Barth as a certified public accountant and another as the holder of a certificate in financial forensics. No photographs or personal items are in evidence. In one corner a hat stand bears a tan trench coat and a somewhat shapeless trilby hat, both reflecting the styles and tastes of a past era.

The desk is business-like and clear of clutter, with a neat stack of files to one side, a plain onyx pen set positioned front and center, an imposing printing calculator that dominates the right-hand side and the ubiquitous in-out basket that stands at the left front corner. There are no items in the "out" tray, and only a single sheet of paper in the "in" tray. A brass nameplate at the front of the desk reads "Jeremy Barth, VP-Internal Audits."

Behind Barth is an oak credenza. Like the bookcase it matches the desk, all plainly purchased as a set many years ago. On its surface are a keyboard, a monitor and mouse. To one side is a plain dark-gray multi-line phone and beside it is a yellow legal pad with black and red ballpoint pens arrayed along one side.

Above the credenza is a window framing a view typical of those afforded to mid-level executives in the crowded Financial District where skyscrapers stand hip-to-elbow. It's apparently a rainy day because the light is wan and wraiths of mist float in the dim urban canyon outside Barth's window as he sits contemplating his realm.

He glances at the clock again. Four thirty-six now. Nearly time. Barth lowers his arms and leans forward to the desk, the worn out bearings of the chair squawking a protest. He opens the pencil drawer in the center of the desk and begins to sort through the items it contains. There are more black and red ballpoint pens, paper clips and pads of sticky notes. He leaves them there taking only a Parker fountain pen, which he clips into his inside coat pocket, and a plain black comb. Barth runs the comb carelessly through the fringe of graying hair that surrounds his balding head then tosses it into his wastebasket with a shrug.

Rising to his feet he steps over to the side chair and picks up the briefcase, opening it and setting it on the desk. Returning to the complaining chair he opens the right-hand file drawer of the desk and riffles through folders. He removes several and places them in the briefcase. After a few minutes he smiles slightly, closes the drawer and snaps the briefcase shut, leaving it on the desk.

Barth looks at the clock. Four fifty-one.

He reaches for the in basket and picks up the single sheet of paper that lies there. He glances at it briefly before plucking a fountain pen from the onyx set to sign the document. He studies it again for a moment before placing it ceremoniously into the "out" tray.

A shadow appears at the door and Barth looks up to see his executive assistant looking in at him. As usual for her, a mousy Italian-American from Queens, she seems subdued, even hesitant. She smiles tentatively.

"Come in Carla," he says, gesturing to one of the guest chairs. "We have a couple of minutes don't we?"

Ignoring his invitation to sit she takes a step into the office and looks around uneasily

"Mr. Barth, we've known each other for a long time," she says, her voice vague and with a distinctive Bronx accent. Her eyes shift from the desktop to the bookcase and from there to the dismal view outside the gloomy window.

"Yes, Carla, that's true," he agrees. He smiles but adds nothing. She has been his assistant for more than a decade.

"Well," she says, glancing down at the desktop again, "I just wanted to say goodbye, you know, personally…"

"Thank you Carla. That's very nice of you." Barth straightens the stack of folders on his desk and gives her an inquiring look.

Over the years he's never revealed anything of himself to this woman, never shared a lunch, never asked about her family, never even chatted with her about the events of the day, whether the Yankees would win the pennant or whether it would rain or snow. Now he smiles again, a wry sort of smile as if he's savoring a private joke.

"Well, that's all I wanted to say," Carla murmurs after a moment. "Don't worry, I'll pack and ship your personal effects as you instructed in your memo. Come on now, everything's ready." She backs through the door, turns and disappears.

Barth continues to sit for a moment, his nose offended by the lingering stench of her cheap perfume. God does he hate that smell. He sighs and spins the chair around to face the window. The bearings squeak. He glances at the clock again, at its plain black hands on a plain white face now pointing to five o'clock.

It's time. His retirement is at hand.

Barth stands up and hitches down his vest. He takes the battered trilby from the hat rack and places it carefully on his head, folds the trench coat over one arm and picks up the briefcase. With one quick glance around the glass cubicle he steps into the hall and turns right.

At the end of the passageway he can see Carla waiting at the door to the corner conference room, an impatient look on her face. He nods and strides reluctantly to face the agony of the pathetic ceremony, a sad little affair with Kool-Aid punch, little packaged snacks, and a collection of his henceforth-to-be-former colleagues. There is sure to be a cheap sheet cake inscribed in red frosting with a tacky message about happy years to come.

He's attended many such events through the years; now it's his turn to experience the indignation. Well, at least he's going voluntarily, taking an early buyout package that gives him his freedom at a relatively early age.

Fifty-six, only fifty-six. He's given this company thirty of those years and has perhaps as many left for his own purposes. He knows he'll be well rid of this place.

He comes to the doorway and looks in at the faces of men and women for whom over many years he's maintained well-concealed contempt. He smiles and the faces smile back at him. It's all about keeping up the front, he knows. It's all about being able to put on smiles like Halloween masks.

Someone hands him a plastic cup of Kool-Aid and he smiles and keeps on smiling until the whole awful thing is done with, until the last well-wisher awkwardly shakes his hand, mutters something and slides out the door leaving Barth alone in the conference room with empty cups and snack wrappers and a green jewelry store box in the center of the table.

Barth looks around for a moment then picks up the box. He pops it open on its spring-loaded hinges and gazes at its contents: a watch, the ultimate emblem of the thirty years he gave to this firm. Taking it out of the box he turns it over to examine once again the engraving on the back. Spare tribute indeed, it merely reads "In Recognition of Your Service," followed by two dates. The traditional badge of retirement.

He twists the watch around in his hand. It's a nice watch but not solid gold much less platinum. No solid gold watch for him; those are for the men at the top, the ones who ride in limousines and bank the multi-million dollar bonuses. They wouldn't be caught dead with a piece of trash like this. At least it doesn't have a picture of Mickey Mouse on the front, he thinks with a snort.

Barth sticks the watch in his pocket and drops the jewelry store box into the trash among the offal remaining from the retirement ceremony. He picks up his hat and coat, hefts the briefcase and strolls toward the nearby elevator doors.

Around him the bullpen is humming, a hive of frantic activity, a muted and unending cacophony of sound and fury. There are deals being struck, millions being made in an endless cycle of cold-hearted greed.

He pokes the down button and when the elevator doors slide back he steps in without even a final glance back. The doors close and he punches the G button with a steady finger. The elevator is empty. He looks at his face in the mirrored wall, the face that never stands out, the face that remains anonymous.

He grins, and this time the smile that appears on the reflected image of his face is no facade, no mask, no artifice. This smile is real, an honest expression of inner satisfaction. Now that his retirement is official Barth can return to his desert home to resume full-time the fulfillment of his carefully laid plans. The trial run some months earlier was a great success and he looks forward to future triumphs.

In his pocket he rubs his fingers over the retirement watch he's just received—and another, a Rolex of solid gold, his secret talisman. As the elevator slows a blank mask replaces Barth's smile as he prepares to face the world and launch in earnest his long awaited retirement plan.

David L. Brown

Chapter Seven

Rob Charlton

It's two days before I can leave for Taos, a three-hour drive from Albuquerque. In the meantime I keep busy doing some basic research on the Greenwald killing. My Excel spreadsheet is growing larger but still contains more empty cells and rows of question marks than actual data. I haven't learned much more about the period in the victim's life engraved on the faux watch.

Time is long and memory is short, or at least that's what the philosophers say. I guess it's true.

I also do some sniffing around about detective lieutenant Flores and conclude my instincts about him are sound. He boasts an excellent record having solved a number of major crimes during his career.

My instincts are to go to Flores and offer to act in the case in an unofficial role on behalf of my client. But because of Mrs. Greenwald's harassment I know I need to tread carefully. If an already enraged Flores were to discover I'm horning in on his case at her behest, he'd likely go ballistic. His threat of a court order could be turned against me. He might even be able to get my investigator's license pulled. That would spell a quick end to my embryonic second career. Clearly Flores is one sleeping dog to be left strictly alone.

On a typically clear New Mexico morning I get an early start on the road to Taos, an artsy community built around a thousand-year-old native pueblo. A phone call to Dr. Humphrey has elicited his invitation to meet for lunch at a restaurant near the town Plaza.

I make good time on Interstate 25 as far as Santa Fe then fight traffic to get around the busy state capital and continue north on a winding two-lane highway that follows the course of the Rio Grande River. It's good windshield time and my mind is at work planning how to approach the retired architect.

Clearly, I can't openly discuss the real object of my visit. With that in mind I've had some new business cards printed at an office supply store. While otherwise accurate as far as my identity, address and phone number, the title "freelance writer" appears below my name. It could even be legit, kinda sorta, because I've seriously considered trying my hand as a scrivener. Many of the cases I worked for the FBI could be mined for crime story plots. Even this Greenwald case could be grist for a writer's mill. Hell, if it works for all those other lawyers-cum-novelists, why not for me? It would surely beat rescuing a long parade of Fluffys or spying on various ill-fortuned husbands to testify against in divorce court.

With these thoughts a kind of inner peace emerges. I smile at the passing scenery—rugged rocks, cottonwood trees lining the river's edge, the distant snow-capped peaks of the Sangre de Cristo Mountains—as I approach Taos.

Dr. Humphrey isn't at all as I had imagined him, perhaps as an aging Indiana Jones or wild-haired Einstein. He's a quiet, slender man of modest height with thin lips, heavy eyebrows above clear hazel eyes and unremarkable nose and chin. I note with some irritation that he's still in possession of a full head of hair, worn a bit long in a shaggy cut. He wears a floppy brimmed hat, field boots and jeans supported by red suspenders under a denim jacket. His grip is firm and as he leads me to a private booth near the back of the restaurant I note he's quite spry for an octogenarian.

We sit and a waiter sets glasses of water and menus on the table. I formally introduce myself with certain reservations concerning the truth, presenting one of my new business cards. He sticks it into a shirt pocket with hardly a glance.

We make small talk for a few moments then concentrate on the menus. He suggests a Native American item, so-called Navajo Tacos with ground beef, refried beans, salsa and shredded cheese on thick, plate-sized foundations of frybread. I agree and side salads and glasses of iced tea round out our orders.

"Well, you've come a long way to talk with an old man," he observes, leaving the comment open-ended in a Socratic way. He gazes at me from beneath the abundant eyebrows. I realize I need to step very carefully in dealing with this shrewd intellect.

"It's a pleasant enough way to spend the day," I hazard. "I've been in Taos before, but don't know very much about it."

This opens up a line of conversation that seems to appeal to him. Soon I'm learning more than I care to about the history of the Taos Pueblo, native spirituality, and most of all the architecture. He speaks of many things—adobe walls, *vigas*, hand-carved corbels and *latillas*—as I busily scribble in my notebook, nodding encouragement to reinforce my cover as an interested interviewer.

Our meals arrive and we begin to eat. The food is excellent, no doubt filled with healthy natural ingredients and following recipes handed down from ancient times. He finishes first and pushes aside his empty plate, demonstrating an amazing appetite for a man of his age and physical stature. He watches quietly as I finish off my meal and wipe my mouth with a napkin.

"That was excellent," I remark. "Worth the drive from Albuquerque in itself."

He grins in appreciation. "Glad you liked it. Now let me hear what you want to know about. You told me on the phone that you're interested in the architecture school back in the 1970s. Is that right?"

"Yes," I reply, trotting out my cover story. "I'm planning an article about that phase in the history of New Mexican architecture, and the school was of course at the very center of it all."

He thinks for a moment then asks which publication has commissioned the work. My Googling has prepared me for this very question. I explain that I'm doing the piece on spec and mention several candidate magazines by name. He seems to accept this and begins to describe his recollections of that period of his life.

He came to the university in the late 1960s as an associate professor. At that time he was in his late 30s and had worked as a professional architect and engineer before returning to academia and earning a Ph.D. at Yale. His back–ground in design is strongly backed by expertise in civil engineering and mathematics.

"At that time the school was much smaller than it is today," he tells me. "I think there were fewer than ten of us on the main faculty, but we were full-timers, not like all these part-time adjunct instructors they use these days. I taught structural engineering and design courses at both the undergraduate and graduate levels. I got tenure in 1972 along with a full professorship."

I scribble away as he describes the development of the school's reputation as an important source of architectural innovation, touching on his own contributions. I let him go on for more than a half hour before carefully introducing the question of the students of the time.

"Ah, yes," he says. "We can't forget them, can we? The Academy tends to overlook them these days in the insistence that faculty devote themselves to creating an endless stream of inconsequential papers that only idiots actually read. These days tenured staff can't really call themselves 'teachers' anymore; they do so little of it. Most of the actual instruction's left to adjuncts and graduate assistants. It's a disgrace. In my day we took pride in our teaching."

I nod, thinking how much this scenario resembles today's FBI. Too many paper pushers and desk jockeys, too few actually out in the field doing the grinding day-to-day work that I had loved so much. Hell, I guess the whole world is sliding in the same direction.

I ask him to recall some of his favorite students, hoping that Greenwald's name will come up. He begins to speak of various students, some local New Mexicans, some from faraway countries. He recalls episodes of success and failure and recounts several humorous anecdotes. I keep my pen moving, waiting in vain to hear the name I want to hear on his lips. At last my patience wears out and I raise the subject myself.

"You know," I say, hoping it to sound like an offhand remark, "there was a well-known architect in Albuquerque who was recently murdered. He would have been about the right age to have been in the school in the 70s."

I pause and let an expression of puzzlement pass over my face. "Let's see now, what was his name...? Greenspan? Something like that. Do you know who I mean?"

He hesitates and for a moment I think I've raised the professor's suspicion, but he's merely reaching back into his memory banks.

"It was Greenwald," he murmurs after a moment. "Donald Greenwald. Yes, I knew him. He was one of my graduate students in structural engineering. Don't remember much about him though."

I try to keep on focus, mentioning that the mystery of his former student's death could make an interesting peg for my article. He ponders and throws out a few tidbits from his memory of a long-ago student.

"I remember he was damned ambitious," he declares. "Made a pile of money in the business, or so I seem to recall." I detect a touch of a mentor's pride in the success of a former student—but also a mere hint of jealousy. I wonder if the good professor remembers more than he wants to say about Greenwald.

"Can you tell me a bit more about him?" I ask, pushing doggedly ahead.

"Oh, yes, I remember that he was a good student, straight A's I think. Yes, I remember he graduated at the top of his class. He became quite an accomplished architect. I don't think he was from a rich family, had to work his way through university. You could do that back in those days, you know. It wasn't like it is today, costing an arm and a leg and leaving the poor graduate in debt up to his ass. Or hers, of course. I seem to recall that Greenwald had to hold down several jobs to keep going."

"Doing what?" I inquire.

"Oh, well, I don't know. I remember he had some kind of part-time assistant job at the school and I think he did some other things, too. Can't really remember."

I decide I've pushed hard enough and change the subject to other students and recollections. We talk for another twenty minutes before he looks at his watch and tells me of an appointment in the pueblo. I thank him for his time and reach for the check, but he takes it instead with a bird-like snatch.

"Treat's on me," he says with a grin. "Just remember this when you write that article of yours."

He rises and I join him. As we walk out into the sun-soaked plaza, I make one more attempt, imploring him to call me if he remembers anything else that could round out my article. I emphasize the importance of what might seem like small, personal details, particularly relating to individuals. He assures me that he will, patting the pocket that contains my card. He shakes my hand and strides purposefully away toward the adobe buildings of the nearby pueblo.

I watch him go, still holding my notebook filled with no doubt worthless notes. I sigh as I close it and put it into an inside pocket. My trip to Taos has led me into another dead end.

Chapter Eight

Luis Flores

Lieutenant Luis Flores is attacking the steep trail up the west side of the Sandia Crest mountain as if it's Omaha Beach and he's part of the first wave on D-Day. It's the weekend, his daughter is with his ex-wife, and he's pissed. Vigorous exercise is his way of working off the frustration that's been building in him for months.

He's pissed at a lot of things—his failed marriage, of course, but mostly his lack of progress on the Greenwald case and the clumsy way he handled Mrs. Greenwald. True she was insufferable in her continued harassment, but beneath his resentment Flores understands that she was acting from obsession, driven by her grief and outrage at what happened to her husband. He should have been able to manage it better.

Flores carries a walking stick and as he climbs he swings it viciously at anything the presents itself…weeds, rocks, twigs, and finally a bird that's minding its own business sitting on a branch. Ducking, the bird squawks in protest and flies away.

Disgusted with himself he stops, breathing heavily. He sits down on a nearby rock, leans his stick beside him and reaches for his water bottle. He drinks, then sits back to gaze westward across the city that sprawls below him.

Flores is aware that the frustration has taken control of him, that the same irrational forces that drove Marsha Greenwald are affecting him as well. He takes several more deep breaths and from long habit reaches for his cigarette pack before remembering that he's given them up.

Sighing, he lets his arm go limp and his hand drop back to his lap. A line from an old movie flutters through his memory, an actor saying: "Looks like I picked the wrong week to give up smoking." At this thought he begins to relax, takes several more deep breaths and begins to run over the Greenwald case in his head for perhaps the thousandth time.

Despite the suspicions of Marsha Greenwald, Flores has not given up on the case, despite pressure from his superiors to back off. Yet still he cannot find a thread to follow, a clue to pursue. The case is as cold as a winter day in Canada.

The death has all the earmarks of a serial killing, yet Flores has been unable to find any similar cases. And not for lack of trying—he's combed records from across the nation. Serial killings tend to be essentially motiveless crimes. Unlike ordinary murderers—those that act from uncontrolled rage, jealousy, the desire for financial gain, the urge for revenge, or mental illness—serial killers generally choose victims who are strangers to them. Serial murders cannot be solved merely through investigation of the victim's family, friends and acquaintances, those most often guilty of everyday killings. Serial deaths often occur on an entirely different plane, crimes committed randomly for reasons only the killers can know.

Flores shifts around on the rock and pulls out a stick of gum, a poor substitute for his much-lamented Marlboros. He unwraps it with care, places the minty-tasting gum into his mouth and systematically folds the aluminum foil again and again until it's reduced to a little square packet. This goes into his pocket as he settles back and lets his eyes travel across the landscape. Beneath him, snaking down from the mountains to the north, is the winding path of the Rio Grande with its skirt of cottonwood trees, the so-called "Bosque" that meanders through Albuquerque like a broad green highway.

As his eyes explore the scene his mind is elsewhere, tugging and poking at the challenges of his unsolved case.

The evidentiary record of each serial murder contains special details, clues left whether deliberately or from careless habit, that identify it as part of a series and that may eventually connect the crimes with their perpetrators. These are like delicate, tangled threads that can, if unraveled with care and diligence, reveal the identity of the killer.

They can be simple facts about how the perpetrator works, such as the profile of his preferred victims, manner of death, presence of sexual violation or mutilation, location, choice of time and many other factors.

Sometimes serial killers deliberately leave behind markers as special clues, things such as written messages, symbols carved on the victim, or distinctive objects such as a playing card. Others take trophies away with them, sometimes even parts of the victim's bodies.

Another tell of the serial murder is the technique of displaying the victim as was done in the Greenwald case. The corpse was elaborately arranged with care and attention to detail, almost as a mortician would prepare a cadaver for viewing in a casket. The dead man was dressed and groomed as if ready for an important business meeting. For lack of similar reference cases Flores cannot tell what if any details of this case may be critical clues, yet they are suggestive of serial murder.

He knows that the lack of parallel cases could mean

several things. An obvious possibility is that this is only the first in a new series of crimes. That's his biggest concern: that more gruesome killings are to come—yet if true why have six long months gone by without a repeat?

With each passing week it becomes more likely the killing is not part of a serial killing spree at all, but a carefully planned and executed one-off murder carried out for a specific and personal purpose. That would mean the choice of victim was far from random. The killer might have set up the death scene to mimic the methods of serial murderers precisely in order to provide cover for a very real underlying motive.

With that in mind Flores has dug into the victim's past in search of possible cause for a vengeful killing, or one aimed at providing the killer with some advantage, such as business opportunity. Drawing boxes and lines on a large piece of construction paper the detective has created a diagram of Greenwald's friends, relatives and associates, scribing lines to connect each interrelationship. The chart, looking much like a spider's web with the box portraying Greenwald as the captured insect at the center, is posted on the wall outside the detective's office and had been annotated by deputies with checkmarks and notations as the investigation progressed.

Focusing on these connections he and his investigative team have spent more than 700 hours of the sheriff's department's time seeking some unsuspected motive that could have driven someone to plan and execute a complex and vicious premeditated murder. Each party had been interviewed, financial records examined, past events reviewed, official noses poked into dozens of private lives and myriad notebooks filled with irrelevant facts.

Not even the least reason for suspicion had been revealed and nothing has been added to the diagram for several weeks. In fact all the deputies assigned to Flores are working other cases and even he is only able to pursue it to the extent of staying alert for a possible break.

The sheriff's detective has by no means dismissed the possibility this is a serial killing, and the lack of evidence pointing to a suspect from among those around Greenwald underscores this hunch. He begins his daily routine each morning by searching crime reports from across the nation. He uses Lexis/Nexis and a focused set of keywords to seek news of any crime with similarities to the Greenwald case. He also searches FBI crime reports and even summaries from Interpol.

Flores knows the lack of follow-up killings doesn't rule out a serial event, especially if this is a first instance. Serial killers often start out slow and build momentum over time so a long delay isn't really unusual, especially if he's dealing with a beginner.

He shudders at the thought of a second murder, or worse, an escalating cascade of killings. The pressure to solve the case will become intense to say the least.

Nothing has panned out and a frustrated Flores sits now gazing across the Rio Grande valley at the distant peaks of long-extinct volcanoes that line the western horizon. The case remains as cold as ever, its prospects as barren as the desert that surrounds him. He can understand Marsha Greenwald's anger at his failure to solve the case, for he shares it himself.

For a moment he ponders whether he should reopen communication with the woman, to apologize for his reaction to her constant calls and demands. He looks down at his feet and idly stirs loose gravel with the end of his stick. No, he decides, better to keep that door closed, at least for now. Meanwhile he's determined to hold the case alive, hoping for a break.

He stands and turns to study the winding trail that leads to the looming ridge-top of the mountain. The aggrieved bird has returned and sits on a more distant branch, watching him resentfully with dark little eyes.

"Sorry," he apologizes, resuming his upward climb. Somehow the trail seems less steep than before.

Chapter Nine

Jeremy Barth

Coffee cup in hand the man with the forgettable face steps out onto the porch of his New Mexico house, the one in which he grew up and that he inherited when his parents died in a mysterious accident. Back at last from the tumult and insanity of Wall Street he gazes with satisfaction toward the rising sun, just now ascending over the Sandia Crest. It spills golden light across nearby fields and a sandy arroyo and warms his upturned face.

Newly retired, Barth is a man with a plan. He sips from the cup and sets it on the porch railing, his mind busy with tasks to be performed and details to be attended to. He glances around the yard, meticulously maintained by a reliable service during his long absences.

The house itself appears ordinary and yet has been kept in top condition, with new roof and windows installed in recent years. The bungalow is painted a luscious pale blue with yellow trim, eye candy among the desert landscape. The driveway passes to the left side to a large detached garage in the rear. Barth's pale tan seven-year-old Kia is parked in the front, still bearing its New York plates and dusty with long highway miles. There are no other houses nearby, just empty desert with a mixture of junipers, cacti and various other plants.

Barth picks up the cup and drains the last of the coffee. He turns and goes back into the house, stopping in the efficient little kitchen to refill the cup. The house is laid out in shotgun style with a central hallway leading back and rooms to each side. In the front are a dining room on the left and living room on the right. Beyond lies the kitchen on the left, connecting with the dining room through swinging double cafe doors. On the right facing the kitchen are a utility and laundry room and a large storage room and pantry.

Next in line are a locked door on the left beyond the kitchen, followed by a little den and a bathroom on the left. A guest bedroom is on the right, followed by two more bedrooms flanking the rear of the house. Except for the utility and storage spaces, each room has windows with pleasant views and roll-down privacy shades. The house is isolated, surrounded on all sides by a quarter-mile or more of desert.

Barth walks toward the back of the house and pauses at the locked door that stands between the kitchen and den. It's a steel door with heavy hinges and thick protective plates around the high-security lock. The door is set in heavy steel framing and has a no-nonsense look designed to intimidate any who dared break into this house. At the side is a keypad to control an alarm system.

Barth punches in a code on the electronic pad. A green light blinks and he turns a key to unlock the door. As he swings it open lights come on, revealing a stairway descending to the basement. Barth goes down, stepping carefully to keep from spilling his coffee.

The basement is spacious, underlying nearly the full house, and has been partitioned into several rooms. The main room is a large study that lies beneath the front half of the house. It's a comfortable space richly finished with wood paneling and expensive carpeting. An antique desk dominates one end and bookshelves line an entire wall. In an opposite corner sit a tan leather couch and matching chair, each flanked by side tables with crystal table lamps. There are fine paintings and some pieces of sculpture collected over the years, many from New York galleries.

Although he's kept a low profile throughout his life, Barth is not without means. As an internal auditor having increasing power within one of Wall Street's leading investment banks, it had been a trivial task for him to amass a war chest of secret funds. In relatively tiny increments and over a period of years, riding on the coattails of multi-billion dollar transactions, he'd diverted and squirreled away more than twenty million dollars, well-concealed in offshore accounts. Some of the funds had been invested over a period of several years in preparation for his retirement plans.

Barth passes through the study to a short hallway that leads further back into the basement. He enters a side room that's outfitted as a workroom or shop. Here is a long bench backed with tools arrayed in order on perforated wallboard. A small metal lathe, a bench-mounted vice, a band saw and a drill press stand ready for use.

On the opposite wall is a work area with a small foreman's desk and tall swivel chair. Behind the chair stands a substantial gun safe nearly five feet wide and with both key and combination locks. Sitting, Barth wheels the chair around to face the safe. He inserts and turns the key then spins the wheel to unlock it. Inside is a tall space intended for long guns and indeed several rifles and shotguns are racked there. To one side is a row of pigeonholes to hold handguns or ammunition. Each is occupied. Below are several drawers, including a tall, deep one that extends the full width of the safe.

Barth slides that drawer open to reveal a row of book-like record boxes intended for the storage of accounting records. The boxes are ranked across the drawer with their spines facing up.

He sits for a moment merely gazing at the boxes. There are more than twenty of them, each carefully labeled on its spine with names and dates. He lightly runs his fingers over them, first to the right then back, stopping on the first box at the far left. He caresses the label. It reads: "Donald Greenwald, June 14, 1975." Gently he lifts the box from the drawer and turns to place it almost reverently on the little desk. He opens it.

Inside are a number of documents, some old, some new. A top sheet contains a list of the contents, which include copies of birth certificates, voter registrations, tax returns, credit reports and notes of personal observations made of the target over a period of many years. In this particular box there are also photographs, images of a man laid out on the sand of a desert.

Barth sits back to contemplate his triumph. In his mind he travels back in time to the clear, frozen memory of the event that placed Greenwald at the top of the things-to-do list for Barth's retirement plan.

It's June 1975. Barth is a graduate student at UNM, about to receive his MBA degree. Struggling to overcome his shy, geeky nature he's at last worked up the courage to ask one of his fellow students for a dinner date. Shelly Richards is a slender brunette with a nice figure, large, liquid eyes and full lips. Quick to smile, she has a ringing laugh that signals her good humor.

For months Barth has hungered for the attention of this woman. She appears to be popular yet doesn't seem to have any steady attachment. Surely she would never entertain dating such an ordinary man as he, and yet her attraction continues to draw on him. At last he makes a move.

They happen to be seated side-by-side in a class on corporate finance. Both are busily writing notes as the presenter delves into the arcane art of advanced accounting. Despite his interest in the subject, Barth finds it hard to concentrate. He imagines a glow of warmth emanating from the woman at his side, although she appears to pay him no attention. At last the class draws to an end and the students begin to stir.

Barth watches as the woman moves to put her notes away in her backpack. Suddenly, on impulse and before she can get up he turns to her with an appealing gaze. He feels like a peasant before a queen and yet he cannot stop himself.

"Ms. Richards..." He pauses, almost chokes. "Shelly..."

She turns to look at him, curious. Her eyebrows rise in query.

"Yes, Jeremy?"

"Would you, that is, could you..." He pauses again as he feels the betraying flush rise up his neck. Somehow he finds the power to surge ahead. "That is, could I buy you dinner sometime?"

Shelly gazes at him for a moment, then her smile appears and she laughs. Barth's heart seems to stop. That laugh is like a knife, cutting to the quick. He begins to turn away, the flush now rising to his cheeks. His hands begin to shake and he can feel sweat popping out on his back. It's a disaster, even worse than he feared. And yet, suddenly the situation changes.

"Jeremy, please don't be embarrassed," she

says, placing her left hand on his forearm. "I'd be glad to have dinner with you."

Barth is stunned and for an instant he can't find words.

"Really?" he manages at last. "You're really serious?"

Shelly laughs again, her eyes twinkling. "Of course I'm serious. What did you have in mind?"

Barth's mind swirls. He hasn't really thought it out that far. His en–treaty was on the spur of the moment and for once he's caught without a plan. With virtually no experience as a social creature he knows little about the restaurant scene. Images flutter through his brain, pictures of restaurant ads, newspaper reviews, scenes of elaborate dining rooms with linen cloths, silver and crystal, cocktails and wine with gourmet meals.

"Why, er, how about Bruno's Bistro?" he blurts out. "On Saturday?"

In the 1970s Bruno's was top-ranked as perhaps the finest and most expensive restaurant in Albuquerque. Barth had once paused to read the menu posted beside the door and to gaze through the glass at candle-lit tables, a room filled with gaily dressed women and men in dark suits being served by uniformed waiters.

Shelly smiles again and nods. "Yes, sure, that would be wonderful. Thank you for asking me Jeremy." She rises and picks up her backpack. "Do you want to meet there or pick me up at my apartment?"

Again Barth is caught off guard, having no idea of the proper etiquette for a first date. His car is practically a wreck, nearly 20 years old and such an embarrassment that he makes a habit of parking it some distance away from the campus to assure it will never be seen. And yet, the thought of picking up his date is compelling. He realizes that he can rent a car for the occasion, and quickly agrees to provide transportation. They agree on a time and she gives him her address and phone number.

Giving him a parting smile Shelly walks away leaving Barth in a state of agitation at the consequences of his sudden conquest. His mind is whirling with plans. He'll need to buy a new suit, and a good one at that. He needs a haircut—no, not that, a style job, a first for him. And, better have his nails done. New shoes, of course. And arrange to rent a car. What should he get? A sports car perhaps, maybe a Corvette. Could it be possible to rent such an exotic machine? He doesn't know, but he'll find out.

Saturday night comes and at seven o'clock Barth stops in front of Shelly Richards' apartment building driving a modest but new Buick hardtop coupe, rented that afternoon. He's wearing a muted gray pinstriped three-piece suit with a white shirt and maroon tie featuring tiny flying ducks. Such agonies he's subjected himself to in making these decisions. He shudders at the thought that some oversight or misstep will make him appear foolish or even stupid on this night of nights.

Shelly is waiting in the lobby and comes out immediately. Barth jumps from the car and hurries around to open the door for her. To his hungry eyes she's a radiant dream, an angel dressed in a frilly pastel dress with matching shoes. Her hair is gleaming and has been arranged with a tortoiseshell comb. A simple strand of pearls and matching earrings are her only jewelry. She takes her seat, looking around the car with approval, and as he returns to the driver's seat she turns to him and smiles.

"Why Jeremy, I had no idea! You could be on the cover of GQ."

GQ? Barth isn't sure what that means but takes it as a compliment. He manages a weak grin and puts the car into gear without a word. Shelly sits back and watches the traffic as he drives. The silence draws out until it becomes uncomfortable for them. Shelly decides to launch a conversation.

"So, Jeremy, I don't know much about you I guess." She turns toward him again and places a hand on his elbow. "Tell me about yourself."

Barth feels the telltale flush take root in his neck and begin to rise. Here is his greatest fear, the traumatic moment he's dreaded. But he's prepared for it and now he brings forth his story. Stumbling at first he describes growing up in Albuquerque as the town itself grew into a city. He tells of boyhood hobbies—ham radio, rockets, collecting leaves and flowers—the details of a happy if mostly fictional youth.

"What sports did you play?" she asks, drawing a suspicious glance from Barth. He was president of the high school chess club and he tells her so before realizing what a geek he's painting himself as. But she surprises him with her response.

"I played some chess myself. It's fun. I like people with more brains than brawn."

Barth feels the flush receding and his spirits

rise a few millimeters. He talks of his college days, how he earned magna cum laude status with his B.S. in accounting. He talks of his plans to take the CPA exams after finishing his MBA.

"And what about you?" he ventures. "You seem to be on a similar track for an MBA. Are you going for a CPA or into management?"

"Well, I'm not sure yet. Yes, I am taking some advanced accounting and statistics, but I like the management courses and may go in that direction." She fidgets with her pearl string and looks away. "My father's a big shot in aeronautics, a senior VP with one of the companies that makes military jets. I'm thinking of adding a degree in a technology field and going into product development and marketing."

"Oh," Barth says and lapses back into silence, pondering how far more glamorous such a career would be compared with his own goal of becoming a boring, everyday, plain vanilla certified public accountant. They drive on without further words, arriving at the restaurant a few minutes later. He turns the car keys over to an attendant with a flourish and hands the youth a dollar.

Inside they're met by a headwaiter wearing an elegant tuxedo and with pomaded hair that almost looks like it could be made of plastic. His matching mustache could have been glued on just moments ago. This vision of authority stands behind a mahogany lectern, running his finger down the appointment list. He looks up expectantly.

"Good evening sir, and welcome to Bruno's Bistro. Do you have a reservation?"

Nervously, Barth shakes his head. He fumbles in his pocket and hands the headwaiter two dollars. A look of surprise passes quickly over the maitre'd's face as he makes the bills disappear.

"We can seat you now," he says with a smirk. "Please come this way." He picks up two menus and a leather bound wine list and leads them toward a banquette table about halfway down the left wall. The seats are butter-soft red leather and the walls are covered in flocked red cloth with a gold pattern of fleur-de-lis. Low-key lighting illuminates the setting for two, complete with fine china and crystal. A waiter appears behind the headwaiter and steps forward as the other withdraws.

"Good evening. My name is Donald and I'll be your waiter tonight," the young man tells them. "Kind of a corny line, isn't it, but that's what we're told to say," he adds with a grin. "Can I get you a cocktail to start?"

Barth looks at Shelly for a cue. She seems to think for an instant before ordering a whisky sour. Barth asks for the same and the waiter departs. An assistant appears to fill their water glasses and place a basket of bread on the table. He disappears and Barth and Shelly look around the room. Silence once again descends. Barth's on edge, knowing he should be talking but finding it hard to put words together.

"This is really nice," Shelly says at last, unfolding her napkin and placing it in her lap. "I've never been in such a fine restaurant."

Barth starts to tell her that he hasn't, either, but chokes it off and tries to look nonchalant. Following her lead he unfolds his napkin too then nervously shuffles the salt and pepper shakers to clear some space on the table. He picks up the menus and hands her one with a flourish. This isn't going well, he thinks, resolving to turn the tides of his fortune.

"Well, I've been wanting to try Bruno's for some time," he offers vaguely. "It's got five stars in the guidebooks, so it should be good. Let's see what's on the menu." He opens his and begins to study it and after gazing at him for a moment Richards follows suit.

"Oh," she remarks. "They have oysters on the half shell. Do you like those? I love them."

Barth has never eaten an oyster and wonders if he could possibly like them, but throwing caution aside he nods in agreement.

"We'd like two orders of oysters on the half shell," he calls out to a passing busboy. The youth looks at him almost in fear, mutters something and shuffles quickly away.

"Well, what's up with him," Barth remarks. "Maybe this place isn't all it's supposed to be. That waiter was rude."

Shelly says nothing and in an instant Donald appears at Barth's elbow.

"Are you ready to order?" he asks. Barth thinks of complaining about the busboy's supposed slight but catches himself.

"Yes, we'd like two orders of oysters," he says. The waiter makes a note on his pad and looks up expectantly. "We haven't made up our mind about a main course," Barth adds and the waiter disappears.

After studying the menu again they decide on entrees. Shelly chooses a stuffed pork chop with rice and mushrooms served with a side order of spinach. Barth decides on a T-bone steak with baked potato and a plain salad. Many of the dishes have French names and Barth is hesitant to try anything he doesn't understand. Donald appears once more to ask whether they've made a wine selection.

Barth glances at the heavy leather-bound wine list and knows that it contains mysteries far beyond his ken. He extends a hesitant hand to pick up the tome, then pauses and looks up at the waiter searchingly.

"We have a number of fine house selections," Donald says, smoothly picking up on the cue. "That includes a number of red wines that would go well with your choices."

Lunging at this easy solution to his dilemma Barth pulls back his hand and asserts: "We'll have a bottle of your best house bordello."

The waiter goggles at Barth for a moment then despite himself he begins to snicker. A couple at a nearby table have overhead and the man begins to laugh. His companion leans forward and he whispers something to her whereupon she also begins to laugh, sneaking a look at Barth. The assistant waiter appears and when Donald tells him what Barth has just said he laughs out loud.

Drawn by the laughter other waiters appear and after whispering among themselves begin to join in the hilarity. Barth hears someone several tables away say to his date, "That man just ordered a bottle of bordello," followed by more laughter. Patrons at several other tables begin to spread the report of Barth's faux pas *and within seconds almost the entire room fills with mirth.*

Barth knows he's done something wrong but is too naive to know what. He glances at Shelly, glad to see she's keeping her face in a neutral expression. He looks back to the waiter beseechingly.

"Well, sir, that was sure a good one," Donald asserts.

Barth looks confused. "I don't understand," he manages to say. "Don't you have any bordello?"

The waiter looks around at what has become an audience and proclaims in a voice loud enough to be heard several tables away: "No, sir, I'm afraid our wine list does not include any Italian houses of ill repute." He begins to laugh again.

At this Shelly can no longer hold back and begins to snicker, joined by a chorus of fellow diners and several waiters and assistants that have gathered around the humorous patron.

At Shelly's laugh Barth freezes like a rabbit sensing the shadow of an eagle. A few days earlier he imagined her laugh as a knife, cutting into his guts. Now he knows that feeling for real. He knows he's screwed up somehow, but this waiter, this man, this...Donald something has made a fool of him, has publicly humiliated him in front of Shelly Richards. And, he realizes, she'll be certain to tell this story to everyone at UNM. This is a disaster of untold magnitude.

Barth almost shrinks in his chair as the laughter dies away. The other servers leave and diners turn back to their meals.

"Would you like to order some actual wine?" the waiter inquires. Despite his normal reserve he cannot keep a sarcastic note from his voice. He grins and Barth's face becomes a mask of hatred.

"No, God damn you," Barth hisses through gritted teeth. "I don't want anything from you." He stands up, throws his napkin onto the table and begins to walk rapidly toward the exit. Both Shelly and the waiter stare after him open-mouthed.

Halfway across the room Barth stops and spins around. He stalks back and confronts the waiter face to face from only two feet. His lips curl and his eyes are flashing with hate.

"So, Mr. Donald," Barth snarls. "What's your real name, your full name?"

Startled, Donald Greenwald takes a step back. He regrets what's happened but has no inkling that his reaction to this man has set in motion a silent vendetta that will lead to his own death more than three decades later. At that instant he becomes a marked man.

Barth's mind brings him back to the present and he looks down at the open file box with satisfaction. He lifts the cover sheet and reaches for a red pen. Carefully he writes across the sheet "CASE CLOSED." He takes the Rolex from his pocket and places it into the box both as trophy and evidence of success. He closes the box and returns it to the drawer.

Once again he runs his fingertips across the row of boxes, more than twenty new cases to be pursued. Each is a perceived insult to be avenged, a suppurating wound in his twisted soul that has eaten at him during decades of careful planning and preparation for vengeance.

Sighing happily he reaches for the next box in line, the next enemy to receive the badge of retirement.

Chapter Ten

Rob Charlton

Although I'm working on another case the mystery of Greenwald's murder still dominates my thoughts. The new job is a step above the usual assignments to spy on misbehaving husbands, but it uses relatively few brain cells. I'm sitting in my maroon baby staking out a warehouse store where valuable merchandise has been disappearing at an alarming rate. The manager is convinced that some of his employees are to blame. My task is to identify how they're doing it.

Stakeouts are probably the most boring part of law enforcement work. I hadn't been involved in one since early in my FBI career and I'd forgotten how mind-sucking it is to sit in a dark car with a pair of binoculars, a thermos of coffee and a box of donuts. Well at least I'm beyond donuts now. Through exquisite tactical planning I've prepared a supply of chicken salad sandwiches, some hard-boiled eggs and a large Polish pickle, all safely preserved in a little soft-sided cooler that sits on the seat beside me. I have some bottles of water in there, too, but can't consume too much without challenging my aging, ever-shrinking bladder.

The good part of stakeout work is that it gives you a lot of time to think. Back in the day, as a young pup I used to spend the time contemplating the mysteries of baseball, women, ways to get out of stakeout work, and women. Huh. Here I am nearly three decades later with no woman in my life, sitting in a lonely car doing exactly what I had wanted to avoid. At least I still have baseball but damn those Rangers! I might as well go whole hog on sports angst and become a Cubs fan. Yeah, that'll be the day.

I'm parked halfway up a small hill about a block away from the loading dock area behind the store, far enough not to be noticed but near enough to scan the area with my image stabilized ten-power binoculars. My windows are tinted all around and it's nighttime so nobody can see me lurking in here. I've got at least two more hours to go before the night staff leaves. That's when things might get interesting. I fill the time thinking about Greenwald.

It would be nice to know the details of the sheriff's department investigation, to examine the evidence in the case file and compare it with the few things I've gleaned in my own investigation. Without context nothing I've learned appears to have any evidentiary value. If only I had something solid to use for barter—and if my client hadn't fucked with Flores' head—that would be a possibility. But I've got nada so if I showed up on his doorstep the detective would not only invite me to leave, but might even bring charges for interfering with a criminal investigation.

Big bummer. It was probably a fat mistake to get involved in this. Maybe I should return Mrs. Greenwald's retainer and beg off.

And yet the case appeals as a challenge to my detecting skills for the very fact of its mysterious nature. It has the earmarks of a classic episode in the annals of crime, perhaps even to compare with the cases of David Berkowitz the "Son of Sam," Ted Bundy, or even the unsolved Boston Strangler or Zodiac cases.

The elaborate display of the victim's body is unique in my experience, leaving no doubt in my mind that it was the work of an obsessed serial murderer, perhaps a beginner just starting to get his boots on. And the enigma of the engraved watch with its "retirement" message is suggestive of something…but what?

I fill my time reviewing what I remember about the nature of serial killers, gleaned from training at the FBI's Quantico profiling center and personal observations from cases I worked. Serial killers are rarely stupid, at least the successful ones who generally have IQ's significantly above average. That would have to be true in this case for to conduct such a complex killing without leaving a single meaningful clue was clearly a *tour de force*, the work of a high level criminal mind.

In general, serial killers are frequently bullied as children and likely come from troubled or broken families. Many are abused and engage in sadism and fire buggery as children. As adults, many have trouble holding jobs and tend to do menial work.

And yet there are no hard and fast rules, for according to FBI profilers some serial killers appear perfectly normal and lead apparently unremarkable lives. In a way individuals in this category are leading two completely separate existences, with a second, secret life that's carefully disguised and hidden. Ted Bundy, for example, was to all appearances a good citizen, often dating women whom he treated with respect, a gentleman. He was a charismatic law student who was active in campus politics, and yet also a monster that kidnapped young women with whom he had no connection to rape, torture and murder.

I set down the binoculars and reach into my cooler for a sandwich. Just as I take a bite my cell phone goes off, not with the theme from *The Untouchables* but in vibe mode.

One early lesson for stakeout personnel is to avoid anything that might call attention to you and ringing cell phones can be the suck. I set down the sandwich and fumble in my pocket. Extracting the phone I answer with my practiced happy persona.

"Hello, Rob Charlton Investigations. How may I help you?"

Oops. Too late I glance at the caller ID and notice that it's the retired professor from Taos, the one who thinks—make that thought—that I'm a freelance writer.

There's a moment of silence then Humphrey's voice comes over the airwaves. He sounds tentative, definitely suspicious.

"Mr. Charlton? This is Willard Humphrey. I thought you were a writer?"

Thinking fast I manage to catch the ball just before it sails over the centerfield fence.

"Yes sir, I am. I specialize in investigative reporting."

This is only a slight deviation from the facts, kind of like the legal distinctions surrounding the meaning of the word "is". I do investigate, and I do write reports, so my statement is completely true while also being grossly misleading. Sheep, meet wolf.

"Oh." The Professor seems to mull over my answer for a moment before continuing. "I see," he says at last. "I hope I'm not calling too late?" I assure him he isn't and he goes on: "Well, you asked me to call if I could think of any more information you could use for your article. I did come up with a few things and made some notes. Is this a good time?"

I say it's fine, put the phone on speaker and pull out my notebook. He begins to relate some minor details about goings-on at the architecture school during the 1970s, including anecdotes and facts about several of his fellow faculty members. He talks of some engineering challenges that were encountered and how features of ancient pueblo construction were being integrated into modern house design. I listen patiently. It seems like a waste of time but one thing I've learned is never to pass up the chance to gain information that might bear on a case, no matter how unlikely it is.

After about ten minutes he begins to run down and pauses for a moment before adding in an uncertain tone: "Oh, and I remembered something about that student you were interested in, Donald Greenwald, the one who was murdered..."

My ears perk up like those of a fast dog that's just spotted a slow rabbit.

"Oh, it probably isn't important," he goes on, about to blow it off. I murmur something about one never knowing and he continues.

"Well, you seemed interested in him and how I told you he had been working his way through university. I remembered something about one of the jobs he had. He was a waiter in a restaurant."

Hmm. Another useless factoid? Probably, but I push ahead, asking for details.

"I happened to be having dinner one night with the dean and his wife and Greenwald was our waiter. He seemed to be a bit embarrassed, but I remember he did an excellent job of serving us."

"When would this have been?"

"Oh, I don't know. Sometime in the mid-70s. I couldn't say for sure."

"What's the name of the restaurant?" I'm scrawling in my notebook by the dim light of a distant streetlamp. He hesitates, apparently stumped, probably wondering what difference it makes. After a moment of reflection he says he can't remember the name.

"I don't think it's still around," he adds. "It was a fancy

joint that used to be over on Central, a French restaurant now that I think about it. You know, uniformed waiters, impressive decor, imported wine, that kind of thing. It wasn't the sort of place I usually went to. The dean chose it and he used to enjoy living large as they say. Lord I still remember that night."

He laughs. "First time I ate snails. Never did it again either." He starts to expand on the subject of exotic foods but realizes he's blathering and curbs his tongue. I wait to see if there's any more but he's apparently run the well of his memory dry. I thank him and we end the call.

Hmm. I close my notebook and tuck it back in my pocket. So Greenwald was a restaurant waiter. So what. Big whoopie doo. It could have been during the time of the date on the watch, June 14, 1975—but it's most likely unrelated to the bizarre killing. I'll have to check it out just because that's the way I work, but I don't hold out much hope for this possible lead.

Sighing I pick up my sandwich and take another bite. What a hell of a way to spend the evening, when I could have gone to the Isotopes game. As ball players go they're not very hot shakes, but it's the only game in town. At least they could probably beat the Cubbies about four games out of five, so there's that.

Chapter Eleven

Jeremy Barth

It's late afternoon as Barth steps back to the front porch of his house. He's holding a crystal glass and a bottle of French Bordeaux. During his adult life he's overcome his ignorance of the mysteries of the vine. In one corner of his kitchen is a built-in climate-controlled wine cabinet holding an eclectic selection of fine wines, some laid down a decade or more ago.

Now permanently reestablished in New Mexico, Barth is preparing to launch the next phase of his retirement plan. Much has already been done, key elements laid into place over several years. His methods have been successfully tested with the retirement of Donald Greenwald. Barth is excited for at last he's ready to put the full plan into operation, a plan that has been in the making for more than two decades.

Deeming this an appropriate time to celebrate his return, Barth has opened a bottle of Haut Brion 2000 vintage and let it breathe for an hour on the little sampling table in one corner of the kitchen. Now he pours the glass half full and holds it up toward the sky. He tips it gently to let the ruby wine swirl around the crystal, raises it to his nose and inhales deeply. He takes a sip and rolls it around his tongue, sighing with pleasure.

To one side stand a pair of wooden Adirondack chairs Barth had purchased some years before during a trip to Maine. The original paint has been stripped and redone in the same pale blue as the siding of the house. Barth settles happily into the left-hand chair, placing the bottle and glass beside him on a low bench. He gazes up at the cerulean New Mexican sky, unblemished by clouds. The sun descending into the west bathes his face with golden light. Barth is content. He reaches for the glass and takes another sip.

He's spent the day reviewing files and planning his next move. As always his program is meticulously organized. The details of each planned retirement are laid out in a professional project planning software program. Barth approaches his plan with the dedication and skill that a competent CEO would bring to a billion dollar corporation. Presently he's nearly completed working out the details for another half-dozen of his twenty-some retirement candidates.

His program already represents years of effort. A major achievement has been to create an organization with several layers of deception. To this end he's recruited three partners, investing some of the millions extorted from his employer to set up each associate with the least possible connection with himself. From years on Wall Street, Barth knows that with sufficient funds almost anything is possible and he has spared none of his former employer's money in the effort.

Each partner has been provided with a false identity, including official birth certificates, bank accounts, credit cards, social security numbers, passports, even ownership of real estate and careers. To further muddy the picture, false records have been created all the way back to kindergarten and grade school.

The first key partner in what Barth humorously likes

to think of as Retirement Consultants, Inc., is Jake Wilson, who appears in public records as a technical rep for a software firm. The company is in fact a shell formed by Barth along with several others during a "holiday" trip to the Bahamas some years earlier.

The authorities would have to dig deep and hard to discover that Wilson is not what he seems. He earns a six-figure salary direct deposited each month in his bank account, where it's augmented every December by a handsome bonus. Each April federal and state tax returns are filed in his name through a reputable CPA firm.

According to the records, Wilson is an accomplished marksman, hunter and former Special Forces officer. He owns a house in the outskirts of Albuquerque but is seldom seen by neighbors and is believed to spend a lot of time traveling on business. His travel expenses are paid through a complex chain of faked documentation, dozens of airline tickets and hotel bills paid from a San Francisco bank account in the name of an offshore company.

Wilson drives a three-year-old beige commercial van, the kind with no windows in the rear and a large sliding door on the right side. The ordinary looking van is kept in a garage behind his house, located on an isolated lot surrounded by overgrown brush and trees and chosen in part for the very fact of its isolation.

Wilson's taste in clothing runs to cowboy boots and jeans with flannel shirts and a wide belt with a silver buckle. Like all of Barth's associates Wilson is a loner who keeps to himself. Although seldom in residence he is sometimes seen hiking in the nearby desert, always alone.

Although he's been part of Barth's organization for six years, the two have never been seen in public together. The only visible connection between the two is a slender thread, the infrequent sight of Barth's Kia driving down a dusty, deserted lane to Wilson's house to be immediately hidden away from curious eyes inside the double garage.

Barth's two other associates have been provided with similarly complete backgrounds. The second to join the program was Jim Craig, now a purported petroleum engineer who lives in Oklahoma City but is often believed to be away working consulting jobs in places such as Nigeria or on the North Slope. Craig owns a condo and keeps a vintage white Stingray hardtop in addition to a dull gray van. He's known to enjoy country-western music and was once seen playing the slots at a nearby Indian casino.

The third of Barth's partners, Robert Singleton, is based in Colorado and like the others is seldom present at his home, a neat little house in a secluded location on the Front Range about twenty miles west of Denver. Singleton is purported to be a management consultant who spends months at a time on overseas assignments in Europe and the Far East. Because of his exotic travel some of his neighbors suspect he's a CIA operative. Although there's absolutely no evidence to support this idea, through subtle suggestions Singleton has carefully planted that seed of speculation.

Singleton owns a metallic blue Chevrolet Bronco 4WD as well as a chocolate colored panel van. He's known to enjoy classical music and video gaming.

Like Wilson, Craig and Singleton draw salaries. Although paid for by Barth via a series of electronic funds transfers through investment fronts set up as channels for his financial dealings, the properties and vehicles are owned outright in the partners' names.

There are definite pecuniary advantages to being an accomplished forensic auditor with connections at the highest level of international finance. Rising to a position of trust in charge of internal audits at a major investment bank, Barth has made full use of these opportunities to set up his network. During the preparation phase of his plan he's used Wilson, Craig and Singleton to research potential retirees, scout locations, and perform certain tasks when Barth doesn't want to be directly involved.

Now that his retirement plan is going into full operation his partners will take more active roles, including the performance of retirements. For this reason he's provided each with a panel van, the kidnapper's vehicle of choice. By operating with his associates as a coordinated "gang," but one made up of loners with no apparent connection between its members, Barth is spreading a fog of uncertainty around his program of crime, both to confuse the authorities and to give him wide freedom of action.

He intends to minimize his personal footprint while acting in turn through his three associates to perform the carefully planned and coordinated retirements. Sometimes he will act through Wilson, other times Craig or Singleton. It was Wilson, in fact, who had performed Donald Greenwald's retirement. But no matter who actually performs the act, behind each retirement will be the vengeful Barth himself.

He drains the glass and pours more of the wine. As before he raises the crystal to the sky, admiring the ruddy color of the Bordeaux, now accentuated by the warm glow of the setting sun. The sight of the gently swirling wine holds a strange fascination for him as his subconscious mind revels in recognition of the age-old affinity between red wine and sacrificial blood, a connection that has deep roots in human psychology.

He lowers the glass to his lips and drinks.

David L. Brown

Chapter Twelve

Rob Charlton

I solve the mystery of the disappearing inventory and the thieves are locked up and charged with grand theft. They were pretty clever, I'll give them that. They re-packed expensive electronics and other high-value products into empty boxes of cheap bulk items such as toilet paper. The "empty" boxes were carried to dumpsters and picked up later at night along with their valuable contents.

I observe and videotape the pick-up from my maroon baby then follow the thieves to a house in a less than upscale part of town. Following my tip, a short time later the Albuquerque police raid the joint and discover a trove of stolen merchandise. Case closed.

After being on the job almost all night I sleep in, waking just in time to grab breakfast at my favorite diner. I go whole hog: biscuits with gravy, bacon, two eggs over easy, hash browns and OJ with a pot of coffee to get my eyes open.

Satisfied, I push back and pat my tummy. Hmm, is it getting a little softer lately? Gotta get back into those tummy-stretching exercises before I have to start investing in a new and more expansive wardrobe. Hate to think if those biscuits and gravy have anything to do with it. Nah,

I've been eating them for years with no problem, so that can't be it.

Back at my lair I sink into my comfy swivel chair and ponder the desk pad calendar in front of me. It features lots of empty spaces. My only open case is the Greenwald investigation, which has pretty much run aground and is probably in the process of sinking.

At least Marsha's been true to her promise not to call me six times a day like she did with poor old Flores. I'll bet the temptation to do so is eating her alive. The thought brings a little smile to my face and a warm feeling inside. Sometimes I wonder about myself.

Recalling last night's phone call from the retired professor I open my spreadsheet and enter the information about Donald Greenwald's work as a restaurant waiter. A slender reed indeed, and it's the only thing I have left to pursue. Not a very fertile investigation. Again I consider whether I shouldn't return Marsha's retainer and walk away. Well, no, that's not the Charlton style. I turn on my computer and begin to Google.

I soon learn that in the 1970s there was a French restaurant on Central called Bruno's Bistro. It was closed in 1998 with the retirement of the owner, Bruno Bisset. I learn from old newspaper reviews that Bisset was an accomplished French chef, a graduate of the Cordon Bleu school in Paris and winner of many ribbons and medals for his culinary skills.

Lord only knows what drew him to New Mexico. Maybe it was the climate, if he preferred dusty deserts and sunny days to the gloomy skies and bright lights of Paris. Perhaps it resulted from an *affaire de coeur*, for who knows about the motivations and strange doings of Frenchmen? I shrug off the thought.

Further research reveals that the former restaurant has been split up into several parts and is now home to a used clothing store, a bike shop and a computer repair joint. Obviously that part of Central has come down in the world. Talk about a dead-end lead. It hardly seems worth pursuing.

But I soldier on in the belief that a few more minutes will lead me to a blank wall. I savor the thought of closing the door on this tiny glimmer, kissing off Marsha and going on with my life. But no such luck. I do a Yahoo people search for Bruno Bisset and *voila!* I learn that a person of that name lives in the area. There's even a phone number. I pick up my iPhone, turn on the speaker and dial.

It rings six times before a voice comes on the line, a woman with a Hispanic accent. I ask for Mr. Bisset and she informs me that "El Patron" is having a nap and cannot be disturbed. Hmm, I seem to have tracked down Greenwald's former boss, for all the good it will do me. Thanking her I leave my number and ring off.

I spend some time paying bills and balancing my incredible shrinking checkbook then exercise my creativity by putting my feet on the desk and pondering the wall. Once again I meditate on my floundering career as a private investigator. I thought it might let me relive my glory days as a Fed, applying my knowledge and skills to bring justice to the world. Instead I've learned that private eyes spend most of their time skating a few dollars away from poverty.

Not only that, there's little sign of the kind of respect I was accustomed to when the full power of the United States government stood behind my badge. Now there's only Rob, alone with no badge and nothing behind except wide-open spaces. It's a whole different world out there than I'd realized.

Thank goodness for my pension and meager savings, but even that's being drained by the negative cash flow

I've incurred. The outrageous rent on this office comes every month as regular as clockwork, along with bills for electricity, internet and phone service, malpractice and liability insurance, advertising, payments on the equipment and furnishings I've bought on a credit card, gas for the maroon baby, and every fee and charge the city, county, state and federal governments can think up. My dream of a glamorous new career has led me into a money pit.

Maybe I should really think about the idea of becoming a writer. I could dump this place and set up a little workplace in one corner of my guest bedroom. I've already got everything I need, for what does a writer require but a computer for word processing? Hell, in the old days all it took was a goose quill and a bottle of ink. That was good enough for Shakespeare. I can make ends meet on the pension checks, so there wouldn't be much pressure to turn my golden words into the real thing.

But then again, could I live like that, hunched over a keyboard every day? I love investigating, following clues in the real world. Could I find satisfaction from fictional sleuthing? They say that truth is stranger than fiction, and it's definitely a lot more interesting, to me at least.

Here I am, feet up on my desk and leaning back in my chair, fingers intertwined behind my head and gazing at the wall. A question for the ages and I've got no idea which way to go.

My reverie is broken by the sound of my phone playing the rollicking notes of *The Untouchables* theme. I sit up and punch it on speaker.

"Hello, Rob Charlton Investigations. How may I help you?" In microseconds I transform myself from moody old washed-up detective to instant Mr. Congeniality. Of course it's all an act, but how much in life isn't?

"'Allo? This is Mr. Charlton?" It's the quavering voice

of an older man. The accent is French and the caller ID says "Bisset."

"Yes, thank you for calling back Mr. Bisset." I gather my thoughts for a moment, trying to decide how to approach this without sounding like an idiot. I decide on the direct approach. "I wanted to ask you some questions about your restaurant."

"*Quoi*? The restaurant she has been many years closed." He pronounces the last word as two syllables with emphasis on the -ed.

"Yes, I know. I'm a writer doing research for an article about Albuquerque in the 1970s. Your restaurant was important on the social scene back then. Could we meet for a few minutes to talk about your experiences?"

"I am the retired person now," he informs me, pronouncing it retire-ed. "I don't see how my restaurant she could be important this day."

I'm winging it to keep him on the line. I decide to pull out the card I've got hidden up my sleeve. It could turn out to be the joker.

"Actually," I tell him, "I'm writing about a man who used to work for you and who was recently murdered. His name was Donald Greenwald."

Bisset is silent for a long moment. I can hear him breathing into the phone. I expect he's vainly trying to recall my client's husband. During the years he operated Bruno's Bistro he must have had hundreds of employees. But I'm surprised.

"Ah, it is the tragedy," he murmurs. "*Oui*, quite well I remember Donald. He designed this house for me when he was a famous architect. It is a good house and he was *un homme bon*."

I've struck the right vein. Bisset agrees to see me and we set a time for the day after tomorrow at his place. I thank him, press the "end call" button and enter the appointment in my phone's calendar. This slender thread of a lead may still have some possibilities. I'm not sure if I'm even happy about that, but as Bisset would no doubt say, *c'est la vie.*

Putting my feet back on the desk I return to my inner conversation on the subject of Rob's uncertain future. Sometimes I wonder why I ever left Costa Rica with its gentle surf, pristine beaches, vibrant women and, oh yeah, the cheap booze. I was happy there, wasn't I? I ask the wall but it holds its secrets close.

Chapter Thirteen

Jeremy Barth

Barth catches an early morning flight to Denver and picks up a rental car. Within an hour he arrives at Robert Singleton's house. Barth is setting in motion the next in his planned series of retirements.

The neat bungalow is set among tall pines with a spectacular view along the Front Range toward Pikes Peak. Barth sits at the kitchen table to drink coffee and eat an early lunch with whole wheat bread, cold cuts, cheese and butter.

His rental car is locked away in the large garage at the back of the property and Singleton's panel van is parked in front of the house. The ordinary looking van is equipped with a concealed compartment built into the floor and which contains some of the tools of the retirement trade. They include ropes, chains, handcuffs and rolls of duct tape. There are no rear seats and the floor of the van is covered with a thick plastic sheet.

The candidate for retirement lives about an hour away in Boulder, home of the University of Colorado. A former acquaintance of Barth's in New York, he's now a visiting professor of finance at the university's business school. His carefully organized retirement is set for this evening, with Singleton officiating.

At about 11 a.m. a FedEx delivery truck comes up the lane and stops in front of the house. Singleton greets the deliveryman at the front door and signs for an overnight express box. It was shipped the previous day from Albuquerque on an account belonging to one of Barth's offshore front companies.

The box is placed on the kitchen table where Barth strips open one end to withdraw several items, each sealed in a plastic bag and cradled in bubble wrap. They include a compact .22 caliber pistol; a clamshell case containing three pre-loaded hypodermic syringes like those carried by diabetics; and a gold watch.

Satisfied that everything is in order, Barth moves to an easy chair in the living room and begins to review in his mind the details of today's retirement program. The subject is Morton J. Drake, a Harvard-educated former financial manager some years younger than Barth. The mistake that put him high on the list of retirement candidates was to disparage Barth during a nasty campaign for the office of president of the New York Financial Club more than twenty years before.

Barth had served the club faithfully as secretary and vice-president and was in line to become president. It would have been an important achievement, boosting his career trajectory at the Wall Street firm where he was a rising star in the finance department. Drake, an ego-driven Young Turk at a leading accounting firm, challenged Barth's nomination and launched his campaign through subtle attacks on Barth. Pretending to be merely joking he ridiculed Barth's lack of charisma and social polish. He mocked Barth's New Mexico degrees while touting his own Harvard pedigree. He wined and dined influential members to win their support for the presidency, always managing to denigrate Barth with a dismissing laugh.

When the vote was taken and Barth lost to the young

upstart, he had no reaction other than to submit his one-line written resignation from the club. A few days later Drake's name was added to an informal list Barth had begun, joining a growing coterie of those who had crossed Barth in some way and thus earned places in his retirement plan.

After more than two decades Drake's time has come. Barth has followed him carefully and knows his rigid patterns. Estranged from his wife, Drake lives alone in a condominium near the UC campus. He follows an unvarying schedule of activities, including a weekly poker game at a club located on the other side of Boulder. The game is set for tonight.

Singleton has reconnoitered the club, going so far as to buy a membership so that he could closely observe Drake. On several occasions he actually joined in the card game, thus making himself familiar to the object of his surveillance.

He'd observed that the obsessively punctual professor always arrives almost precisely at 8:30, a half-hour before the poker play begins. He'd noted the parking lot behind the club is almost always deserted at that time, and Drake's habit of parking his car by itself far in the poorly-lighted rear of the parking lot, perhaps to avoid dings from other car doors. As in everything else Drake is fastidious about his car, a late-model Lincoln that always looks as if it was just driven out of the showroom.

Through his rigid and obsessive patterns, Drake has set the stage for his own bizarre "retirement." Now, relaxing in his easy chair, Barth goes over each detail of the evening's plan. It's simplicity itself. He plays the action in his mind like a movie clip.

As Drake parks his Lincoln, Singleton pulls up beside it in the van. He jumps out and approaches

Drake as he gets out of his car, calling to him by name as if to an old friend. He reaches out to shake Drake's hand, holding a syringe hidden in his left. As they clasp hands Singleton suddenly pulls Drake toward him and there's a quick jab of a needle.

The syringe, filled with the same narcotic used to incapacitate wild animals, penetrates Drake's neck causing him to almost immediately become unconscious as the chemical reaches his brain. Singleton restrains his victim for the moment it takes for the drug to act then lets him slump to the ground. He looks around to be sure no one can see what he's doing. He slides open the side door of the van and stoops to quickly lift the limp body and hoist it inside. He slides the door shut, goes around to the driver's side door, gets in and drives away.

Barth plays the movie through his mind several times without finding any flaw. Now he rises, yawns and retires to the bedroom. The weather report is good, promising Singleton an easy drive to Boulder. Barth takes off his shoes and curls up on the bed for a restful nap.

Chapter Fourteen

Luis Flores

It's two days later and detective Flores is running his daily keyword search of the Internet, seeking possible connections to the Greenwald case. Sipping black coffee he scrolls through Lexis/Nexis files of current news. He flicks past an item from *The Denver Post,* hesitates then clicks back. The headline that catches his attention reads:

Cops Say Body Displayed
In Boulder Mystery Killing

The story is long on speculation and short on facts, but Flores learns that Morton Drake, a professor and finance expert from UC, was found dead in the nearby forest. The body is neatly displayed, lying on its back with hands on chest. The cause of death is a shot to the forehead with a small caliber bullet.

Flores reads the news item several times then jots down a few notes. The display of the body and shot to the head match the case of Greenwald, so there are two points of reference. He reaches for the telephone and dials information to get the number for the Boulder Police. In a few moments he's speaking with the detective assigned to the Drake murder, sergeant Robert Walton. He introduces himself and asks for details about the case. Walton resists at first, but after Flores describes the similarities between his case and the earlier killing in New Mexico he opens up.

"It's the strangest thing I've ever seen," he tells Flores. "That body was positioned like a cadaver in a funeral home, neat as a pin. The vic looked like he'd just decided to lie down and take a nap, as if he'd stand up and walk away just any minute now."

Flores tells him that was also true in the Greenwald case, adding that in that instance no useful evidence such as prints, trace or DNA was found.

"Yeah, same here," Walton replies. "Forensics did a complete workup and found nada. It's like the guy just dropped out of the sky. Hey, you don't think this was one of those UFO abductions do you?"

Flores denies the likelihood of that and pushes for more information. After discussing some additional observations they agree it's possible the killings are part of a series. Flores is about to end the conversation when Walton remembers one more thing.

"Funny thing, we found a wristwatch on the victim that was inscribed with some retirement message. It was the date that caught my eye."

"A watch?" Flores isn't very interested. "What made you notice that?"

"Well, the date didn't make sense. Here, let me check my notes again." There's a long pause, then: "Yeah, here it is, a gold Movado, and the inscription reads: 'To Dr. Morton J. Drake, Happy Retirement, November 12, 1989.' How's that for strange? The guy was still in his 20's then, so how could he have been retired?"

Flores is silent for a moment, writing in his own notebook. The watch probably doesn't mean anything but as a careful investigator he documents everything. He asks Walton to forward him a copy of the case file, thanks him and hangs up the phone.

He sits back in his chair for a moment, thinking. The mode of the Colorado killing is similar enough that it may be related to his case, and that would validate his perception of the Greenwald death as the work of a serial murderer. To Flores' relief the killer seems to have moved to another jurisdiction.

"Better Walton's cross to bear than mine," he murmurs as he puts his notebook back in the case file beside his computer, unaware that just a few miles away the perpetrator is enjoying breakfast.

Who would take so much trouble to send a message? he asks himself. That question calls for further investigation, but for now he has more pressing work to do. Shrugging he puts away the notebook and opens the file on a current case involving a fatal stabbing at a county park south of the city, the apparent result of a drug deal gone wrong.

David L. Brown

Chapter Fifteen

Rob Charlton

I'm a little early for my ten o'clock appointment with Bruno Bisset so I cruise the area in my maroon baby to kill some time, starting with a pass by the Bisset chateau. This is definitely an upscale neighborhood but Bisset's house stands out even among its hoity-toity neighbors. There must be some good bucks to be made serving up French dishes.

The building vaguely reminds me of something from a fairy tale, with a kind of watchtower on one end and a winding stairway leading to a huge, carved wood front door. The stucco walls are a pastel no doubt named something like "dusky pink" or "desert rose." The roof is Mexican tile and the large lot is lavishly landscaped with a variety of mature bushes and a few specimen trees.

After circling a few blocks I pull up and park in front of the house, ascend the winding steps and push on the bell. Inside I faintly hear chimes playing a passage I recognize from La Marseillaise, the French national anthem. Old Bruno may have spent most of his life as a New Mexican, but he's still a Frenchman to the end. I hear footsteps coming to the door. It opens and a woman wearing a maid's uniform looks out inquiringly. I identify myself and she gestures for me to enter.

The entrance hall is wide and long with pegged plank flooring and stucco walls. The space is tall, rising to skylights more than 20 feet above. It reminds me of the entrance at Marsha Greenwald's house, and then I remember Bisset saying that Greenwald designed this house, as he surely did his own. Donald must have had a thing for dramatic entrances. At the end of the hall a large Tricolor flag hangs as a reminder that this is home to a Frenchman.

Saying nothing the maid leads me to a side door and waves me into what could only be called a drawing room. It's at least thirty-five feet by twenty with rich wood paneling and a massive river rock fireplace at one side. Tall, narrow windows look out upon the landscaping.

A large painting above the carved fireplace mantle pictures Napoleon Bonaparte wearing splendid full dress uniform and mounted on a white horse. One hand is tucked inside his coat in his special personal style. In the background are glimpses of a battlefield scattered with broken gun carriages and the bodies of men and horses. No doubt the scene of some great victory for La Belle France.

Furniture is arranged in two conversation areas, one larger one with pairs of leather couches and chairs in front of the fireplace and the other an intimate space in one corner with two high-backed chairs facing each other across a small table. A bottle of wine stands open on the table along with two glasses, a plate of cheese and a loaf of bread. Hmm, a bit early in the day for drinking but it won't be my first time. After all it's always five o'clock somewhere. Hell, when I was in Costa Rica I even had a clock that was all fives.

The door opens and Bisset bustles into the room. A portly gentleman of about 80 he looks the part of an aging but well-fed chef, with extra chins and a round belly. His hair's gray but his blue eyes are bright and piercing. He shakes my hand and guides me to the little tasting table. I offer one of my freelance writer cards and take a seat.

He sits down opposite me and smiles. He's actually beaming. I'm reminded of statues of the Laughing Buddha, round and filled with jollity. Goodness, I've seldom felt so welcome. Without asking he pours wine into a glass and places it in front of me. He pours for himself and raises his glass.

"As you know, *monsieur*, wine is very important to we French people. There is an old saying in my country, *'Un jour sans vin est comme un jour sans soleil'*. It means in English 'A day without the wine is like a day without the sunshine'. Thank heavens for *le vin*, for without it we could not be French, *oui*?"

We click glasses and I take a sip. It's excellent, rich with flavor and without the bitter aftertaste of so many of the everyday bottles I buy at Marv's.

"And so we also enjoy *le pain*, or as you call it, bread, the staff of life," Bisset continues, tearing off a piece of the loaf and handing it to me. "This came from my oven just before a half hour," he adds.

Indeed the bread is still warm and tastes delightful. He cuts a wedge of cheese and for a moment I enjoy the wine-and-cheese treat. Maybe there's something to this French cuisine stuff. Bisset watches me, his face wreathed in smiles, delighting in my pleasure. With his infectious love for food and drink I can begin to see why he was such a successful restaurateur.

"And so, Mr. Charlton, from your name may I guess that you are also at least a bit French?"

"Alas, the name is Welsh, from the old Celtic," I admit. "But I do have some French blood, on my mother's side of the family. Some great grandfather, I think, who was from Dijon."

"Ah, *c'est magnifique*!" he exclaims. I am myself from that region. We are perhaps distant cousins, *non*?" He laughs heartily.

I agree it's possible and turn the conversation to the purpose of my visit. He tells me some of the history of his restaurant, often wandering from the subject to describe some splendid dish or other. I'm fascinated to learn that he earned an international reputation for adapting traditional French recipes to what's available in Southwestern markets, for example replacing wild boar with javalina, a pig-like animal indigenous to the area. He also created dishes using native blue corn, green chilies and other regional foods while still retaining the French style.

I ask him why he closed his restaurant instead of selling it to someone else. He shrugs and murmurs, "Who else could do what I do? Without Bruno there can be no Bruno's Bistro." I see his point and steer him to the subject of Greenwald. His smile fades.

"Ah, *c'est tragique*," he murmurs. "Donald became my friend. I was so sorry for Marsha. Over his coffin we wept together."

He describes his early impressions of the young Greenwald, a university student who served first as an assistant and later as a first tier waiter at Bruno's Bistro. A disciplined worker with a sharp sense of individual tastes, he had the instincts to guide patrons unerringly to choices that left them satisfied and happy. His tips reflected this ability.

"So, Greenwald was always well-liked?" I ask. "No friction with other staff? No arguments with clients?"

"*Oui*, he was always *très populaire*," Bisset responds at once. But then his smile fades a bit and I make a little motion with my left hand to encourage him to go on.

"Once only did he have some troubles," Bisset muses, looking down at the table and toying with a piece of bread. "It was a misunderstanding with a diner, a very stupid man. This person, this idiot, he makes the ass of himself and Donald he cannot help from laughing. The man he jumps up, shouts at Donald and walks out. He is so angry he is leaving his woman at the table. I come from the kitchen, but too late. Donald he is very upset. I tell him to go home. We never spoke of it again, but I know it was something for which he was very asham-ed."

Hmm, could be something here, but not likely. Everyone has experiences like that, and if every such episode led to bloody murder the human race would have been long since extinct. I push Bisset for more details but he can't remember anything more.

I raise the question of the date from the watch engraving, June 14, 1975, asking if Greenwald worked at the restaurant at that time. Bisset thinks for a moment before answering.

"It may be so, *monsieur*. Much time is gone past, but I think he came to me in the year of 1974 and was surely there for at least two years."

"Would he have been a full waiter on that date I mentioned?"

Again he thinks for a moment before nodding agreement. I make a few notes and draw the interview to a close. We stand up and he escorts me to the door that leads into the entrance hall.

"Maria!" he calls out as we enter the foyer. "*Le pain!*" The maid appears bearing a basket in which a second fresh loaf of bread is peeping out from beneath a checkered napkin. She hands it to Bisset who turns and presents it to me with a flourish.

"In France, it is sometimes our tradition to make a parting gift of bread. Please to enjoy."

I accept the gift with a little bow, murmuring my thanks. Maria opens the front door and I'm nearly through it when Bisset calls out, "*Un moment monsieur*." I pause and he steps forward.

"You are interested in this special date, this June 14, *oui*?" I nod. "Well, there is perhaps something more you can know. I have all the daily records for my restaurant, each reservation book, every receipt, all stored away safe in the boxes. Does this have interest for you?"

Umm, that sounds like a lot of work. Except perhaps for stakeouts, there may be nothing I hate more than document searches. But I hesitate for only an instant. If I'm going to keep this investigation on life support I shouldn't pass up even the thinnest thread.

"Where are these records? Do you have them here?"

"Ah, no *monsieur*. They are in the restaurant."

I look confused and Bisset laughs.

"No, I am mistake, the restaurant she is clos-ed. But still I own the building where she lived. There is a storage room inside and *voila!* there are all the records."

He tells me to call him if I want to examine the files and I promise to think about it. We shake hands once more and I descend to my maroon baby carrying the basket and its contents like a trophy of war. A delicious odor rises from the freshly baked loaf, making me feel right with the world.

Chapter Sixteen

Jeremy Barth

Reveling in the success of the Drake retirement, Barth has returned to Albuquerque. It's the next morning and he's sipping coffee and nibbling on a croissant as he reviews the Drake file in his downstairs lair. The file box is filled with documents about Drake's life, and now Barth adds an account of his death at the hands of Singleton, writing with a fountain pen on sheets of fine linen writing paper.

The abduction goes just as planned, catching the finance professor off guard in the dimly lit parking lot behind his club. Singleton lifts the unconscious victim into the van and shuts the door. He picks up Drake's car keys, dropped when he was struck in the neck with the syringe. He climbs into the driver's seat of his van and starts the engine. As he drives away he activates the remote on Drake's key ring, watching in the rear view mirror as the Lincoln's lights flash twice to signal the doors are locked and the alarm set. He keeps the keys as a trophy and they now sit at one side of Barth's little desk beside a gold watch.

Now Barth writes a meticulous account of the killing.

After driving to a remote clearing in the nearby

Arapaho National Forest Singleton parks and turns off the lights. After chaining Drake around the waist to a steel ring inside the van he waits, sipping from a bottle of water and occasionally humming. He's wearing medical gloves and a silk smock that covers most of his clothing. His shoes are the most common brand available at discount stores.

After about an hour his retiree begins to stir. Singleton turns him onto his back and splashes cold water onto his face. Sputtering, Drake begins to waken.

"Wha, whazzit," he cries. Singleton splashes more water and his prisoner comes fully alert.

"What the hell," he croaks. "What's going on here?" He tries to struggle up but the chains pull him back. Singleton watches silently in the dark, preparing for his carefully rehearsed ceremony.

After a moment Drake manages to rise into a sitting position, back braced against the sidewall of the van. He squints, trying to make out his assailant but all he can see is a dim shadow. Filled with anger and resentment Drake rants, but after a moment his rage runs its course and dissolves into fear. He sinks back against the steel wall.

"Why are you doing this?" he asks, his voice now flat, resigned. "What do you want from me? I have money…"

Singleton moves now, reaching to turn on the overhead light. He watches the reaction as Drake recognizes him.

"Robert? Bob…?" Drake manages. "What are we doing here?"

Singleton leans closer and speaks at last.

"Hello Morton, remember me?"

Drake goggles for a moment.

"Yes, of course," he manages. "It's Bob, Bob Singleton. You're a management consultant. I just said. What are you doing?"

"No, Morton, It's not what you think. I'm your retirement counselor. It's time for you to retire."

"What! Retire? What do you mean, retire?"

Singleton smiles and reaches into a small backpack. He pulls out a gold watch, the badge of retirement.

"Of course you want to retire, Morton," he says in a soothing voice. "Look what I have for you. It's a gold wristwatch, just like yours but with a personal inscription." He studies the professor's confused expression for a moment. He holds out the watch and Drake hesitatingly takes it and raises it to the light.

"My God," he breathes. "What's it mean?"

"Go ahead, read the inscription. It's for you. For your retirement."

"But...I'm not retiring," Drake protests. His eyes remain locked on the watch. His fingers run nervously around the band.

"No, really, you are. Read the inscription. I insist."

Cautiously Drake lifts the watch and peers at the back. There's an engraved message. His eyes go wide as he reads.

"What does this mean?" he demands, looking at Singleton with startled eyes. "This is bullshit. It has the date all wrong; it says November 12, 1989. What are you up to you bastard?"

Singleton gazes regretfully at Drake's anxious face.

"Morton, I must say I'm disappointed in you," he announces. "Swearing is the last resort of the uncouth. And for you, a Harvard man no less, to use such crude language. Tosh. I'm deeply offended."

"Who the hell are you?" Drake demands, his voice rising. "Singleton? I don't really know you, do I?"

Singleton smiles benevolently.

"Let's just say I'm a messenger, bearing a message from your past. Think back Morton. It's early November, 1989. The 12th day of the month. A Tuesday. What were you doing then?"

Confused, Drake lets the watch drop into his lap and stares at Singleton.

"I, why, I d-don't know," he stutters. "That was a long time ago."

Singleton sighs gently and leans back.

"Again, I'm disappointed in you Morton. So very, very disappointed. How could you have forgotten? It was an important day for you, a career-changing event. There was a fine banquet. You were the guest of honor. There was someone else, someone who wasn't there. Surely you remember."

Drake seems to be straining to recall. A gleam of recognition comes onto his face.

"Was it the New York Financial Club? The inaugural dinner? Is that it?"

Singleton nods.

"What does that have to do with anything?" Raging again, Drake almost screams. "What the hell do you think you're doing? That was more than 25 years ago! I hardly remember anything about that time in my life."

Singleton smiles and pats Drake almost lovingly on the shoulder. His victim shrinks back, quivering with terror.

"Calm down now, Morton. This is your retirement we're celebrating here. It's no time to be emotional. Look what a fine retirement present you've earned."

"Earned! But I already have a watch!"

"Why yes, of course, but this one is special. You're more than deserving of this reward. It's a retirement watch. A mark of achievement. Think of it! What an appropriate symbol for a lifetime of work. You should be proud."

Drake is more confused than ever. He struggles briefly against the chains before sinking back.

"What do you want?" he asks, his voice again flat, resigned.

"Want? Why only to help you celebrate your retirement, just as it says in the inscription." Singleton gazes regretfully at his victim. "Have you still no idea how you've earned your place in history?"

Drake stares blindly back, his mouth sagging open in bewilderment.

"Who are you?" he asks again. "Just who the fuck are you?"

"Ah! ah! ah! There goes that dirty mouth again." Singleton shakes a finger in Drake's face. "I wonder what we should do with such a bad boy." He resumes gazing for a moment then speaks a name: "Jeremy Barth. Don't you remember him? He's my employer."

Drake doesn't react, the expression of confusion still on his face. He looks searchingly at his captor.

"So, Morton, you don't even remember that name," Singleton remarks in an almost offhand way. "What a pity that your brain's so cluttered with its own thoughts of self-grandeur that you cannot remember the name of a man whose reputation you tried to destroy. I am so disap–pointed. It's almost heartbreaking to see you're such a shell of a man." He affects a deep sigh of regret. "But I must say I'm not surprised. You always were an asshole, Morton." He watches as the puzzled Drake searches his memory.

"Barth? Jeremy Barth? I seem to remember that name from somewhere..."

"As well you should, Morton my friend. He was a former associate of yours in the New York Financial Club. It was Jeremy Barth who stood in line to become president of the club, the rightful recipient of that honor. Does that ring any little bells with you Morton?"

The professor's face turns chalk white as long-suppressed memories come flooding back. "My God," he breathes. "And you're here to rub my nose in it. What are you, Singleton, a hired thug? Well, you've made your point. You can report back to this Jeremy Barth that you've scared the bloody hell out of me. I've learned my lesson and you can let me go now."

Singleton smiles, a broad, Cheshire Cat kind of smile.

"Oh, Morton, so sorry, but like diamonds this retirement is forever. There'll be no double-dipping on this one."

Everything else is anti-climax. Singleton stabs a second syringe of incapacitating drug into Drake's neck and goes to work on the final stage of the retirement ceremony. The chains are loosened and the limp prisoner lifted from the van. Carefully Singleton lays him on the ground, aligning his feet toward Polaris, twinkling high in the northern sky. He removes his victim's watch and puts the nearly identical fake on his wrist. He produces a clothes brush and cloth from the backpack and proceeds to wipe down Drake's shoes and brush his clothing, straightening his arms and legs. He wipes a bit of spittle from the lips and busies himself with smoothing the collar, tucking in the shirt and making sure the shirtsleeve cuffs are pulled down and even. He buttons the coat jacket and brushes it gently to remove all traces of dust. He withdraws a small hairbrush and fixes Drake's hair.

Satisfied at last he steps back to make a final check then removes a digital camera from the backpack and takes several flash pictures of the arranged body, still alive but not for long.

Finally he produces the .22 caliber pistol and checks the magazine. It's loaded with low velocity cartridges, the kind that will penetrate the skull but not powerful enough to pass through the other side.

He lays a doubled cloth gently over Drake's face to protect it from powder marks. He lowers the barrel of the pistol to a precise point on the center of the forehead. He folds part of the cloth over the pistol to catch the empty cartridge. He smiles and straightens a stray wisp of the man's hair.

"Have a nice retirement, Morton," he tells the unconscious man. "Many happy returns." He pulls the trigger. Paralyzed by the drug, Drake's body doesn't even twitch as the killing shot enters

his brain and bounces back from the rear of his skull. Death is almost instantaneous.

Singleton lifts the cloth and examines his work. A few drops of blood ooze from the entry wound. He uses the cloth to gently wipe them away. He puts the shell casing in his pocket, steps back for a final look then turns, gets into the van and drives slowly away.

Bent over his foreman's desk like some modern-day Bob Cratchit at his accounts, Barth completes his written report, reads it over carefully then places it in the file box. He picks up the watch and the car keys on a ring with Drake's Phi Beta Kappa key and adds the trophies to the collection along with the spent shell casing. Digital photo prints of the retirement display have already been placed in the file.

He lifts the cover sheet and using a red ink pen he marks the file on Morton J. Drake, Ph.D. as officially closed. Barth smiles to himself and reaches for another box.

Chapter Seventeen

Rob Charlton

For maybe the hundredth time I'm asking myself why I keep digging on the Greenwald case. It's not really Marsha's money that motivates me, and in fact I kind of resent the hold that gives her over me. No, my obsession comes from within. I just cannot let a challenge go. That trait has gotten me into trouble before. And the real truth is that the case fascinates me. Solving murders is what I did during most of my years at the Bureau, and it's hard to give up on something that's been an important part of what you are.

This time I'm starting to get that creepy feeling that I'm acting out of line, and it's a dangerous place to be. The murder of Donald Greenwald is the subject of an on-going official investigation, and neither I nor anyone else has the right to interfere in a criminal case. On the other hand, am I actually interfering? Not really, I try to convince myself. Almost everything I've done is fairly innocent, and since I'm acting as a consultant to Mrs. Greenwald there's a thin layer of legitimacy in what I've done.

I'm sitting in my office chair once again, communing with the wall, which as usual is keeping mum. As far as I can figure, none of the information I've uncovered has any bearing on the case. It consists merely of random facts about Greenwald's life. As far as I know there's no connection whatsoever to his murder—except for that one mysterious date and the word "retirement" engraved on the fake gold watch.

That one bothers me because even though it's led me nowhere, it still may have some importance. The lead investigator and his team likely missed that clue and it was discovered only by chance by Marsha and me. One could argue that Flores dropped the ball and by cutting off Mrs. Greenwald he left her with no inclination to cooperate with him.

But I'm bothered by the fact that the watch could mean something in the context of the official investigation, if linked with facts to which I'm not privy. Unknowingly, I could be harming the case by holding back that information. Should I give up and turn the information over to Flores? The wall is silent on this question.

Again I examine my position. In ordinary circum-stances I would've gone to him immediately, and only decided against it because of the way he froze out Marsha, even threatening her with a restraining order. Now that I'm pretty much out of options, maybe it's time to step aside, resign the assignment and advise Marsha to turn the watch over to Flores. Let him figure out what, if anything, it might mean. No matter what happens, I know that eventually I'm going to have to share everything I've learned with the detective.

This private eye business isn't turning out well for me. It's not at all like the days when I was with the Bureau. Then I was part of a large, coordinated organization with every imaginable resource at hand, all paid for by Uncle Sugar. Now it's just me, the wall and a pile of bills.

Well, there's one tiny loose end and I guess I'd better tie it up before figuring out how to wriggle out of this mess with my skin intact. I pick up the phone and call

Bruno Bisset about the records stored in his former restaurant building.

Within an hour I'm parking the maroon baby on Central and checking out the storefronts in Bisset's building. Bisset has directed me to the owner of the computer place, who has access to the storage area in the back of the building.

He's expecting me and immediately leads the way through his workroom and down a passageway. At the end is a locked door for which he produces a key. He swings the door open and turns on the lights. Inside are four rows of industrial shelving and several hundred sealed file boxes. I take one look and groan.

It turns out the challenge isn't that great, thanks to Bisset's excellent organization. Each box represents the records from one month, and inside are pocket folders for each day. His accountant must have loved Bruno. Within minutes I've located the box for June, 1975 and extracted the folder for the 14th. I carry the trophy triumphantly back to the maroon baby and take it to my office for study.

In the front of the folder is the reservations log with times, names and checkmarks to indicate the guests had arrived and been seated. There were 113 parties registered that day. In most cases the assigned table and waiter are also noted. There's also a worksheet listing tips added to credit cards and paid out to staff. Don Greenwald's name is on the list and I note he'd earned a paltry amount that day, less than twenty bucks.

Most of the rest consists of duplicate sales slips or credit card receipts. For once I can put that mute wall to actual use. Using sticky tape I sort and organize the contents by placing each receipt on the wall, sorting by time stamps or receipt numbers. This takes me almost an hour. When I've finished there's a river of paper across the wall approximating a timeline.

The display begins on the left side of my wall with the earliest receipts from about 11:30 a.m., presumably when the Bistro opened its doors. As the luncheon hour progresses the flow of paper across the wall rapidly grows to a large bump like the one in a python that swallowed a pig. This peaks at about 1 p.m. then trails off to nothing sometime after 2 o'clock. The next bump starts a little after four and rises more slowly than the noontime rush. It peaks at about 8 p.m. then slowly dwindles until the last receipt of the day shortly before midnight.

I sit back for a moment and examine my handiwork. Jeez, this isn't the kind of work I enjoy. It's going on to noon so I decide to give it a rest and go out for an early lunch. There's a little bar and grill nearby called Sally's Place and even from several blocks away I can feel the attractive force of Sally's excellent cheeseburgers.

I decide to walk, leaving the maroon baby to fend for herself. Maybe the exercise will help tighten up those sagging tummy muscles. At the very least it may help offset the effect of the burger I'll soon be consuming. And probably with a cold brew. Oh well, when it comes to middle-age spread it's generally a losing battle, and I don't mean losing weight either.

The little bar has a dining area that would politely be called intimate. I call it crowded and prefer to sit at the bar instead of at one of the tiny tables. The owner, Sally Birch, is also the bartender and waitress while in the kitchen Bob, her short order cook, flips a mean burger. The menu's pretty limited, offering various species of burger, french-fries, onion rings and coleslaw. Bruno Bisset would no doubt be horrified, but it suits me just fine. I slip onto a barstool and lay my iPhone on the bar beside me. It's too early for the usual lunch crowd and I'm the only one in the place.

"Well hello big guy," Sally calls out from the other end

where she's wiping down a glass with a towel. "Long time no see."

"Yeah, hi yourself," I reply. "Been busy but I got an emergency signal from my tummy. Seems to be desperate for one of your burgers."

Sally chuckles, puts the glass on the back bar and comes down to shake my hand. "Good to see you Rob."

She's a stocky woman of a certain age—I'd guess she's pushing the big five-oh, not that I'd ever ask—but dresses like a hippy and wears her long blonde hair bound in a ponytail that hangs halfway down her back. In fact, Sally once admitted to me that she really was a hippy in her younger days and even lived on a commune in California for several months before giving up the weed-sex-and-LSD lifestyle and going back to college.

"The usual?" she asks, cocking one eyebrow at me.

I nod. For me "the usual" is a half-pound burger on a whole-wheat poppy seed bun, grilled medium-rare and topped with cheddar, grilled onion, pickles and jalapeno peppers, with fries on the side and plenty of catsup. I like to eat a healthy, balanced diet and this meets all the requirements of the Department of Agriculture's dietary guidelines, with servings of meat, dairy, bread and four veg's. Five if you count the catsup. Couldn't go wrong with that. To be sure I get all my vitamins and minerals I order a bottle of Modelo Especial.

Sally shouts my food order back to Bob and pops the brewski, handing me the bottle without a glass. Why people want to drink beer from glasses when it comes ready-to-drink in a nice cold bottle is beyond me. I take a swig and set the bottle down. From the back I hear the sizzling sound of an all-beef patty hitting the hot grill. Ah, this is the life.

Sally and I chat for a while, comparing observations about the state of the nation and the weather. She knows

I'm a Rangers fan and being from Chicago she favors the ill-fortuned Cubbies, so in the interest of peace in our time we avoid the subject of baseball.

"So what's keepin' you so busy," Sally asks, setting my platter of health food down on the bar in front of me. "That PI business of yours starting to pick up? It's about time."

I don't reply right away, focused on pouring catsup, dipping a fry and popping it in my mouth.

"Um, kinda," I offer. She gives me a look that says I'm expected to be more responsive.

"Yeah, I've been working on a couple of things," I add, licking my fingers and reaching for another fry. "Nothing too exciting though. Frankly, Sally, I've been wondering whether it wasn't a big mistake to think I could make a go of it as a private investigator." I pick up the burger and take a big bite. Juice runs down my chin.

Sally studies me for a moment then hands me a napkin.

"Rob, you were a top FBI agent. What could be so hard about doing private work?" Sally used to be a police dispatcher and she knows something about the law enforcement game. As a bartender she knows about human nature, too. For that reason she keeps a baseball bat and a .38 behind the bar.

I chew on my burger for a moment, thinking about her question.

"You know, that might be the problem," I tell her. "When I was with the Bureau I worked on big cases. Being a PI is all about little stuff, cases that aren't really interesting to me. Most of them are actually humiliating if you want to know the God's truth."

A couple of guys come in and sit down near the other end of the bar so Sally goes to take their orders, leaving me to munch on my burger and fries. I wipe my fingers on the napkin and take another swig of the smooth Mexican beer. I look at myself in the mirror behind the bar and go into contemplative mode.

As a creative tool the mirror proves far superior to my office wall because it actually speaks to me, kinda sorta. It does this not through speech but by letting me see myself, something the wall has never done.

What I see is a middle-aged man in a rumpled suit and loosened tie. There's a spot of grease on the tie. He has all the early warning signs of someone that's going to pot, including the hint of a double chin and receding hair gone gray around the temples. It's a guy I recognize, but he's not the Rob of old, the one who laughed at fate and took on whatever the world dished up. His life has drifted a bit off course, but as any motivational speaker will tell you, nothing's impossible if you set your mind to it. You can be whatever you want, but it has to be the right thing.

I must face that what I just said to Sally is true, that crappy assignments such as spying on errant husbands are personally humiliating to me.

I come to a moment of clarity: If I'm going to continue in this business, it can't be by accepting that kind of work. For my own self-respect I gotta do meaningful stuff, and if I want to build a successful career I must set myself above the hacks that creep around motels with video cameras and testify in divorce courts.

I realize that if I can't establish a reputation for being able to handle the toughest cases, and thus earn the right to gain that class of assignment, I don't want to be in this game at all.

I take another hit from the bottle and return to the burger. It's funny how sometimes the sharp instincts of a good bartender can light the way to self-realization. With just a few well-chosen words Sally has opened my mind. Not that I haven't had the same thoughts myself, but hearing them from someone else somehow makes things snap into focus.

I've glimpsed the possibility of a better, brighter future, one in which I can regain the respect I once had, and the Greenwald case is the key. I must soldier on, solve the mystery and identify the murderer. After all, that's what I do best and handling penny ante cases is not only a waste of my talents, it's a toxic drain on my own self-esteem. By breaking the Greenwald case I can establish myself as the go-to guy for the toughest cases, the ones no ordinary PI could begin to handle.

I push back the empty platter, drain the last of the beer and lay money on the bar. I smile and wave at Sally as I head for the door. In my brief visit to this intimate little bar I seem to have re-discovered the old Rob. I even imagine there's a hint of a spring in my step as I stride back to my office, shoulders back and head held high. I'm also painfully aware that I'm taking shallow breaths, struggling to hold in my gut.

Chapter Eighteen

Rob Charlton

Back in my office I begin the tedious task of analyzing the trove of information from Bisset's records room. I start by making a mark-up copy of the reservations sheets. I put the copy on a clipboard and begin at the left side of the wall to try to correlate the entries with the receipts I've organized into a rough timeline, making notes as I go.

I soon discover there are more receipts than entries on the list. I conclude this must be due to walk-ins, individuals or groups that arrived with no reservations and were immediately seated without being noted on the reservations log.

The biggest problem is to try to correlate the receipts with the log. None of the cash receipts bear names to compare with the listing, and a number of the credit card slips are for corporations or in names that do not appear on the list. This is a painful task, perhaps a waste of time.

After about an hour I take a break to catch up on my email. Great news. I discover that I've won sizeable amounts of money from various lotteries I never entered. I'm also invited to help two troubled widows from African nations by transferring their late husbands' millions into my bank account. What a wonderful world we live in, with opportunity at every turn. I also learn of several sure-fire non-medical methods guaranteed to increase my sexual prowess, but figure I don't need any help with that. Not yet anyway, but it's good to know they'll be there when I need them.

There's only one personal email in my in-box. It's from my ex-wife and it's filled with her usual complaints about the unfair nature of life. I want to write back asking if she'd like some cheese with that whine, but choose the high road instead. I learned from long experience not to taunt dangerous animals and the last thing I need right now is a flame war with Greta. We've been divorced for nearly 20 years and why she can't just go on with her life is one mystery I've never been able to solve. Thank goodness she lives far, far away in a galaxy called Boston. Greta's location is one reason why I'd decided to settle in the Southwest.

I decide not to respond until later and return to my task. I've marked up the duplicate reservations sheet and have notes scrawled on a yellow-dog legal pad. After contemplating my progress I decide to enter the data in a spreadsheet. I launch Excel and in the first column set up rows across for each 15-minute increment during the day. In the second column I enter all the reservation names for each time period then begin to add receipts in a third column based on the timestamps on the cash receipts or credit card slips.

It takes me a half-hour to realize this approach is fruitless. There are so many discontinuities in the data that nothing wants to match. And it makes sense, not only because so many receipts have no names or different names, but also because there's no correlation between the times. If a party has a reservation for 7 p.m., for example, and if they spend two hours enjoying their meal, the receipt would be time stamped at about 9:00 p.m. It could have been earlier or later depending on how long they spent at their meal. Hmm, this isn't working. I close the spreadsheet and put my noodle to work again.

After some thought I decide that the only thing I can do is rely on my time-proven intuition, so I begin studying the receipts with the old eagle eyes, looking for anything that might provide a relevant clue to what may have occurred that night.

First I locate any reference to Greenwald, figuring that should narrow my search. Some of the reservations entries bear the initials DG and someone has written the initials on some of the charge slips, probably to calculate the tips. Yes, when I check the tips worksheet I find these figures match the amounts on the charge slips and that DG indeed stands for Donald Greenwald.

I soon notice something else: that there are no DG entries during the lunch period. From that I conclude he didn't work the noon shift, which eliminates the entire lunchtime part of the timeline. Good. I remove the lunch receipts from the wall and set them aside.

The first reference to Greenwald, as indicated by his initials on the headwaiter's reservations log, comes at around 5:40 p.m. and several others quickly follow. By 7:30 he's been assigned to about a dozen tables, and then something strange happens: There are no further notations for him. He apparently did not finish the shift.

I remember Bisset's anecdote about Greenwald's encounter with the angry client, and how the waiter was told to take the rest of the night off. This could be a connection between that event and the date engraved on the watch, evidence that I'm on the right track.

Following my nose I focus on the reservations entries assigned to Greenwald from 6:30 to the last one at about 7:30. I carefully note them down on a fresh sheet of paper, feeling that little tingle I sometimes get when a breakthrough may be near. This list could include the name of the man with whom Greenwald clashed, someone who might be motivated to take revenge and leave the date of June 14, 1975 as a calling card.

I study the list carefully. It contains nine names. Most are surnames only, sometimes with a title. Three are preceded by the appellation "Dr." and another named Smith has a first initial for further identification. It reads like a cross-section of America. Here's what I wrote:

Roberts
Collins
Dr. Westwood
R. Smith
Williams
Dr. Garcia
Miller
Dr. Stuart
Albertson

Now at last I have something to work with. Next I go to the receipts and try to match something to each name. I find credit card slips in the names of Collins, R. Smith, Williams and Garcia. These give me more information, including first names for the individuals. I learn that Collins is a woman, Cynthia; that the R before Smith's name stands for Rupert; that Williams' first name is Stephen; and that Garcia's is Jose.

There are no receipts for the other five names on the list.

I sit back and think for a moment. There's a chance I can identify Westwood and Stuart by their titles, but this isn't going to be easy. After all, how many people named Roberts could there be in Albuquerque? A hundred? Two hundred? More? And what about Miller and Albertson?

Those are all fairly common names and a long time has passed since that night in 1975. People move, change their names, die and sometimes even disappear without a trace.

I sigh in frustration. Obviously I've got my work cut out for me to follow up on these leads.

I set aside the receipts concerning the nine possible suspects, then with the usual Rob persistence I decide to go over the entire remaining receipts one more time with my intuition antennae tuned to high.

They all seem irrelevant, except for one that stands out for its difference. Instead of a paid cash or charge receipt it's a sheet from a waiter's order pad. It lists two cocktails and two orders of oysters, and I recognize Greenwald's handwriting.

Across the middle of the sheet someone else has marked "Cancelled" and the initials BB that I take to be Bisset's. Then at the very bottom is a scrawled signature.

I squint and hold the sheet closer to make out the name. It's a woman's, something like Shirley or Sarah perhaps. And the last name is Ricardo or Richards. I squint some more, trying to visualize the actual letters behind the squiggles. Shelly, it's Shelly. And it's Richards, not Ricardo. Shelly Richards.

Why was this order cancelled? It might fit the story Bisset told. Could this be the name of the angry client's companion? Who is she?

I turn to my computer and open Google. I type in the name plus "Albuquerque" and "New Mexico" then hit the Enter button. A long string of hits appears and I begin to scroll down the index entries. About halfway down the first screen something catches my eye. It's an old news report from *The Albuquerque Tribune,* a now-defunct newspaper. I click to open the file.

Accident Claims Life
Of UNM Student

Shelly Richards, 22, a graduate student in business administration at UNM died late last night in an apparent freak accident at the apartment building where she lived in the 1200 block of Carlyle Street.

According to Albuquerque Police spokeswoman Anita Rodriguez Ms. Richards apparently slipped on a staircase and fell, suffering a traumatic blow to her head.

The victim was discovered by another tenant in the building at approximately 11:22 p.m. yesterday and pronounced dead at the UNM Hospital.

A native of Connecticut, Ms. Richards was well-liked among fellow students and faculty. Her advisor, Prof. Henry Michaels, told *The Tribune* she was a brilliant student who had a bright future ahead of her.

"It's a tragedy for such a vibrant, talented young woman to lose her life at such an early age," Michaels said. "She was very popular and will be greatly missed. We have cancelled all the department's classes tomorrow to let our students come to terms with her loss."

The body will be returned to Connecticut for burial. Contributions in her memory can be made to the UNM department of finance and business administration scholarship fund.

Almost certain what I'll find, I scroll to the top and check the date. The article appeared on June 15, 1975. Shelly Richards died on the night of June 14, the date inscribed on the watch left on the body of Donald Greenwald more than 30 years later.

Oh, yeah Rob, you're on the trail of a killer all right, and he's a slippery one. Odds are overwhelming that the mystery man from Bruno's Bistro is connected to the death of this woman—and that connects him with Greenwald. I've got a solid lead now, and the names of nine potential suspects to pursue.

As Sherlock used to say to Watson, the game's afoot.

Chapter Nineteen

Rob Charlton

Now that I've got some solid leads I figure it's time to share what I've got with Flores. If I hold back this information—the connection between Greenwald and the event in the restaurant on June 14, 1975—I really will be interfering with his investigation. I punch on my phone and dial the sheriff's department. In a moment Flores comes on the line.

I introduce myself, mentioning the Greenwald case and my FBI career. At that point Flores interrupts.

"So what're you saying? The Feds are taking my case?"

"No, of course not. I'm retired from the Bureau and working as a PI. I've been retained by Marsha Greenwald to look into the death of her husband."

There's a long silence then an outburst.

"I do not fucking believe this!" I can almost hear the spittle hitting the phone's mike. I've touched a nerve here, that's for sure. Momma used to tell me silence is golden and for once I follow her advice.

"So let me get this straight," Flores continues, "that woman can't get enough of harassing my ass so she hires some snoop to pick up where she left off. Is that it?"

"No, of course not," I murmur. I realize I'm starting to sound like a parrot.

"Well, what is it then? I don't have time for this."

"I'm serving as a consultant to Mrs. Greenwald," I inform him, keeping my voice calm. "I've done a little informal checking around and I think you may need to know what I've learned."

Silence.

"It may help you," I suggest. "I don't have the full picture of your investigation, but what I've come across could fit with information you've got."

Silence

"Worth a few minutes of your time," I add.

Silence. Then, calmly: "What was your name again?" I tell him and hear the clicking sound of typing on a keyboard. There's a long silence. He's apparently checking me out.

"Says here you've only been in the investigations biz for a few months," Flores says at last, an accusatory note in his voice. "You weren't even living here when Greenwald was killed."

My goodness the sheriff's department already has a file on me. I confirm his statement but add that I was with the Bureau for three decades as a murder investigator and as a SAC. That slows him down and we share another long silence.

"OK," Flores says at last, his voice now approximating a normal tone. "I could spare you a few minutes. When can we meet?"

"Any time you want," I tell him. "I'd prefer somewhere discreet, not your office. And I want this unofficial. I'm not trying to steal your thunder, but I want you to know I plan to continue to dig on this."

Flores raises his voice an octave. He's almost hissing.

"Listen, snoop, I wanna make this clear. I'll hear you out, but then I want you off my back. I've had it with Marsha Greenwald, and I've had it with you. Got that?"

I murmur something noncommittal that may sound like "yes" and wait for him to continue.

"I can meet you this afternoon," he comes back, voice calm but cold.

I suggest 3 o'clock at Sally's Place and he agrees. He hangs up first and I hear the receiver bang onto the cradle of his phone like he was killing a rat. Hmm, maybe he kinda was, and I'm the rat. Oh well, after what my client put him through I can understand where he's coming from. Rob the Rat. Has a nice ring to it. I resist the temptation to squeak at my friend the wall.

I've got a half-hour until my date with destiny. I spend it typing out a brief summary of my investigation and printing a copy to give to Flores. I've already made a duplicate set of my notes. I decide to walk to Sally's Place again and to take my briefcase to carry the evidence file and a tape recorder in case we want to record our meeting.

When I get to the bar there's a black unmarked patrol car parked in front and a tall Hispanic man is standing beside it, watching me approach with his arms crossed on his chest.

"Lieutenant," I murmur, holding out my hand. He ignores it and spins away without even saying hello. My gracious. I follow him into the bar. Sally greets us with a querulous look but sensing the tension in the air she says nothing. Flores leads the way to the furthest table and sits down with his back to the wall. I take the chair opposite him. We look at each other, he glaring ominously, me trying to hold a neutral expression and forcing just a friendly glimpse of a smile. I feel like a kid that's been called to the principal's office. I try not to squirm in my seat.

Sally stays behind the bar but keeps looking for a signal. I glance her way and give a little shake of my head so she goes back to arranging bottles and polishing glasses. Bartending is a lot like detecting, lots of boring routine interspersed with peaks of excitement.

Flores speaks at last.

"So you're Charlton," he observes, demonstrating his astonishing powers of deduction. I nod and say nothing. "OK, whatcha got?"

I start out with a bit of my personal background. He listens with a hint of bored impatience as I describe my education, culminating in a law degree at Ohio State. I tell him how I was recruited for the Bureau and briefly mention some of my exploits, murders I solved, the thrill of the hunt. As a brother investigator I hope this will draw him out, but he affects indifference and slouches back, apparently unimpressed.

"OK, I get it," he interrupts after a couple of minutes, "you're Super Dick. Let's get on with it."

My goodness. This guy's got a chip on his shoulder the size of a Ponderosa log. I settle back in my own chair and glance around the empty room. Sally's moved to the far end of the bar, pretending to pay us no attention. I turn my eyes back to meet his. The glare's still turned on to medium-high and his arms are crossed in the plainest body language there is. He might as well just come out and say it: "I don't like you and hope you die painfully and soon."

Well, frankly asshole, I don't like you either now that you bring it up. But I keep my mouth shut and my arms at my sides, letting my little phony smile continue to peek through. I take a slow, deep breath.

"All right, if you want it that way I'll just say what I have to say and you can get on with whatever's more important to you. I've been poking around in the public record, checking out Greenwald's past, conducting some interviews. I've discovered a connection to something that happened on June 14, 1975."

I pause, watching to see if there's a reaction. I've wondered whether or not Flores had noticed the engraving on the watch and made any speculations about it. He apparently hadn't because his face registers only mild confusion.

"Wait," he interjects. "What the hell kind of a clue is that? How does something that happened years ago relate to Greenwald's murder? And how the hell did you find out about it, whatever it is."

He's sitting up straight in his chair again and the glare has faded to medium-low. I estimate it's about equivalent to a 65-watt bulb.

I hesitate for a moment, wondering how to negotiate the minefield that lies between us. When he learns of the watch, and finds out that he missed what may be an important clue, he's going to do one of two things. Either he's going to go Krakatoa on me, or the scales will be lifted from his eyes. Based on his attitude so far I'm putting all my chips on alternative number one.

I play for a moment of time. I reach down to my lawyer's briefcase on the floor beside me, snap it open and pull out a bulky file. I fumble with the papers inside, mostly copies of my notes and the summary I'd prepared for him. The watch is in there, too, and I slowly pull it out and set it on the table in front of me. His eyes are drawn to it. I've obviously aroused his curiosity but he says nothing. I decide to approach this with the assumption that he's fully aware of the inscription and has made it part of his case file.

"The only clue I had to work with is Greenwald's watch," I inform him. I say no more, leaving the watch on my side of the table. He stares at it for a moment then raises his eyes to mine. The poor goof has no idea what I'm talking about.

"As I'm sure you recall," I offer tactfully, "that date is inscribed on the back of the watch. I thought it might mean something so I followed up on that slender thread. Everything I've got is tied to the information from the watch."

Flores reaches slowly across the table and picks up the watch. He draws it toward him, turns it over and as he reads the inscription I almost imagine I can see his pupils expand. He stares at it for a long moment then back at me.

"As I'm also sure you know, the watch is a fake," I inform him. "Made in China. My guess is the killer kept Greenwald's Rolex as a trophy and left this one as a message. You'd probably know more about that."

Flores leans forward, placing his elbows on the table. He lays the watch down carefully next to a napkin dispenser and condiments. For a moment he stares at it. I hear a little sound that seems to be coming from his throat. I wait, wondering what's going through his head and what he'll do next. Is Krakatoa about to blow?

He looks up and the glare has been turned to zero. For a brief instant he reminds me of the proverbial deer in the headlights but then he straightens up in the chair. He calls out to Sally.

"Bartender, can we have some coffee here?"

He glances at me. "You want some?" I nod. The danger has passed and Krakatoa will remain dormant for another day.

Chapter Twenty

Rob Charlton

Sally brings cups, cream, sugar and a pot of coffee to the table. She pours and Flores motions for her to leave the pot. She withdraws to the bar and for a moment we engage in pouring and stirring. I take a sip and set down my cup. Flores does likewise before speaking.

"Charlton, I've gotta tell you, I plain missed it." He grimaces. "The watch. I don't even remember seeing that inscription, and if I did I musta figured it was an old watch that someone else received for a retirement gift, maybe Greenwald's father. I never even entered it into evidence. The fact is I should have checked it out and I didn't."

I shrug and murmur something about how Marsha Greenwald should have noticed the inscription when he went over the personal effects with her. Flores picks up his cup and takes another sip. He reaches for the sugar and adds another hit of sucrose.

"Apparently you think this is important," I suggest, pointing to the watch. "Maybe you know something else?"

He nods.

"You said the inscription might fit together with facts from my investigation," he volunteers. "Well, you're right." He reaches inside his jacket, pulls out a notebook and sets it on the table. "I figured from the first that this might be a serial killing and I've been looking for connections to other crimes. Turns out there was a death a few days ago up in Colorado that I thought might fit the pattern." He picks up the watch and sets it beside the notebook. "This confirms it."

"What's the connection?

Referring to his notes Flores explains about the mystery of the retirement inscription on the back of a Movado watch. His conclusion: When added to the other similarities between the death of Morton Drake and the Greenwald killing it's impossible to believe the two aren't related. I agree.

"So, you've got a serial killer with an obsession about retirement, who literally 'retires' his victims." I muse for a moment before continuing. "That doesn't fit the typical serial pattern. These aren't random deaths but more like deliberate revenge killings. I think he knows his victims and is resentful about some real or perceived harm they've done to him."

Frowning in concentration Flores takes another sip of coffee before replying.

"Yeah," he murmurs at last. "You may have something there."

"It fits with what I've learned," I continue and proceed to describe the nasty confrontation between Greenwald and an unidentified patron at Bruno's Bistro. He thinks about this for a moment.

"So you think this guy committed this bloody murder in retribution for being embarrassed by a waiter a long time ago? Seems kinda improbable."

I smile and reach into my packet of notes. I hand him a copy of the waiter's order sheet marked "Cancelled" and signed at the bottom in a woman's hand.

"That order book page is from Bruno's Bistro on the

evening of June 14, 1975, the date on the watch. Note the initials DG at the top. That stands for the waiter, Donald Greenwald. The signature at the bottom is by a woman named Shelly Richards."

Flores studies the page for a moment then glances up at me.

"So, what's the significance of this?"

I purse my lips grimly and pull out another piece of paper.

"It's something I discovered just today. It caused me to call you and ask for this meeting." I hand him a copy of the newspaper story about the death of Shelly Richards. "The date on that news clipping is June 15, 1975."

Flores holds the two pieces of paper, one in each hand, his eyes flicking back and forth.

"Jesus," he breathes.

"Exactly what I thought," I tell him.

"The perp killed the woman the same night and then waited more than thirty years to take his revenge on Greenwald. That's incredible."

"Yep, that's the way I figure it."

Flores sits back in his chair and gazes out a nearby window. I sip coffee and wait as he processes this information. At last he speaks.

"Listen, Charlton, I'm not happy about the way you've gotten involved in this case." I start to open my mouth but he holds up a hand to stop me from speaking. "But, I can understand your reluctance to contact me after the way I blew off Marsha Greenwald."

"She's a very difficult woman," I interject. "Frankly I wouldn't have taken the consult except for the fact that you threatened her with a court order. That gave me justification."

Flores sighs. "That was another mistake on my part, one I've regretted ever since."

"I know she was harassing you pretty badly. She admitted she was calling you as much as five or six times a day, both at the office and on your personal phone."

"Yeah, she was. Actually I think her record was twelve calls. Look, I'm going through a rough stretch in my life. My wife and I divorced a few months ago and I get custody of my daughter on most weekends. That's supposed to be special time for us. But I can't shut off my phone—the department needs to be able to get ahold of me—and her calls just drove me up the wall. Hell, did you know I actually changed my cell phone and in about two days she'd gotten the new number?"

"Yes, so she said. I told her it was a mistake on her part, that it constituted harassment. I can understand your reaction."

"How're you getting along with her?" he asks with a curious expression. "I can't imagine a more difficult client. She must be driving you crazy, too."

I grin. "No, actually she's being very good. I told her I'd call her only if and when I know something firm, and that in the meantime if I hear a single peep out of her I'll immediately resign and return the balance of my retainer. She's left me strictly alone. I've sent her brief daily emails to confirm I'm working the case, but giving no details."

"Wish I'd had that option," Flores murmurs with a frown. "Look, Charlton, I'm sorry about the hard-assed way I treated you today. Frankly, just the mention of Marsha Greenwald was enough to make me blow my stack, and I apologize."

"No harm," I tell him.

"Well, there is harm. I've let my emotions interfere with the way I've handled this case. I feel ashamed. And I'm truly sorry I refused to shake your hand out there," he adds, nodding toward the bar's front door. He extends his hand now and I accept it.

"Apology accepted," I offer, "and I owe you one, too, for poking around in your case without telling you. I'm just glad we've finally connected. And please, call me Rob."

"And I'm Luis. Thanks for understanding."

"The question is, where do we go from here. We've both made some progress but this case is a long way from being solved. As I told you I intend to keep working this on behalf of Mrs. Greenwald and I agree to share everything I find with you. I'd also like to be kept informed about anything you discover." I smile before continuing: "In return I'll agree to keep Marsha on a short leash so you'll never have to deal with her."

A broad smile breaks out on Flores' face.

"Say, that's music to my ears," he exclaims.

Chapter Twenty-One

Jeremy Barth

Barth is busy in his basement room, preparing for another retirement. He's been at it since early in the morning. The contents of a retirement file are spread out on his little work desk and he's been making notes. Now he stands and stretches, satisfied with his progress.

The next retirement is set to take place in Texas and Jim Craig, Barth's Oklahoma City associate, has the assignment. The subject is Brent Fitzgerald, an old acquaintance of Barth's who will soon be visiting his daughter and grand–children in Denton, just north of Dallas-Fort Worth. Preparations are well under way and Craig's instructions are nearly complete.

Fitzgerald, a retired New York investment broker who lives in Connecticut, is targeted for his involvement in an investment scheme through which Barth had lost a considerable sum of money. The long-ago event involved the sale to Barth of shares in a real estate investment trust. The REIT was set up to manage a portfolio of commercial buildings and shopping centers and Fitzgerald had pushed Barth hard to invest. As a financier Barth knew the tax advantages could save him money thanks to depreciation and write-downs as the actual value of the properties continued to rise.

Giving in to Fitzgerald's aggressive salesmanship, Barth eventually bought a $50,000 tranche in what turned out to be a scam. The modern office buildings, apartment complexes and shopping centers pictured in the elaborate printed investment proposal turned out to be bogus. Instead of the prime property described in the prospectus, the REIT owned a collection of run-down buildings, many of which were virtually worthless and some even vacant and in a state of ruin.

Most of the money received from investors was swallowed up by management fees and, as Barth discovered later, outrageous sales commissions paid to brokers such as Fitzgerald, who pocketed twenty-five percent of the money Barth put up. The general partners of the REIT turned out to be front companies registered in the Bahamas.

When after two years the REIT declared insolvency Barth learned he'd lost the entire investment, a major part of his personal wealth at that time. When he confronted Fitzgerald the man actually laughed in his face, asserting it had been up to Barth to perform due diligence and suggesting he should have personally investigated the properties before investing. He pointed to the web of codicils and statements of indemnity in the fine print of the contract Barth had signed.

It was legal theft and Barth had no recourse other than to swallow the loss. But there was something else he could do, and that was to add Fitzgerald's name to his growing retirement list where it had remained a source of great satisfaction.

Barth planned to retire Fitzgerald in a manner appropriate to his crime, displaying his corpse in an abandoned office building in Dallas that was part of the REIT's bogus portfolio. As in the case of Greenwald the retirement gift will be a watch, an expensive gold Piaget. Barth has already purchased a Chinese knock-off of the watch Fitzgerald wears and used his laser machine to engrave the message. It reads: Happy Retirement to Brent Fitzgerald, November 17, 1991. The date is the one that appeared on the REIT purchase agreement Barth signed.

The watch, wrapped in a piece of flannel, is part of the file. Now he unfolds the cloth and picks up the watch. He smiles and fondles it for a moment. It will be carefully cleaned of any fingerprints before Craig places it on the victim's wrist, but for now he revels in the tactile feeling of the engraving on the back. After a moment he folds it back into the cloth and slides it into the file box. He places the file into the drawer with the others and locks the safe.

Chapter Twenty-Two

Rob Charlton

Flores and I agree to work together on an unofficial basis. His resources at the Sheriff's department are spread thin so he's glad to have my support, especially since my fees will come from Mrs. Greenwald instead of his limited budget. He agrees to learn more about the Colorado killing and for my part I'll follow up on the names I've gleaned from Bisset's records.

It's the next morning and I'm back at my office thumbing through my notes to find the list I'd written. Now that I've discovered the connection between the cancelled food order and the late Shelly Richards I can eliminate the names for which there are credit card slips. Since their orders were paid they couldn't be involved. There are four: Cynthia Collins, Rupert Smith, Stephen Williams and Jose Garcia. I draw a line through those names, leaving five from the reservations book for which I've been unable to find payment receipts.

Roberts

~~Collins (Cynthia)~~

Dr. Westwood

~~R. Smith (Rupert)~~

~~Williams (Stephen)~~

~~Dr. Garcia (Jose)~~

Miller

Dr. Stuart

Albertson

It's possible one of these is the killer, but there's another reason for trying to find them: They may be witnesses, possibly able to describe Shelly Richards' mysterious companion and likely murderer. It's a long shot but from Bisset's description of the confrontation it might have left deep impressions on observers. If there's even the slightest chance one of these individuals can provide a bit of evidence, it's worth pursuing. For that reason I realize I must also try to locate the four subjects I've eliminated as suspects. In fact, they'll be easiest to find because I've got first names for them.

This is going to be a difficult and perhaps fruitless task, but I can't see any way out of it. I decide to check with Bisset in case he remembers anything that could help ID the names. Some may have been regulars. I punch on my iPhone and dial. His maid answers and in a moment he comes on the line. I fill him in on what I've learned and tell him about the list of patrons served by Greenwald that night. Perhaps, I suggest, some of the names might be familiar to him.

"Ah, *c'est possible,* but it has been many years," he responds.

I read the list to him, pausing after each name as he makes notes. When I finish there's silence as he searches his memory of long-ago events.

"*Mon amie,* I can little recall these names," he informs me at last. "There are so many in my head. *Oui,* some may have familiarity, but what can I say?"

I imagine the Gallic shrug that accompanies this statement. He continues.

"I do think there was a Cynthia that used to come often to dine. *C'est possible* she is this Collins you mention, but about her I know nothing. And this Doctor Westwood, I think I knew someone like that. I picture a pompous man with the red hair and a large nose; he was perhaps a surgeon. About the others, *non*, there is nothing I can say."

I push for more information and learn that Collins was a stout woman around 40 years old who was usually accompanied by another woman.

"They perhaps were lovers, or as you say now, partners," Bisset volunteers.

He recalls Westwood as tall, thin and probably about fifty years old.

If those ages are correct, after more than 35 years Collins would be in her 70's and Westwood would be well into his 80's. I begin to fully appreciate the difficulty of my quest for information. I thank Bisset, mentioning my enjoyment of the gift of fresh-baked bread, and hang up.

I do a little Google searching and learn that a Dr. Walter Westwood, a retired surgeon who practiced here in Albuquerque, died three years ago, age 87. Scratch one probable witness. I find several people named Cynthia Collins in New Mexico but none in the target age range. I run a Yahoo people search program and find many more individuals of that name scattered across the country. It would be like looking for that old needle in the haystack. I search for Dr. Jose Garcia with similar discouraging results.

I do similar searches for Rupert Smith and Stephen Williams, the only remaining entries on the list for which I have first names. People search shows well over a hundred Rupert Smiths, if you can believe it, and several hundred Stephen Williams's. More needles.

That leaves only Roberts, Miller, Dr. Stuart and Albertson. Of those, the only hope would be to find the doctor, since there will be hundreds or thousands of people with the common surnames and I have no first names to narrow down the search. I punch "Dr. Stuart" and "New Mexico" into the Google search field and find a possibility. A Dr. Brian Stuart is endocrinologist here in the city.

A few more keystrokes and I learn that in 1975 he was doing his residency at the UNM medical school. The campus is less than eight blocks from Bisset's building, so it seems likely I've found my potential witness. I call his office and after being put on music hold for what seems an eternity and with a little abject begging and pleading I manage to obtain a 15-minute appointment with him for the following day.

I decide to hang it up for now and get some grub. My inner compass directs me once again to Sally's Place, the neighborhood health food and refreshment center. It's only 11:15 and Sally is alone in the bar when I arrive, puffing a little from the exertion of power walking the last three blocks while holding in my gut. I wheeze my way onto a stool and plant my elbows on the bar.

Sally's polishing glassware as usual. I'm sure she'll eventually rub holes in all the glasses and customers will find their drinks dribbling down their shirtfronts. She looks at me like she would something her cat might have found in the back alley. I try on a grin and she shakes her head somberly then laughs.

"What's with you?" I inquire.

Sally puts down the bar towel and walks over to stand opposite me.

"You're up to something," she suggests. "That was a pretty serious meet-and-greet you had with that cop yesterday."

"Howd'ya know he was a cop?" I counter.

She laughs again in the way that says "you've gotta be kidding me".

"Well, one clue was that big black unmarked parked right in front of my door, scaring away my afternoon customers."

"Oh, yeah, that."

"Yeah, that. Plus the cop mustache, bulge in the left armpit, arrogant attitude, sunglasses. Could've spotted the guy a mile away. Plain clothes my left foot. So who's he?"

"A sheriff's detective," I admit, seeing I wasn't about to put anything over on Sally. "We're working on something together."

"Yeah, I saw how your meeting started out. Looked like you were working on something all right, maybe a duel to the death or fifteen rounds of cage fighting."

I chuckle and point at a menu to indicate my usual. Without asking she pops the cap on a cold Modelo and sets it in front of me on a cardboard coaster. I raise no objection.

"Thought your kind didn't work with the cops," she says. "After the air temperature cooled down back there you two were thick as thieves."

"Uh, yeah. I've been working for a client whose husband was killed and he's the lead investigator on the case." I attempt to gloss over the details but Sally's interest has been awakened.

"Look," I explain, "I can't let any of this get out, so whatever I tell you hasta be strictly between us. You see and hear a lot of stuff and you've been around, so maybe you can help." I take a sip from the bottle. She's looking like she expects me to say more, so I make a bold leap and add: "Frankly, I need someone to talk things over with, just to keep me sane."

"That's what bartenders are for," she replies, flipping

her ponytail as she turns to shout my order back to the kitchen.

While my lunch is cooking I give her a rough outline of the case, leaving out names and details. She listens with all the patience and supportive facial expressions of a professional bartender. A bell rings to inform us that my food's ready. She sets it on the bar and I break off my narrative to launch an assault on the freshly fried potatoes, dripping with healthy grease. I taste one and reach for the salt.

"Sounds like you've got a bitch of a case," Sally remarks. "And a likewise client, too."

"She's not really so bad," I say between bites. I'm surprised to hear myself defending Mrs. Greenwald, but it's really true. Her mistreatment of Flores came out of frustration and the stress of her loss, not from any malicious intent. "She needs closure, and I'm trying to give it to her."

I chew on a bite of burger before continuing.

"That cop's really trying, too. We're on the same page on this now, so between us maybe we'll get somewhere."

The door opens and a couple of guys walk in. They look like marginally successful accountants or insurance salesmen, wearing cheap suits and ties that went out of style a decade ago. They take the table in the far corner that Flores and I had shared the day before. Sally goes to take their orders, leaving me to finish devastating my platter of food. The temptation is great but I decide against a piece of Sally's famous banana cream pie. I make the healthier choice, apple pie a la mode. That last part is French so I figure Bisset would approve.

Chapter Twenty-Three

Rob Charlton

I'm up early the next morning, not due to any lack of sloth but because Dr. Stuart has stuck me with a 7:30 appointment. It's well-known that doctors have no concept of the importance of healthful rest, prancing around at all hours of the day and night. It's enough to make anyone nervous in their presence. In fact, as he greets me I'm informed he's been up for several hours doing hospital rounds and preparing for his appointments. I express my congratulations and thanks for a bit of his valuable time. He apparently fails to see the irony behind my words.

He's a pleasant enough man, slender and with a flat little tummy. Poor guy doesn't have enough meat on his bones. What if he takes sick, as even doctors do? He won't have any bodily resources to see him through his illness. Must not be eating right. Probably do him some good to chow down on a few platters of Sally's burgers and some biscuits and sausage gravy. I decide against mentioning this.

He meets me in the reception area and leads me to a crowded little office. There's the usual desk and chairs and stacks of medical journals, patient jackets and books. He offers me coffee from a thermos pitcher and I gladly accept.

We make small talk for a moment before I begin to give him the background for my quest. I figure the chances are I'll get a blank look and the interview will be over. But, surprise, as I begin to describe the scene in the restaurant I see a little smile come over his face. Could I be hitting the jackpot? I stop talking and look at him inquiringly.

"How interesting," he comments. "It's nothing short of amazing but yes, I actually do recall that event. In fact, I think of it from time to time. It was quite a scene."

Dr. Stuart tells me that he and his wife were seated at a table adjacent to the banquette where the mystery diner acted out the drama with the waiter, Donald Greenwald. He describes the happening as if it were yesterday, adding several details that I hadn't gotten from Bisset.

"It was hilarious, like the best of Charlie Chaplin," he summarized. "Whoever he was, that guy could have been a great comedian."

"Well, it wasn't so funny for the woman he was with," I inform him. "She died that night, an apparent accidental fall but now we think she was probably murdered."

His smile evaporates and he sits back in his chair, startled.

"Murdered? Over that?"

"Yes, and we think the waiter has now been killed as well. I'm cooperating with the Sheriff's department on the investigation into his murder."

"My God," he breathes. "That's terrible. I feel awful. I've always had this fond memory of something tremendously comedic, and now to find out that it turned to tragedy…" He stops mid-sentence and fumbles with his coffee cup for a moment. "Well, now I'm embarrassed," he admits.

We drink coffee for a moment while he absorbs this information. After a moment I speak.

"I'd appreciate it if you don't mention this to anyone, " I say. "It's part of an ongoing investigation."

"Oh of course," he agrees. "Wouldn't think of it. I suppose you'd like to know anything I can remember about the man?"

I nod and he takes another sip of coffee as he plumbs his memory.

"OK," he says after a moment, "I can sort of picture him. You've got to take into account that it was many years ago, but I've often been told that I never forget a patient. I have a pretty good recollection about people."

I pull out my notebook and pen and prepare to take notes.

"I can't say there was anything really memorable about him," he continues. "Kind of an average sort of guy as I recall. He was really nicely dressed, though, pin-striped three-piece suit, white shirt, could have been a banker. Fairly young, though. In fact, now that I think about it he looked way over-dressed for his age. Of course I got the feeling from his actions that he was inexperienced and naive, which didn't fit with his appearance."

"Yeah, I see that. Can you describe him physically?"

He thinks for a minute.

"Can't say I can be much help there," he muses. "I'd have to say he was a plain vanilla kind of guy, average size, average looks. A Caucasian, of course. Definitely not Hispanic. I think his hair was medium colored, maybe light brown and worn short. I'm afraid I'm not being much help."

"No, this is very helpful doctor," I encourage him. "This is the first description we've had of the individual, so everything you've said is useful. Anything else?"

He thinks for a bit longer before answering.

"Well, he had a kind of nervous mannerism. You can probably tell that from the way the conversation went. The guy was obviously uncomfortable. I'd guess he'd never been in a fine restaurant before, that he was trying to impress his date but was in way over his head."

"Yeah, that fits."

"I remember the girl saying something about the nice car he had, a Buick or Olds if I remember correctly. I'm kind of embarrassed to say but my wife and I were listening to their conversation. It wasn't that we were trying to be nosy, but they were talking pretty loudly and we were sitting there about eight feet away. You know how it is…"

I give a little wave of my hand both to assure him I understand and to continue. I'm getting an interesting picture, of a well-dressed man who drives a nice car, but uncertain and nervous. A study in contradictions. Is the doctor correct in his guess the killer was trying to impress his date and had gone overboard in the effort?

"I remember they were talking about the menu and he didn't seem to know much about French cuisine. I think he told her he was going to order a steak and baked potato. Lord, what a waste at a restaurant like that."

"I've met Bruno Bisset and I gather he was a fine chef," I tell him.

"Oh you have no idea. This town hasn't seen anything like it since he closed his restaurant. Many of we regulars were heartbroken when we learned he was retiring."

"Do you remember anything more about the way the event went down? For example, anything else that was said, body language, things like that?"

"Not really. I just remember the way the waiters and others laughed at his *faux pas*. I have to admit we chuckled a bit, too. As I said, it was almost like a comedic act. But then he exploded, got up and left the restaurant in a huff."

He stopped, then continued: "No, that's not entirely correct. I remember now that he started to walk out, then came back and asked the waiter for his name. He was very angry. Then he left. His date was just sitting there in shock. Talk about embarrassment. Damn, I'm sorry to hear what happened to her..."

"Yeah, it sucks. From everything I've learned the fault was entirely with him. Bisset told me the waiter was devastated about how he broke out laughing and made a sarcastic comment. Apparently it was completely unlike him. He was one of the best waiters Bisset had."

"Yeah, I remember the guy. He was good. Worked there for a year or so and then I didn't see him again."

"He was a student," I explain.

"Sure, most of those guys were smart. Say, it wasn't that architect that was murdered a few months ago was it?"

I say nothing but give a little nod.

"Damn!" Stuart slaps his hand on the arm of his chair. "What a shame."

"Yeah," I agree. "Anything else you can remember?

He thinks for a moment then shakes his head.

"Well, thanks. This's been helpful." I start to rise but he stops me with a wave.

"You know," he says pensively, "I can't be sure but I distinctly got the impression that the two were students together, the man and his date. There was something they said, I don't know, some mention of a professor at the university, a class, something like that. As I say, I can't really pin it down, just an impression."

I sit back down and open my notebook again.

"Doctor, you've just given me a possible link." I scribble in my notebook and ask for more details, but after a moment it's clear I've drained the well of his memory. I thank him and leave.

It's not even eight o'clock and already several patients are sitting in his waiting room. They're leafing through tattered magazines, some of which may date to the Nixon administration. I shudder at the thought of being caught up in the jaws of the medical-industrial complex. These people are like zombie sheep, waiting to be sheared. I guess that's why they call them patients—it must take a lot of patience to submit to the indignities of a medical waiting room. Yeah, I know, different words. Bad pun. Sorry.

It's still early and I haven't had my breakfast. Elated that my long shot's paid off with a slender thread to follow, I head for a nearby diner to celebrate. I once heard a motivational speaker say something about starting the day off right with a good hot breakfast. I wanted to hug the guy.

Chapter Twenty-Four

Jim Craig

The nondescript van with Oklahoma plates is parked in a side street about two blocks from the secluded house on the outskirts of Denton, Texas where Brent Fitzgerald is visiting his daughter and grandsons. Margie Logan is divorced and lives with her two sons, 14 and 16. In the van, Jim Craig is preparing the former broker's permanent retirement.

It's nearly sundown and Craig's target will soon be alone in the house. He knows this because a few weeks earlier he placed two tiny transmitters on windows of the house, one covering the kitchen and one at the living room. The bugs are stuck with adhesive directly onto the glass, picking up conversations inside the rooms and sending them to a mil-spec repeater hidden in a tree a few dozen yards away. The repeater sends them on through a cell phone connection to a sound-activated recorder.

Early that morning Craig listened as the mother and sons made plans to attend a high school basketball game. Discussing this over breakfast, Fitzgerald tells them he's tired from his travels and will stay to catch up on his rest. It's the perfect setup for which Craig has waited.

Now they're eating an early dinner and in about half an hour mother and sons will leave for the game. Craig monitors the conversations directly through an earpiece headset. Fitzgerald repeats his plan to stay in the house and relax in an easy chair. It's game on for the retirement.

As he waits Craig goes over the plan in his mind. After a careful reconnoiter he'll arrive at the door of the Logan house wearing coveralls and a cap bearing the logo of Denton Municipal Electric, the city-owned power company. When Fitzgerald comes to the door he'll be informed of a possible electrical short at the house. The van will be parked directly in front with a magnetic sign identifying the power company on the side facing the house.

With Fitzgerald's suspicions laid to rest, Craig will lure him onto the porch, restrain him, slap duct tape across his mouth and frog march him to the van. There he'll chain the victim, remove the magnetic sign and drive away to the chosen retirement place.

It's a sure-fire plan, one of Barth's best efforts.

Now Craig hears the family preparing to leave. There's the sound of dishes clattering into a sink, doors slamming, footsteps on stairs. Goodbyes are said and at last Fitzgerald is alone. Craig hears the TV set come on and the broken sound bites of channels being surfed. In a moment the set settles on a football game, the ravings of a hyperactive color announcer and the background roar of a crowd. The time has come. Craig starts the engine and begins to move.

It's a half-hour later and everything has gone according to plan. Craig has driven his chained and gagged victim to an abandoned building on the outskirts of Ft. Worth. Once an apartment block built in the early 1950s and empty since being condemned over a decade ago, the place is a dump, reeking of mildew and rat feces. Craig unchains Fitzgerald and pushes him to his feet with a pistol held to his neck. When the broker attempts to squirm away he receives a blow to his right temple from the barrel of the pistol.

"If you struggle, you'll suffer," Craig informs him in a cold, impersonal whisper. "Now move."

Pointing the way with the beam from a pocket flashlight he leads Fitzgerald into the empty ruin and down a hallway to an open room. There are sounds of squeaking and the scurrying of little feet. Fitzgerald is thrown onto the floor against a wall. Craig sets down a small shoulder bag and takes out a battery-powered lantern. He turns it on and sets it on the floor beside them. He crouches before his victim, gazing implacably into his face. Wide-eyed, the doomed broker stares back at him, trying to work his mouth against the restraint of the gray metallic tape.

"Now, Mr. Fitzgerald," Craig begins, much as a CEO might call his directors to order, "we're here for a very important reason." He pauses before continuing.

"You're wondering why you've been called to this meeting, and I will explain. Let me introduce myself. I'm your retirement counselor and this is your retirement day."

The victim begins to shake his head violently. Craig reaches to grasp one end of the tape.

"It seems you have something you want to say," he whispers. "I'll remove the tape if you swear not to start yelling. If you do, you'll suffer." He waits for a response and after a moment Fitzgerald nods in agreement. The tape is ripped away. Craig pushes the pistol forward against the broker's chest.

"You can talk," he says in a flat tone.

"I...I won't yell," the man whispers. "What's this about retirement. Are you nuts? I retired several years ago."

Craig smiles.

"Yes, but that was a temporary retirement. We're talking about something more permanent here."

Again he waits as Fitzgerald absorbs his meaning.

"You're going to kill me." It's not a question. "Why, why in Heaven? I've done nothing to you!"

Craig sits back on his haunches like a resting Buddha, contemplating his subject.

"You've done harm to hundreds," he informs the man. "You enriched yourself at the expense of your clients. You lied and cheated your way to wealth and lived high for decades by stealing from those who trusted you. That's the why of this, the way you earned this retirement."

Fitzgerald's face turns white. He begins to shake uncontrollably as if taken with a sudden chill. His mouth moves but only gibbering sounds emerge. Craig observes with satisfaction.

"So, Mr. Big Shot New York broker, I've got something for you." He reaches into his pocket and removes a shining gold watch. He holds it out and Fitzgerald notices the hand is wearing a surgical glove. He focuses on the familiar watch.

"That's mine…" he croaks, "But no…" He raises his left arm to see that his own Piaget is still in place on his wrist. "What's this about?"

"It's your retirement watch," Craig tells him. "Here, take off your old one and put this on. You'll want to read the inscription first. It's quite touching."

Fitzgerald takes the watch and holds it up to the light, straining his eyes to read the engraving on its back. He looks up with eyebrows raised.

"This is nuts," he declares. "What's this date, sometime in 1991? That's more than twenty years ago!"

"It's the day you earned your retirement. The one time you cheated someone who cared enough to do something about it. Now go on, put on the watch."

The broker sinks back, letting the watch fall onto his lap. Craig raises the pistol threateningly.

"I said put it on," he hisses. "Right now." He pokes the pistol into Fitzgerald's chest.

Fumbling, Fitzgerald removes his own Piaget and straps on the replacement. He lets his arm fall and looks up helplessly.

"Now what are you going to do?" he whimpers, shrinking back against the wall.

Craig withdraws the pistol and resumes his Buddha-like position. He gazes calmly at the frightened man.

"Why now, of course, it's time for your retirement. The last chickens are coming home to roost."

He begins to rise and is caught off balance as Fitz–gerald kicks out with his left foot, striking Craig in the thigh and causing him to fall. Attempting to catch himself he loses his grip on the pistol and it spins away into the darkness. He falls heavily, striking his head against the wall. He's momentarily disoriented.

"You son-of-a-bitch!" In a rage Fitzgerald springs to his feet and towers over Craig. He kicks out with a heavy shoe, catching the assailant in the solar plexus. His breath knocked out of him, Craig involuntarily folds into a fetal position, moaning with pain. Another kick to the head and suddenly Fitzgerald is gone, the sound of his running feet echoing down the empty hallway.

"Shit, oh shit," Craig moans, rolling onto his back and attempting to rise. He knows he's too late. His quarry is gone, taking the retirement watch with him.

After a time he's able to rise, wheezing and clutching his chest. He staggers to the van, throws the bag into the back and climbs in. In a moment he's driving swiftly away from the scene, knowing there's no chance of catching Fitzgerald in the dark wasteland that surrounds the desolate and abandoned building.

Raging, he pounds on the steering wheel, cursing the man and his own carelessness. The retirement has failed.

Chapter Twenty-five

Rob Charlton

It's been a quiet couple of days but that's about to change. I just get to my office and start to check my email when the merry theme from *The Untouchables* announces an incoming call on my iPhone. I hit the green button and put it on speaker. It's Luis Flores. He's in no talkative mood apparently, doesn't even let me finish saying hello before he starts to speak.

"Rob, we need to meet." His voice is crisp and he's obviously already hopped up on his morning coffee. Mine is still going through whatever it is that Mr. Coffee does with all his slurping and dripping.

"Um...OK," I respond with my usual early-morning up-and-at-'em enthusiasm. I'd been up late the night before going over a list of business and finance students from Shelly Richards' classes and was hoping to clear my desk and go out for an early lunch.

"How about that bar, Sally's Place?" Flores suggests. I say nothing and after a moment he adds, "I'll park around the corner this time." I'd mentioned Sally's displeasure.

"Sounds fine to me," I agree. "She's usually open by now so any time is fine."

"I'll see you in fifteen minutes," Flores announces and hangs up without waiting for my reply.

Hmm, something must be up. Hoping Sally has her coffee pot going I regretfully put Mr. Coffee back to sleep and gather my case files. I decide to drive this time. My maroon baby has been feeling neglected and I figure if there's something to the admonition that Hell hath no fury like a woman scorned it probably applies to automobiles, too. And, yes, I've always thought of my cars as of the feminine persuasion, just as sea captains regard their ships. Yeah, I know, it's probably nuts but I've seen lots of guys dis their rides and end up on the phone to triple-A. Sucks for them.

I arrive just as Sally unlocks the door and turns around the CLOSED sign. A couple of shabby characters are waiting on the sidewalk for a mid-morning shot of Ol' Devil Rum. They practically knock her down getting into the bar. Sally shrugs and makes a little facial expression that says a lot about the tribulations of the bartending life. She puts her hands on her hips and regards me with a questioning look.

"Grill's not on yet, and you're not the kind to start drinking before decent people are even out of bed," she tells me. "And don't tell me you want a burger for breakfast."

"Coffee on?" I ask, putting on a hopeful hound kind of face. She laughs and stands aside to let me in.

"I'm meeting that sheriff's detective," I inform her. "He promised to park around the corner so we won't make any trouble for you."

She says something under her breath that I can't quite make out but that might have been unladylike.

"Got any of those healthy Danish to go with the coffee?"

"You mean the ones with the pineapple goo on them?" she asks with a smirk. "Or the ones with the cherry goo?"

"Yeah, give me one of each."

Armed with coffee and Danish I stake out the table in the far corner. Just as I arrange my snack Flores arrives and bustles over to join me without even glancing around. The two guys are at the far end of the bar sipping their morning shots-and-beers. Flores looks at my plate and tries vainly to hold back a look of revulsion.

"How can you eat that crap?" he asks.

I shrug and take a bite of the one with the pineapple goo. Apparently Flores is not aware that pineapple has lots of healthy antioxidants and that the Danish rolls also feature cream cheese, which adds a dairy portion to the mix. There's wheat flour of course, and sugar, both known for their energy-boosting effects. They may not be as nutritious as one of Sally's special burgers, but they meet many of the demands of the USDA Food Pyramid.

"Want some coffee?" I say around a mouthful of goodness. He nods and I get Sally's attention, pointing at my cup and gesturing at Flores. She hurries over with a cup. Her early birds are calling for refills so she leaves the pot on the table and goes to attend to their needs.

I look at Flores and raise one eyebrow in a meaningful way I've developed over the years. It always had a good effect when I was interrogating suspected felons, and it works in other situations, too. Hardboiled detective that he is he ignores me and opens a folder stuffed with documents.

"It looks like our guy's tried another one," he tells me. I can tell he's excited, but at the same time there's an undertone of disappointment in his attitude.

"Tell me about it," I respond and he begins his report, referring to the papers in his folder.

I learn that in Denton, Texas a man named Brent Fitzgerald was kidnapped two nights earlier and taken to an abandoned building. The kidnapper had prepared to kill him, describing it as a "retirement".

"The thing that definitely ties it to our case is that the perp actually produced a fake watch with engraving just like on Greenwald's," Flores informs me. "He actually made Fitzgerald put it on his wrist, but then the guy escaped."

Flores continues to relate details of the incident. Fitzgerald not only escaped unharmed, he got the license plate number of the kidnapper's van and gave it to police. It was registered to an Oklahoma address in the name of James Craig. The interstate nature of the crime caused the Denton PD to call the FBI. The Oke City PD swat team and FBI agents conducted an early-morning raid on a condo allegedly belonging to the aforesaid Craig.

"Great!" I exclaim. "Sounds like our killer's toast. Did they catch him or is he on the run?"

Flores isn't smiling.

"Apparently, neither of the above," he reports. "The condo was clean, like no one had ever lived there. They found a few articles of clothing and some makeup in the bedroom but the rest of the place was empty. There was no food in the fridge, no booze in the bar, nothing to indicate that anyone actually lived there."

"Huh." I take a sip of coffee and attack the second Danish. Cherries are also good sources of antioxidants, as any health-conscious consumer knows. "So they think this Craig guy took a powder? Hell, he could be in Brazil by now."

Flores gazes at his documents for a moment before answering. He shakes his head.

"According to the FBI, there's no evidence that any such person ever existed. His birth certificate is phony and everything else is based on that. He had credit cards that go to dead ends, a bank account that gets money from some offshore company that turns out to be a front for something else and so forth. Bills are satisfied through auto-pay from a bank in San Francisco. There's no 'there' there."

I sit back in my chair and think for a moment.

"So, whoever it is has created a completely fictitious existence," I muse. "But it's a pretty extreme example since even the condo was a front. Obviously the guy actually lived someplace else and had that extra layer of deception in place. That had to be expensive."

"Very," Flores agrees. "It makes me wonder what's going on here. This is starting to look like a lot more than just your everyday serial killer at work."

"Did they find any identifying evidence? Prints? DNA?"

Flores looks glum.

"They found the van late last night at the Dallas-Fort Worth airport, in long-term parking. Both it and the condo were completely clean. The vic noticed the guy was wearing flesh-colored surgical gloves and had on some kind of smock. Looks like he's being very careful."

"Hmm, that's remarkable. I've never heard of a case where there was no trace evidence to connect the killer to the crime. It seems to invalidate Locard's principle."

The early 20th century French detective Edmond Locard proposed that every contact between a criminal and his or her victim or crime scene leaves a trace. Our killer apparently knew this and was avoiding the consequences.

"No, Locard's law still holds," Flores tells me. "The FBI found a few hairs that were apparently from Craig. They're going to run DNA tests on them. But of course the DNA database is seriously limited. It could help make a positive ID once we catch the guy, but probably won't help us identify him now."

I finish off the cherry Danish and wash it down with coffee. I chew thoughtfully, enjoying the sugar rush.

"Now that the FBI is in it, does that mean they're going to take over the Greenwald and Drake cases?" I ask.

"Not yet," Flores tells me. "I've made them aware of the similarities to the Denton attack, coordinating with the Colorado detective, but they aren't convinced there's a connection to what happened in Texas."

"Hmm, sounds like the typical FBI stance," I remark. "They're always reluctant to get into cases unless and until they have definite grounds under the law, such as interstate or federal crimes. The rule is to leave cases of violent crime to local authorities unless absolutely necessary."

"Well, speaking of that, don't our case and the one in Colorado involve kidnapping?" Flores asks. "That's a federal crime, right?"

"No. Unless ransom is demanded the Feds don't consider it kidnapping."

Flores thinks about that for a moment.

"Yeah, I knew that," he says. "Lots of crimes involve snatching the victim…rapes, murders, you name it. If the Feds gave a broad definition to kidnapping they'd be getting their noses into practically every violent crime in the nation."

"And we'd need to expand the FBI to about a hundred times what it is. That would drive the state's rights people and Libertarians into hysterics. Never gonna happen."

"So you think we're going to be left alone for now?"

"Yes, unless there's more evidence to pull them in. The connection between our case and the one in Colorado could give them justification because of the interstate factor, but as I said they're reluctant to get into things like this. They'd need a lot more to want to jump in."

"Well, I'll keep them informed," Flores concludes. "How about you? Making any progress?"

"I got that list of students you requested from the

university and spent a few hours last night trying to spot anything. Trouble is, there were a lot of kids in those classes back in 1975. More than two hundred shared classes with Shelly Richards, and there were many more enrolled in the business school at the time.

"Even when I cut it down by removing the women, there're still several hundred possibilities. I'll try to run down the students from her classes and see if they remember anything. It could give us a clue, but it's a long shot."

Flores puts on his glum face again.

"OK," he says at last. "Wish I had the resources to help on that, but as long as Marcia Greenwald is willing to pay you, keep it up. How's that working out, by the way?"

"Oh, I'm still keeping her on a short leash," I report with a mischievous grin. "I'm going to run through her advance in a few days, though, and she may opt not to continue. Actually, though, I think she's gonna stick with it."

"Good." Flores picks up his reports and begins to put them back into the folder. "I'll have these scanned and emailed to you in about an hour."

I leave a Hamilton on the table and we get up and walk toward the door. Sally's busy pouring a third round for her morning clients and I merely nod to her as we go out onto the sidewalk. My maroon baby is parked nearby and as I walk toward her Flores turns the other way to where his unmarked is concealed around the corner.

"See you later, Amigo," he calls out.

"Later, Gator," I reply with a laugh.

The baby's glad to see me. She chirps happily when I hit the unlock button on the key fob.

Chapter Twenty-six

Rob Charlton

I spend the rest of the day trying to run down classmates of Shelly Richards. It's like spending a week in Frustration City, and although I manage to speak with a dozen or so, none have anything to offer the investigation. Most of them vaguely recall Shelly's death, but only one even remembers her name. I leave messages with several others when the calls go through to voicemail.

That magic hour is approaching when the twilight is gloaming or whatever the poets would say so I decide to hang it up. I set the alarm and lock my lair, pausing in the parking lot to check the weather.

If there's one thing about New Mexico it's that the weather is about as predictable as dirt. In fact, dirt has a lot to do with it. This afternoon the winds are blowing up desert sand and grit and the sky has a brown tint. The maroon baby's covered with a thin layer of tan dust. I can taste the stuff in my mouth.

There's a sure-fire cure for a mouth full of dust and that's a mouth full of beer, so I drive the three blocks to Sally's Place and plunk myself down at the bar. Sally's busy with several thirsty patrons and takes a minute to get to me. I make choking gestures and she laughs as she pops the top on a cold Modelo, twists a chunk of lime onto the rim and sets it in front of me. I snatch it, throw the lime onto the bar and take a long swig.

"You're a real life saver," I tell her, wiping my mouth with the back of my hand.

"What, a peppermint breath mint?" she comes back.

"No, honey, not that kind. The real ones."

"Oh, you mean an ugly ring with a rope attached to it? Thanks a lot." Some people can't resist being smartasses. I give her a wry look and she returns a cheeky grin.

"How's the case coming?" she inquires, turning serious.

"Oh, shit, don't even ask." I take another swig of the beer, slouch forward with my elbows on the bar and lower my voice. "I can't talk about it with an audience," I murmur, rotating my head to indicate the crowd of fellow bar-flies. "I'll come for an early lunch tomorrow." She nods and steps away to serve another customer.

I sit and sip, keeping an eye on myself in the mirror behind the bar. Liquor bottles are lined up on the back bar and it gives me the appearance of looking over a picket fence. Crap, I gotta do something about those jowls. I ponder possible actions, wondering if my government health insurance will cover a face-lift. Maybe there's a new drug that melts away jowls quickly and painlessly. Hell, if there is it probably has some terrible side effect, like causing you to become impotent. Maybe jowls aren't the worst thing that can happen to a man. I should think of them as marks of success and maturity. Probably.

I drain the bottle and wave the empty bottle at Sally.

Settling down for the second inning of my evening I start to go into my creative mode, trying to figure out how to pan some gold from that useless list of former students. If we're right, one of them is our killer, but which one? I pick up a napkin and begin making little diagrams. It seems fruitless to continue to cold-call people about something that happened so many years ago. None of them are likely to remember anything that would help us identify the bad guy.

Something sparks in my brain. The murder van was found at the airport in Texas, which almost certainly means the killer abandoned it and flew out of Dallas-Fort Worth. He must have known he'd been made and obviously wasn't going back to Oklahoma.

It seems the killer's been working under a fake identity. He may have used the Jim Craig alias to buy a ticket, but perhaps not. Let's say we get a list of all the passengers who flew out of that airport around the time the van was dropped off. There are two possibilities. First, if he flew under the Craig name we can learn where he went. No doubt the FBI is already doing that.

But there's another possibility, and that's that the perp may have bought a ticket under his real name. He would want to cover his trail, so it's just possible he did that. After all, he has no reason to suspect we have any way to connect him to the crimes.

So if we compare the names of the airline passengers with the ones from the university class, we might just find our killer. Traveling under his own name could be the mistake that will let us ID him.

This is exciting. I feel the rush I used to get on a hot trail back when I was an FBI agent. I can almost smell it—the guy's slowly coming into focus for me. Yes, there's a definite possibility I can nail this guy. He's out there, and sooner or later he'll fall into my hands.

I finish my beer and drive back to my lair, surprising a roadrunner that's lurking around the parking lot looking for bugs or lizards. Startled, he does his swhoooosh thing and I can't help but think about the old cartoons and how my case kinda sorta matches that epic duel between bird and beast. Yeah, I may be the coyote in this story, but no way I'm gonna take the long dive into the canyon. This time the coyote's going to play it smart.

Chapter Twenty-seven

Jeremy Barth

Barth rages. He stands on the porch of his house staring wildly around the desert landscape. His hands are curled into fists, one clutching a wireless telephone as if to crush it. His eyes are wild, his lips trembling with anger and...with something else. Could it be fear?

Not only has the retirement of Brent Fitzgerald gone wrong, the authorities have tied the attempt to Jim Craig. Barth's lost a key member of his dispersed organization. It's a serious blow to what he fancifully thinks of as Retirement Consultants, LLC. Craig was tasked to play significant parts in the carefully planned siege of revenge against Barth's perceived enemies.

But it's something else that's brought him to seething rage: A phone message.

Gritting his teeth he relaxes his hands, lifts the phone and hits the replay button. As a recording begins to sound in his ear for the fourth time he stares grimly at the rugged cliffs of the Sandia Crest.

> *Good morning Mr. Barth. My name is Rob Charlton. I'm a private investigator working in cooperation with the Bernalillo County Sheriffs Department. We're seeking information about a*

UNM student named Shelly Richards who died in 1975. According to the university's records she was a classmate of yours. Please call me at your earliest convenience.

Barth's anger rises as the speaker goes on to leave a phone number and signs off with a cordial thank you. He snarls and lets the phone drop to the floor. He kicks it and it skitters off the porch into a flowerbed.

What the hell is this?

It's never occurred to Barth that the death of Shelly Richards would ever be questioned. That book was closed, a perfect crime long since wiped from the memory of the law. How could that case be raising its head from the mists of time? *And now! Why now?*

Could it be even remotely possible that her death has somehow been connected with the retirement of Donald Greenwald? It's beyond all belief. But if not that, what? The likely possibility seems too great to dismiss.

The white heat of Barth's rage burns out to a glowing ember leaving him shaken and weak. He walks into the yard and picks up the phone from the flowerbed. He turns it on, hears a dial tone, turns it off and slips it into his pocket. As he shakes off the shock of potential discovery his mind begins to work.

Barth realizes there's no reason to believe he's a suspect. Shelly Richards had hundreds of classmates and he'd been careful to conceal any connection with her. He killed her to keep from being humiliated and her death wiped away any connection between them. It was skillfully done, making the authorities believe she had died from an accidental fall. The appearance that her death was accidental was simple and believable, and cops are always ready to accept the simplest solutions. Her death wasn't even investigated as a murder. Case closed.

But something's happened, something to bring her death back under the light of examination. It has to be related to the Greenwald retirement. What if some classmate knew and remembers that she was meeting him that night? Could long-buried facts come out, facts that would not only tie him to her death, but to the more recent killing of the former restaurant waiter?

Barth returns to the porch and sits down in one of his pale blue Adirondack chairs. He closes his eyes and takes several deep breaths. It's time to stop reacting and think about the phone call and what it might mean. Who is this Rob Charlton, the owner of the matter-of-fact voice on the phone? He said he was a private investigator, not a part of law enforcement. What's the meaning of that?

He doesn't know, but he's aware that if Charlton's sniffing on his trail he represents an imminent threat. Barth settles back in the chair and steeples his hands together, fingers touching fingers. He cradles his chin on the tips and lets his eyes focus to infinity into the clear blue sky.

He knows how to deal with threats. He's done it all his life, made it his special skill. No need to panic. This is an opportunity to exercise those skills once more, to demonstrate his superiority.

The ember of has rage grows cold. He rises and goes to the kitchen to make coffee. Carrying his cup he retreats to the secret room. He opens a supply cabinet and selects one of the thin case files used to organize his retirement plans. He sits at the foreman's desk in the high swivel chair and picks up a pen. Carefully he writes a name on the spine of the case and sets it aside.

Making notes on a legal pad he begins to rough out a course of action. He'll follow his usual strategy, a process drawn from years of experience in management. Step one is to learn all pertinent facts through research. Next is to organize, evaluate and analyze those facts. Third is to create a plan to take every advantage from the knowledge obtained. And finally, the culminating execution of the plan.

He smiles as he works, for Barth loves a challenge. He makes a note to find out what kind of watch Charlton wears.

Chapter Twenty-eight

Rob Charlton

I'm one frustrated PI. Everything about the Greenwald case leads to dead ends. I've wasted most of the last two days on the phone trying to track down information about Shelly Richards. After so many years few of her classmates even vaguely remember her and none of my calls yield any leads.

On another front Flores calls to report that the DNA from the hair samples believed to be from Jim Craig turned up a match. He doesn't seem particularly happy.

"Trouble is, the match is to a guy who died several years ago," Flores tells me.

"What?"

"Yeah, my reaction too. Actually the match was to a lifer who died in prison, out in New York State. The FBI guy told me they think it was from a human hair wig. Seems that a lot of prisoners sell their hair to wig makers."

"Hmm, makes sense," I muse. "Well, that tells us something at least. Either Craig is bald or he was disguised. Any hope of tracking the hair?"

"The FBI's attempting to trace it but I have little hope they'll succeed. It seems that human hair goes through brokers and dealers and who knows where before it ends up as wigs."

* * * * *

It's late afternoon and I'm sitting in my swivel chair doing my staring-at-the-wall thing. I've taken down all the receipts from the restaurant and put them away in the file. Although the wall should be grateful, it's being its usual reticent self. No help there.

I give it a resentful glare and turn to my desk, shutting down things for the day. I've developed a sizeable file on the Greenwald case, arranged in folders and stored in my locked filing cabinet. I turn off the computer and wait while it goes through its shutdown cycle. I remove the external backup hard drive and lock it in my little wall safe. I look around one last time before stepping through the tiny reception area to set the alarm inside the front door. It does its reassuring beep-beep-beep thing and I step out, closing and locking the door behind me.

Again I face the empty parking lot and row of defunct stores. The place is looking shabbier than ever. Rubbish has collected in little windrows, mingling with the desert dust. A nest of empty beer cans is scattered in one corner and I see a broken window in one of the storefronts. A neon sign at Marv's Liquors has lost a few letters and the rest is blinking in an annoying way. Even his OPEN sign is flickering as if unsure. Shit, this place is turning into a dump.

I notice one thing different. A panel van's parked about sixty feet from my door at the street side of the lot with its windshield facing me. The windows are blacked out so in the fading light I can't tell if anyone's inside. My antennae give a little twitch. The setup reminds me of a stakeout. Am I being watched? Nah, I'd have to be paranoid to think that.

I step over to the maroon baby and click to wake her up. She sounds happy, so that makes one of us. I shrug, climb in and start the engine. As I begin to drive out of the lot I start to turn left but on a whim turn right instead and pass slowly behind the parked van. It's a New Mexico plate and as I accelerate down the street I use my finger to scrawl the number in the dust on the baby's dashboard. Just a habit from years of being a suspicious lawman.

I cruise around for a while, enjoying the maroon baby's companionship. She's purring like a pussycat. The last light of a colorful tie-dyed sunset is fading in the west and a bright star appears. I figure it's either the planet Venus or one of those UFOs that are so common here. It doesn't seem to be moving so it's probably the planet. I keep driving, letting my mind work.

The clock's ticking on this case. So far there've been lots of hints but no real evidence to point me at a suspect. Jim Craig is almost certainly the killer—although that's obviously not his real name and he's disappeared without a trace. A comparison of the airline lists, obtained for me by Flores through the FBI, has revealed no connection with any of the names from Shelly Richards' UNM classmates. The empty condo and phony identification makes it obvious that the murderer's not only clever but has money he's willing to spend. No telling who Craig is, or where he's gone.

There's a Rangers game tonight and I decide to stop by the sports bar to watch it and grab something to eat. They put on a pretty good burger, not quite up to Sally's but then she doesn't have the big screen TV. I need to get my mind off of this case and baseball has always been my friend. That and beer.

It's after nine and the Rangers are tied with Oakland in the bottom of the seventh when my cell phone rings. I consider letting it go through to voicemail but decide it might be important so I step away from the bar and click to answer. It's a woman at the security company telling me my office alarm has just gone off. I advise her it wasn't me and she hangs up to call the police.

That isn't much assurance. In my experience the cops usually arrive too late to prevent most crimes. The observation "when seconds count the police are only minutes away" is all too true. I throw some money on the bar and hustle out to the maroon baby.

Even though I have no siren or flashing lights I beat the cops to my office by several minutes. The front door has been forced and the alarm is still blaring its indignant complaint. I pull out my Glock and step inside. There's no one in the reception area. Stepping aside to keep from being a target silhouetted against the streetlights outside the door I call out a challenge. No response. Everything's quiet.

Carefully I slip to the door of my inner lair and take a quick peek. Nothing. I reach inside to turn on the lights then step through the door with my gun raised. Empty.

My heart almost stops when I look around. There's only a dust-free rectangle to mark where my computer lived. The electronic files are password protected and backed up on the hard drive in my safe. But the bad news is that the filing cabinet drawers are yawning open. I use a pen to pull the top drawer all the way out. The Greenwald files are gone. Shit.

Now I hear the sound of sirens and a moment later I step outside to greet a squad car with two uniforms, my gun back in its holster. They jump out with hands on their own side arms but relax when they see my hands are empty.

I identify myself and tell them what I've seen. One of the cops goes back to the car and radios for a detective and CSI criminalist. The other officer begins to ask me questions, making notes. I tell him what I've seen. He asks if anything is missing and I mention the computer but hedge my answer, unwilling to reveal the loss of the Greenwald papers.

Presently the detective arrives and introduces himself. The poor guy's name is Harry George. I always feel uneasy around people who have two first names. I'm embarrassed for them. There's something unnatural about it, but he seems like a decent sort. He asks me a few questions then goes to study the crime scene. A CSI tech arrives to blow fingerprint dust all over everything.

Waiting in the parking lot I call the security company and ask them to arrange for a locksmith to secure the office. Then I dial Flores. He sounds a bit grumpy.

"Sorry to call you at home, but my office has just been robbed," I tell him. "They got my case file and computer."

Silence, then "Crap, it's got to be him."

"Yeah, that's what I figured. If it were just the computer it could be anybody, but who else would want the Greenwald file?"

Flores remains silent again for a long moment.

"You know," he says, "this could be a good thing."

"OK," I say dubiously. "And how's that so?"

"Well, it means we're getting close to him. He knows you're after him."

"That's not very reassuring seeing as how he's a stone cold killer and all."

"Well, there is that." He ponders a moment. "Look at it this way: How do you think he found out about you? Unless I'm mistaken it was through the calls you've made to former UNM students."

I let that sink in for a moment. Damn.

"Yeah, you must be right," I agree, "but that may not help us much. He could be one of the people I talked to, or he could have found out through the grapevine. It does narrow our search but I think I've made about sixty or seventy calls."

"There's something else: It means he's here in New Mexico."

"Yeah, that's true for now, but he could also be on the next plane out."

"Somehow I don't think so. We know Retirement Man had connections to this area, was apparently a student at the University. And the first murder took place here. I have a feeling he's somewhere nearby."

Flores and I had begun to refer to the mysterious killer as Retirement Man, and while it doesn't have the panache of "Son of Sam" or "Jack the Ripper" it's OK for our purposes.

Something else occurs to me. I tell Flores about the van I saw earlier in the parking lot as I was leaving, and my suspicion that it might be a stakeout.

"Could be our man," he muses. "Give me the description."

"I can do better than that," I inform him with a chuckle. "I just happened to write down the license plate number." I walk over to the maroon baby and lean in the door to read him the number scrawled in the dust.

"Hold on a moment, I'll be right back." He puts me on hold.

About two minutes pass and Flores comes back on the phone. He's excited.

"DMV has the van registered to a Jake Wilson. He's got a house right here, over on the west side. That could be him."

"How we gonna proceed?"

"Stay put. I'll be there in about ten minutes."

Chapter Twenty-nine

Rob Charlton

True to his word Flores arrives *mucho pronto,* his siren wailing and the hidden lights behind his car's front grille pulsing red and blue. He pulls up beside the maroon baby and jumps out, looking around at the scene. He's wearing jeans and boots with a golf shirt under a denim jacket. With my practiced eye I notice the bulge of a handgun hidden in the small of his back. I should suggest he needs a size larger on his jackets, but he'd probably take it the wrong way. Some people are sensitive about the size of their bodies.

The responding APD cars are still parked in front of my office and the CSI team is working inside. Waving at me Flores strides over to confer with Harry George, the detective in charge of the case. I start to follow but just then a truck bearing the words "Mike's Lock & Key" pulls in off the street. I've seen Mike before, when he installed the present lock and alarm system. He's got some explaining to do. I turn to greet him as he bounces out of the truck.

"Hi Mr. Charlton," he trills. "Bit of bad luck, huh?"

I give him a few seconds of my second most intense glare but it doesn't seem to register.

"Yeah," I admit, turning toward the door. "Seems your

locks and alarm didn't do much good." I emphasize the "your" but he seems invulnerable to the irony. I look at him sideways expecting a mea culpa, but no, the guy's in serious denial about his ineffective craft. He actually smiles.

"Oh, no sir, the system worked just as it's supposed to. The alarm went off to alert the security office and the cops were on their way."

The horse has left and he's telling me there wasn't much sense closing the barn door in the first place. I maintain a stoic silence but he sticks to his self-serving story, determined to maintain the fiction that his services are somehow useful against would-be miscreants.

"Unless you're talking about a bank safe, nothing can keep out a determined burglar," he tells me with unabashed enthusiasm. I imagine he's reading from a little script in his head, perhaps memorized from a National Association of Locksmith and Alarm Specialists pamphlet titled "How to Bullshit Clients for Fun and Profit."

Actually I know from my years in law enforcement that he's right but it's different somehow when it happens to you. I shrug and turn off my glare. Mike walks over to inspect the door, now covered with fingerprint powder. I stroll along to look over his shoulder. It looks like the door was wrenched out of its frame with a wrecking bar. The deadbolt is finally living up to its name, twisted right out of the door and hanging by a bit of shredded metal, dead like a duck.

"That's nasty," Mike opines. He appears to be trying to hold back a happy grin. "Looks like we'll have to put in a whole new door."

I think I catch a glimpse of dollar signs in his eyes but can't be sure. I turn on the glare again, but he turns back to examine the dimensions of his economic windfall with the oblivious idiocy of a proud new parent.

OK, I think, it's decision time for old Rob. If I have him put in a new door it's probably gonna cost me a grand, maybe two. There goes my budget again. And, hell, after this demonstration of state-of-the-art non-security I should have the door upgraded to something that can't be popped open with a church key like a can of beer. That could cost a lot more.

On the other hand, this place is a dump and I need to reconsider whether to even continue to do business here. Ever since Chan's Qwik-Chow shut down next door there hasn't even been the odor of ginger and overheated oil to add life to the neighborhood. Come to think of it, I've never heard of a Chinese restaurant closing. They seem to have nine lives, like the cats they probably use for their stir-fries. Obviously, this place has some really bad karma.

"Listen, Mike," I tell him, "I need time to think about this. Can you jerry rig something just to keep the door secure until tomorrow? A padlock or something?"

I see the glint of avarice fade in his eyes like a dying swan. He's on to where this is going. He looks around the deserted strip mall and nods glumly.

"Great!" I shine him on like a Harvest Moon, suddenly filled with an odd feeling of release. "Do that and I'll get back to you."

Wow, I feel like I did when I signed the divorce papers with Greta. I've made an executive decision to dump the dump. There'll be plenty of time to decide my future but I know it won't be here in this depressing hole in the wall. I almost feel like breaking into song, something like "I Gotta Be Me" or "Happy Days Are Here Again."

Flores has been standing to one side with a doleful expression on his face. Now I turn to him and we step away to stand beside his unmarked.

"Typical snatch and run," he says. "Did he take anything except the laptop and Greenwald file?"

I grimace and shake my head. "Crap, Luis, I made it easy for him. The files were all neatly labeled, and that locked filing cabinet might as well have been made of cardboard."

Frustrated, I pound a fist into my open left hand.

"Nothing like this could ever have happened at the Bureau," I exclaim.

Flores looks at me for a moment with a wry smile.

"No, I suppose not," he offers wryly. "From what I've seen, at the Bureau most agents can't find their own butts with flashlights and mirrors. A burglar wouldn't have a chance."

I put on a disappointed look and place my hands on my hips in a disapproving manner.

"Luis, I'm offended. You're referring to my former employer. I'll have you know that in thirty years as an agent none of my files went missing." I pause, thinking. "Mostly not," I add. I pause again. "And it wasn't my fault," I conclude with this-subject-is-over certainty. A man has to stand up for his dignity.

"Just kidding," Flores says, chuckling and slapping me on the back. He gestures to the passenger door of his car. We get in and he starts up the engine to run the air conditioning. Our conversation turns serious.

"What should we do, Rob?" Luis asks. "We have the name and address of someone who may have scoped out your office. It could have been Retirement Man but we don't know anything for sure. Hell, the van could have been stolen for all we know."

"Yeah," I agree, "it's just a hunch. The guy could have parked there and walked down to that coffee shop on the corner. There's nothing to tie it to the break-in."

We muse for a while. I gaze at the flickering neon sign at Marv's Liquor, thinking how much I'm not gonna miss this place.

"There was something about that van that raised my hackles," I say at last. "It had the look and smell of a stake-out. I think it was him."

We lapse back into silence for a while.

"I don't suppose you said anything about Greenwald to the responding officers?" Flores asks. I assure him I hadn't and he continues. "Technically, the break-in is their case and we must stand aside. But Retirement Man is our case, and this could be the lead we've been looking for. There's no reason for us to tie the two together, at least not now."

"You're right," I agree. "It's not the break-in that's important; it's what was taken that matters."

Flores reaches a hand to his breast pocket then stops and lets it drop back.

"Ah, crap," he mutters.

I look at him but say nothing. He glances over at me then sighs and turns his eyes away.

"I gave up smoking a couple weeks ago," he informs me in a quiet, embarrassed tone.

I nod with understanding, remembering how it was with me. When I was in law school and during my early days with the Bureau I smoked at least a pack a day. Back then it was almost required adult behavior, or at least it seemed like it. You grew up and at a certain time you were expected to start to smoke. If you weren't walking a mile for a Camel, you were nobody. Back in that antediluvian age of my youth everyone did it, even doctors for crying out loud. You'd think at least they would have had a lick of sense. It's a wonder the entire human race didn't contract lung cancer and go extinct. Remembering my Mom's advice about the golden quality of silence I say nothing.

He sits quietly for a moment. I wonder if he's thinking about our case or still fighting that nicotine demon that's clamoring inside his head. I look out to where the crime scene tech is packing it in. The police detective is making notes on a clipboard and Mike is rooting around in his truck preparing to secure the door to my office.

"Yeah," Flores says at last, "it's our case. Let's check this guy out."

He starts the engine and puts the car in gear.

Chapter Thirty

Jeremy Barth

Barth's been busy since returning from the Jake Wilson house with the stolen file. He's devoted the last hour to a preliminary reading of Charlton's notes. He feels like a Klondike prospector who's just hit the mother lode. It's all here, the information that could lead to him—but is now in his hands. There's nothing to directly implicate him and now this precious information is his to use against his enemies.

The retirement list is about to get longer.

He sits at the tall foreman's desk in his downstairs room, hunched over the stack of files like a vulture on a day-old carcass. On a legal pad he's written down several names: Rob Charlton. Luis Flores. Marsha Greenwald. Bruno Bisset. Three more potential retirees in addition to the ex-FBI agent.

Barth yawns and stretches. He's hungry and realizes that in his excitement he hasn't eaten. He locks away the file and goes upstairs to fix a late supper.

In the kitchen he gently grills a pork tenderloin, tops it with mushroom sauce and tears romaine to make a side salad. He sits at the kitchen table to eat, continuing to think about his plan. He's brought the legal pad upstairs and makes notes as he eats.

The key is Charlton. He's the dangerous one, the dogged investigator who might actually identify Barth. He draws a heavy line beneath Charlton's name. Retiring this one will be his top priority, job number one. The others know things, too, but it's the PI who has all the threads in his hands. Doing the others will merely be cleanup.

He adds two more names to the list: Professor Willard Humphrey. Dr. Brian Stuart. These people are loose ends that will also need to be attended to. It pays to be tho–rough, like a battlefield surgeon debriding a wound then cauterizing it.

Barth makes a cup of espresso and carries it onto the porch. The sky is dark and lights wink through the branches of a nearby shade tree, the stars of the striding giant Orion and Sirius the Dog Star rising from the east.

He sinks into a chair, puts his feet up on the porch railing in front of him and drinks the bitter coffee in a single gulp. The evening air is cool and dry, the blessing of high desert summer when days are hot and nights are cool.

For the first time Barth begins to ponder a diversion from his retirement model. Charlton needs to be dealt with quickly and efficiently. There isn't time to do prepare a formal retirement. Barth's prepared for this possibility.

He smiles in cruel anticipation. Charlton has a sur–prise coming to him, a fatal one.

Barth's in his element now, applying his Wall Street management skills to plan a death. How to proceed? There's the obvious way, to end Charlton's life with a bullet. That would leave no doubt about the event. But wouldn't it be better to create less certainty? Poison? An apparent automobile accident like the one that killed his parents? An engineered fall such as covered the murder of Shelly Richards? Barth ponders the options.

No, he decides, the situation requires direct and

prompt action. A quick bullet is the best way to take care of Charlton. In the chaos that follows he can plan actions against the others and deal with them one by one.

He rises and returns to his basement workshop. The arms safe contains several long guns. He draws out a sniper rifle, the ideal tool for long distance killing. It's a Sako TRG .300 Winchester Magnum, effective at up to more than a quarter mile and fitted with a Weaver 3-15X scope. The bolt-action rifle in dark camouflage colors has the deadly beauty of a venomous snake.

Barth knows this gun well for it's his closely guarded secret that while appearing to be a quiet and harmless accountant he's spent years mastering the tools of his vengeance. He lays the rifle carefully on the workbench and returns to the gun safe.

The next alternative is a matte black Remington model 870 Express tactical shotgun. Firing 12 gauge magnum shells it's a deadly weapon for relatively close-in work. Loaded with double-aught cartridges it can fire up to eight times with its quick pump action, each shot sending nine lead pellets into the target in a hail of death. Barth fondles the shotgun lovingly before placing it beside the rifle.

His next alternative is an automatic pistol, the weapon of choice for concealment and surprise attacks at close range. He selects a matte black .45 caliber Beretta Px4 Storm from one of the pigeon-holes along the right side of the gun safe.

The deadly handgun holds ten fat rounds, nine in the magazine and one in the chamber. It fits in a concealed holster and its reliable action can fire deadly bullets as fast as the trigger is pulled.

He places it with the rifle and shotgun on the bench and stands back to study the tools of death. Satisfied that this choice of weapons is assured to take down Charlton in almost any situation, Barth proceeds to collect boxes of ammunition for each weapon and pack the weapons in carrying cases.

The task itself will be assigned to Jake Wilson.

Chapter Thirty-one

Rob Charlton

We drive past the house belonging to Jake Wilson, the owner of record for the van I saw near my office. It's after 11 p.m. and everything's quiet. I notice the house is isolated from its neighbors. There's a dry arroyo along the right side and scraggly trees and brush enclose the back and sides of the lot, which is large, maybe a couple of acres. We glimpse an outbuilding behind the house.

Flores drives by without slowing and continues for a quarter mile before pulling over onto the shoulder. He puts the unmarked into park and glances at me with an unasked question.

"Let's take a look," I suggest. He nods in agreement and shuts down the engine. We get out and start to walk back toward the house, talking quietly.

"We don't need a warrant just to look around," Flores points out. "We can even knock on the door and see what happens."

"We need a cover story, a reason to be there."

"I'll show my shield and say we had a report of a burglar in the area."

"Yeah, that'll work."

"Think we should call for some backup? I could have a uniformed deputy here in ten or fifteen minutes."

"No, let's not take it to that level."

"OK, we'll play it by ear."

We pause as we come to the driveway. The house was probably built in the 1970s but it's in the Territorial style of the early 1800s when Anglos began to settle in the part of the Spanish Empire that was to become northern New Mexico. It has a pitched metal roof and a wide, open porch across the front. The driveway curves around the left side toward a large detached garage in the rear.

We hear nothing but the gentle sound of the desert breeze. Here at the edge of the city the sky is like a black cloth dotted with diamond specks of light. Yeah, sometimes I let my poetic spirit run away with me. Let's just say it's really dark. Flores has brought a couple of flashlights from his car and he hands me one.

"Let's check around the outside before we approach the front," he whispers.

"I'll go left and you go right. We'll meet at the garage in back."

He grunts in agreement and we begin our careful examination of the property, keeping the flashlights turned off. The ground is sandy and dotted with weeds so I have to pick my way slowly. I move to the right until I come to the edge of the arroyo, a dusty gash in the desert that becomes a running stream only at those rare times when rain falls.

I work my way along the arroyo until I'm even with the side of the house. I stop to study this new perspective. There's no sign of life, neither light nor sound to indicate human occupancy. I wait and listen but hear only the wind and the faint whine of traffic on a distant expressway. The scent of some fragrant desert plant is tickling my nose.

I move on, circling the back of the lot almost by feel in the dim starlight. The garage looms ahead of me and I catch a glimpse of Flores approaching it from the other side. We meet at the double doors at the front. Flores flicks his light briefly and we see the building's secured by a large padlock. Curious.

"Let's check the sides," Flores says.

He moves off to the left. I go right and we circle around. There's a small window on the east side and I stop there and wait for him. We move close and he shines his light through the glass, holding it close and shielding it with his hand. It's no surprise to see a familiar looking panel van parked inside. Flores glances at me and I nod. He flicks off the light and we step away from the window.

"Well, that eliminates the possibility the van was stolen," I whisper.

"Yeah, but it still doesn't prove anything. We've got no connection with the break-in, just that the van was there."

"No," I admit somewhat glumly.

We start to move toward the house, following along beside the sandy driveway. I notice something lying on the ground off to one side. It looks like a piece of paper. I'm drawn to it because my habit is to consider everything as possible evidence. Like thousands of useless things I've picked up over the years it's probably a candy wrapper, but I step over and pick it up by one corner, being careful to preserve fingerprint impressions.

"Whatcha got?" Flores asks, stepping alongside me.

"Not sure. Let's have a look."

We turn our backs to the house and Flores flicks on his flashlight, nearly covering the lens with his fingers to reveal only a tiny beam.

"Bingo," I breathe.

"What?"

I'm holding a cash receipt from Bruno's Bistro dated June 14, 1975. Yellowed with age it's still got a bit of tape on the top edge from when it had graced my office wall.

*****

Back in Flores' car we debate how to proceed. It's a tricky situation because we have evidence that ties Wilson to the break-in at my office, a case belonging to the Albuquerque Police. On the other hand, the receipt may also tie Wilson to the Greenwald murder, Flores' case. We don't want to lose control, but jurisdictional considerations must always be taken into account.

I'm all too familiar with these kinds of mine fields from my days in the FBI. Local authorities are always determined to keep control of cases and resent it when the feds interfere. Same thing applies between competing local law enforcement agencies that sometimes fight like wildcats over who gets to take credit for a case solved, or to pass on the blame for failure.

Flores checks our position with the GPS on his in-car computer and we learn that the Wilson house is located outside the Albuquerque city limits. We agree that gives the Sheriff's Office priority for this site, but still doesn't let us skirt the jurisdictional issue. The break-in definitely happened inside the city.

Now the question is whether Flores has grounds to make an arrest. Again, it's sticky because while Wilson can be directly tied to the burglary, the APD's case, the connection with Greenwald is subject to speculation. We're on shaky ground here.

"I think we gotta share this with APD," Flores concludes. "I'm not happy about it, but I know that detective, Harry George, and I think we can work with him on the burglary aspect and still keep control of our murder case."

Flores gets on his radio to order a team of deputies to put the house under surveillance until we can organize a warrant and make our move. Then he puts his cell phone on speaker and calls APD, asking for George.

We learn that the detective is still on duty but not in the office. Flores identifies himself and obtains George's cell number. In a few minutes Flores has him on the phone and asks for a meeting at a nearby truck stop coffee shop to discuss the break-in.

"What's so important that we gotta meet?" George objects. "It's a penny ante snatch and run case. I've got bigger fish to fry."

"Bigger than cold blooded serial murder?" Flores asks, winking at me. That stops the whining. George agrees to meet us as soon as he can get there.

Chapter Thirty-two

Jeremy Barth

Excited by his decision to assassinate Charlton, Barth decides not to wait until morning to transport his armaments to the Wilson house. He packs them in his Kia along with a pair of night vision binoculars and some other accessories. The stolen files have revealed just how close the detective is to finding the thread that will lead him to Barth. Time is of the essence—he must stop his hunter as quickly as possible.

He already knows where the ex-FBI agent lives and has worked out several scenarios. An obvious plan is to ambush Charlton outside his apartment building and use the sniper rifle or tactical shotgun to take him down. The choice of weapon will depend on the distance.

He's already reconnoitered the large parking lot in the rear of the 60-unit building. It has assigned parking for tenants and he knows from Charlton's unit number where he parks his car. There's plenty of room to set up the killing zone from a location near the back of the lot in an area reserved for visitors. At a distance of less than twenty yards this would be an ideal place for the tactical shotgun, capable of sending Charlton to hell in a storm of lead.

A second scenario would be to set up at Charlton's office, perhaps from the far end of the parking lot.

But Barth's impatient. He decides to engineer a strike by Wilson early in the morning, aimed at catching Charlton in bed. In that plan lock-picks will be used to break into the detective's apartment. The Beretta .45 is the ideal choice for the kill. Three quick shots will do it, the classic double-tap to the chest and an insurance bullet to the brain and Wilson can be down the stairs and away.

He feels a euphoric sense of happiness. He's in his element, managing murder and death. It's true that he gains satisfaction from the long-term careful planning of formal retirements but there's something vital about organizing an assassination, the delivery of sudden, unexpected death. Once the detective has been eliminated he can work out detailed retirement plans for the others on his list, then resume his regular program of retribution.

It's after midnight and Barth hums happily to himself as he drives, savoring the certain pleasure of turning his hunter into the hunted.

As he turns down the winding lane that leads to the Wilson house he catches a glint of reflection in his head–lights. Senses suddenly alert he slows but continues to drive.

He sees a sheriff's patrol car parked off the right side of the road just a quarter mile from the Wilson house, its lights turned off. Barth can see the dim shape of a uniformed officer inside. Coincidence? He hopes so.

Instead of turning into the driveway he continues past the house. In a moment his fear is realized. Just around a bend in the road he comes upon another squad car, parked on the left and facing him in the dark.

Oh, shit!

The house is under surveillance!

Barth feels a cold chill run up his spine. He steps on the accelerator and continues past the lurking deputy.

Knowing that Wilson has been compromised and will

have to be written off, he pounds on the steering wheel and screams with rage.

For nearly an hour Barth continues to drive aimlessly, struggling to calm his anger and frustration. First Craig and now Wilson have been discovered. The fruits of his years of planning and investment are being destroyed before his eyes.

Reaching a deserted area outside the city he pulls off the paved road onto a sandy track and stops. For a long time he sits behind the wheel, letting the anger slowly abate. It's Charlton, he knows instinctively. The bastard is closer than he'd thought. But how? It has to be the van, the only possible connection. Somehow the PI must have spotted it and traced it to Wilson.

Again Barth vents his rage. He should have been more careful. The Wilson van should have been fitted with stolen license plates. He'd thought about it but decided it was too great a risk. He'd taken care to assure there was no video security where the van was parked, but apparently that hadn't been enough.

In time Barth's anger is replaced by a feeling of cold determination. His only remaining base, the Singleton house, is far away in Colorado. Charlton must be killed and it's up to Barth to do the job.

A warm feeling of anticipation begins to replace the cold chill of discovery. He's ready. Tonight Charlton will die.

Chapter Thirty-three

Rob Charlton

It's almost dawn by the time Flores can obtain a warrant and organize a raid on the Jake Wilson house. In the meantime he drops me back at the office to pick up the maroon baby. I check my office door and see that Mike's secured it with a heavy chain and padlock then I drive back in time to witness the planned take-down at the Wilson house.

I park a couple of blocks away and walk to the end of the driveway where Flores' deputies are assembling. Surveillance has revealed no sign of activity in the house and thermal imaging reveals no hot spots indicating possible human occupation. Flores wisely plans to act as if there's someone present.

At six a.m. he orders his men to proceed and leads the way to the front door. APD detective George and I move in to a spot about thirty feet to the left, giving us a clear view of the door. We watch as pairs of SWAT officers circle left and right around the house to secure the back and sides. Two men armed with AR-15 rifles stand to each side as Flores approaches the door. He rings the bell.

There's no response. After ten seconds he rings again, waits another count of ten and steps aside. He motions and a burly officer carrying a heavy ram steps up to the door. The ram swings and the door rips open, its locks shattered and torn out of the frame.

"Sheriff's Department!" Flores shouts. "This is a raid!"

There's no response. The two SWAT officers dodge through the door. One cuts left the other right. Flores holds back for a moment before following.

From our position in the yard we trace the progress of the tactical team from the moving beams of high-intensity helmet lights flickering through the windows. It takes them only a few seconds to sweep the bungalow. Shouts of "Clear" signal that it's been secured. Flores steps back out the door and motions for us to approach.

The house is nearly deserted. Several rooms are empty and there's no sign that anyone has actually lived here. The refrigerator is empty and there's nothing in the little pantry except a few droppings from a no-doubt pissed-off mouse.

The exception is the bedroom where a selection of western style clothing hangs in the closet. There are jeans, shirts with pearl snaps for buttons, and even a Stetson hat. Three pairs of western boots are lined up on the floor of the closet.

The top drawer of a dresser yields a few other items, including a couple of bolo ties, a box of skin-toned surgical gloves and a ginger wig. The bathroom medicine chest houses a selection of theatrical makeup and a pair of heavy horn-rimmed glasses with plain lenses.

There's no sign of my stolen case files.

Flores and I look at each other in dismay. Clearly we've reached another dead end, a front address like the one in Oklahoma City. There's no such person as Jake Wilson and the trail to Retirement Man is cold.

It's a couple hours later and I've managed to roust out Mike the lock service guy to come give me the key to the padlock he put on my office. I spend organize the remains of my files, boxing them up and putting them in the trunk of the maroon baby. I plan to set up in my spare bedroom and will arrange for some guys with a truck to come move my desk, chairs and other stuff.

I phone the landlord to let him know that I plan to renege on my lease, explaining in no uncertain terms that I don't expect any blowback. I generously agree to pay the current rent and forego my deposit. He sounds depressed but accepting.

Next it's off to the Apple store to buy a new computer. I've got a backup hard drive with everything that was on the original machine, even the software, so it should be easy to get up to speed again. I decide to splurge and get the latest model with extra whizbangs and a big, wide screen.

Now it's time for a late breakfast. I feel drawn to the diner with its famous biscuits and gravy but gravitate instead to Sally's. She's just opened for the day and is wiping down the bar with a damp cloth when I come in the door. She looks at me for a moment then shakes her head sadly.

"Jesus, Rob, you look like shit," she tells me.

This is not the greeting I'd hoped for but a glance at myself in the back bar mirror demonstrates the accuracy of her assessment. I mumble something and climb onto a barstool. God, I look pathetic.

"Coffee, I presume?"

I nod and glance down the bar to where the fresh Danish rolls are stacked beneath a clear plastic dome. Sally pours and brings me a selection of pastry. I inhale the first one, the kind with pineapple goo, and take a sip of *cafe noir,* thinking how Bruno would approve of my continental breakfast. Maybe I should invest in a beret and start smoking the stinking cigarettes so popular with those of the French persuasion. No. Go down that path and the next thing you know I'd be hankering for a platter of snails or some frog's legs *du jour*.

Sally's been watching me with concern and as the caffeine hits my bloodstream I manage to smile.

"Just pulled an all-nighter," I explain. She continues to watch without commenting so I start to relate my experiences, starting with the break-in at the office. She listens with the attention of a professional bartender, nodding or shaking her head at appropriate times.

"So you think these two used the condo in Oke City and the house here as fronts?" she asks.

"Yeah, they're not real people. They're like those phony 'legends' that CIA spooks use, complete with counterfeit documents. Obviously this is a big operation, and a costly one. And it's not a serial killer at all, but a conspiracy. There are at least two of them so…"

I catch an inquiring look on Sally's face and stop mid-sentence.

"Yeah?" she murmurs, urging me on.

"Wait. I might be wrong."

"Whatta you mean?

I ponder for a moment, toying with a third pastry. I play back my words in my head. *There are at least two…*

"There might not be two. They could be the same."

I grab my phone and hit the speed dial for Flores. He's been up all night too and from the tone of his voice he has on his grumpy face.

"Listen, Luis," I begin, "I've got a thought about our mystery perps. What if they're the same guy?"

It takes Flores a moment to get up to speed with that.

"What? You mean Craig and Wilson?"

"Yeah."

"Just one guy?" That's ridiculous. Why would you think that?

"Call it a hunch," I explain. I wince at my words. That's the kind of thing my ex used to say, throwing her precious so-called female intuition in my face whenever the facts wouldn't do.

Flores ponders for a moment.

"Well, they're plainly linked," he hazards. "And they both use disguises, so I suppose it's possible." He doesn't sound convinced.

"We can check it," I inform him. Pull up their DMV pictures. Even if they're disguised you should be able to see a resemblance if they're the same guy."

"Huh!" Flores grunts. "You're right." He sounds offended that he hadn't thought of it himself. "I've got them both in my data files and I'm sitting right at my computer."

I hear the clicking of keys followed by a moment of silence.

"Jesus, Mary and Joseph," Flores breathes. "You're right. They don't look the same, but the differences are superficial. It's one guy all right."

"Then we've got a serial killer after all," I point out. "And a very dangerous one indeed."

Chapter Thirty-four

Jeremy Barth

His plans in disarray, Barth returns to his house, his rage turned to cold resolve. The loss of Craig and Wilson is sobering but he revels in the fact that this is exactly why he had created those members of his team. Their purpose was to act when directed and disappear when no longer needed, leaving nothing that can be traced to Barth.

Descending to his hidden lair he gloats at the thought that he's led his enemies, that all-too-clever Rob Charlton and his foolish detective friend Flores, up another blind alley. He imagines the frustration they must be feeling at finding their investigation once again in limbo.

He laughs aloud at the thought that anyone would actually think Barth would allow some other person to savor the pleasure of retiring his enemies. The idea is almost beyond belief to him, but only he knows the intensity of the fires of hate that burn within him.

Of course there never were any actual associates. Craig and Wilson, like Singleton in Colorado, were merely masks for Barth himself to wear, to put on and take off at his whim and to be cast aside without a second thought.

Over the years and using the millions diverted from his employer, Barth had painstakingly created the false identities of the three men with carefully polished profiles, each provided with unique disguises to hide the monster lurking within.

Wilson was the first. To build that persona Barth begun with a careful study of his own appearance and ways of acting then worked to make Wilson different in every possible way. While Barth wore business attire, Wilson affected the cowboy look with jeans, snap-buttoned shirts and Stetson hats. His boots were crafted with thick heels and lifts to add three inches to Barth's height and his shaggy ginger wig was in stark contrast to Barth's own closely trimmed hair.

Barth had studied acting to give his creations their own special traits of body language and speech. While he himself walked in a kind of plodding manner and seemed to blend into any crowd, when disguised as Wilson he walked with an athletic stride, projecting an aura of confidence. He spoke with a carefully cultivated western drawl.

He'd developed different styles for each of his other creations, devoting many hours to practicing their individual manners of speaking and moving. As Singleton, for example, he learned to speak with a barely noticeable lisp and when wearing the Craig identity he walked with a rolling gait apparently due to a slight limp.

Barth the master actor, the wearer of masks, the adept hiding the inner monster beneath layers of secrets like the mysterious core of an unknown planet. Sometimes in moments of whimsy he thought he was deserving of an Academy Award, perhaps a very special one for lifetime achievement.

During the last years of his employment Barth had been busy, devoting nearly all his weekend or vacation days to creating his phantom team. At first he traveled on Wilson's credit cards and passport, arranging details of the slowly developing retirement plan. It was as Wilson that he began the surveillance that added facts to his files, concentrating first on Donald Greenwald. It was as Wilson that he had set up the other two front identities, and performed Greenwald's retirement ceremony.

Having established Craig and Singleton Barth spread his wings further, using all three identities for his activities. To every appearance Barth himself spent most of his non-working time in New York, living a quiet and solitary life. In reality almost every Friday night he flew out of Kennedy Airport as Wilson, Craig or Singleton. On those occasions he tended the garden of his deceit, walking in the desert in the guise of Wilson, playing cards in Colorado as Singleton, or driving a Stingray as Craig. And always he was learning facts about the people on his special list, facts that were carefully added to their files and taken into account for their planned retirements.

Barth's life was built entirely upon a foundation of appearances and masks. To cover the evil thing he had discovered himself to be was as natural as breathing, a skill honed since, as a child, he had first found deep pleasure in pulling wings from butterflies. The instinctive desire to hide his true self reached full bloom after that momentous turning point in his life when at the age of eight he dismembered a neighbor's dog with a hedge pruner and experienced an almost sexual release of pre-pubescent pleasure.

Even at that early age Barth recognized he must present false fronts to hide the monster that dwelled inside his head like a second *him*. To conceal the evil within he did the things that growing boys are supposed to do, collecting stamps, shooting baskets, dabbling with a chemistry set.

Throughout his school years he studied hard because he instinctively knew that knowledge would give him power, and that power would give him the ability to pursue his true calling, the art of helping the living into the realm of the dead. Reading Greek mythology as a ninth grader he was entranced by the story of the River Styx and the ferryman who transported the souls of the newly dead to Hades. He began to think of himself as a kind of reincarnation of Charon, the mythical ferryman emerging in the flesh.

At fourteen he claimed his first human life, that of a schoolmate who had embarrassed Barth in an English class. Even then he planned the death carefully, like an important school report or science project. The boy died slowly and with great suffering as Barth practiced techniques learned from a surgical textbook he'd found in the city library.

The murder took place in a remote grove of desert shrubbery. Under a full moon and wearing a Boy Scout hands-free headlamp he used a carefully honed filleting knife to perform an appendectomy on his bound and gagged victim, removed several fingers one at a time using a pair of garden shears, and finally applied a hacksaw shoplifted from a hardware store to amputate a leg just below the hip.

Barth was disappointed when at that point his victim died from shock and loss of blood, denying him further surgical pleasures. He realized he had much more to learn, not least how to staunch bleeding and control the onset of shock. The boy's disappearance was never solved, the parts of his dismembered body moldering beneath the desert sand in a secret place.

As he grew through his teenage years Barth had kept a tight rein on his macabre desires, knowing the price of overreaching could be discovery. It was more than six years later as a junior at the UNM business school that his first true retirement was planned and executed. The victims were his own parents, deserving of death for the abuse inflicted by his father and the inaction of a mother who could have protected him but did not.

He staged it as an accident, a complex and devious plan involving certain modifications to the family auto. Barth had long indulged an interest in mechanics and it was not remarked upon that he often tuned the engine, adjusted the brakes and performed other work on the family's Chevy station wagon.

Through experiment and study he devised a way to cause the vehicle to engage the accelerator pedal at 70 miles per hour, causing the engine to run away at ever increasing speed. The gearshift was fixed to lock in place and brake lines carefully weakened so that attempting to stop the car against the pull of the engine would cause them to burst.

The result was a fiery crash when the car spun off a sharp curve at more than 100 miles per hour with both his parents aboard. When he received the news of their deaths Barth ejaculated in his trousers and maintained a hard erection for nearly an hour.

As he knew they would the authorities wrote it off as an accident, failing to discover the ways in which the family auto had been made an instrument of death. The police report focused particularly on the autopsy finding that Barth's father had elevated blood alcohol, a normal state for him.

As their only child the 21-year-old Barth inherited the house and modest financial assets, enough to assure he could complete his education.

Now, hunched over his foreman's desk like some monstrous praying mantis he prepares for the next phase of his plan. It will be necessary for him to don the mask of Bob Singleton, the form in which he retired Morton Drake in the Colorado forest. Barth decides to drive north, assume the guise of Singleton and return to pick up where he'd left off before Wilson's discovery.

He begins to gather some things for the driving trip in his unremarkable, dusty Kia. Rob Charlton will get a brief reprieve but his death is still very much at the top of Barth's busy things-to-do list.

Chapter Thirty-five

Rob Charlton

I spend the rest of the day organizing my new home office. The two guys with the truck bring my desk and chairs and I get them to help me move the guestroom bed over against the wall to make room for a workspace. I order a replacement for my ravaged filing cabinet and a few other accessories then set up my new computer. It's easier than I thought and I'm pleased to have time for an afternoon nap.

I wake up around five and bumble around the apartment for a while, trying to get a feel for my new lifestyle as a telecommuter. It feels okay. Aware that I may be the target of an accomplished killer I decide to run a security audit.

I start by examining the front door. It's fairly solid metal but fitted with a typical off-the-shelf lock and combination deadbolt, the kind that might keep out children and men–tally challenged burglars but offer little security against a determined thief or murderer. I pick up the phone and call Mike, the lock guy. Within a half hour he's busy upgrading my first line of defense, installing a pick-resistant lock and deadbolt and securing a heavy steel plate to reinforce the door jamb.

After the locksmith is gone I go over my defense

status, cleaning and lubing my Glock and applying leather conditioner to my shoulder holster to soften it for easy action. I practice my quick draw techniques and do dry fire practice, pointing and clicking the empty pistol at my own image in a mirror.

After a while I root around in my dresser drawer and get out the back-up gun I used to carry in the Bureau. It's a Beretta Tomcat .32 caliber automatic in an ankle holster, a neat little gun that weighs less than a pound. Some say the .32 caliber cartridge doesn't have enough stopping power, insisting on forty-four magnum, forty-five or even fifty caliber cannons, bless their bloody little hearts. I lean to the thought that it's accuracy that counts. A well-placed shot to the heart or brain will stop a subject no matter what the size or weight of the bullet.

I may not be Wyatt Earp but I'm comfortable with a gun in my hand. The Bureau does an excellent job of teaching the fine art of gun fighting. At its Quantico headquarters they have a model town called Hogan's Alley where agents are trained to manage the use of deadly force in almost every conceivable situation. Although I never won trophies I was always a decent shot and easily qualified on the range during semi-annual evaluations. Still, recognizing my skills are a bit rusty I resolve to visit a shooting range as soon as I can. Meanwhile I'll carry both my weapons at all times until the danger is past.

Now it's nearly eight o'clock and hunger stirs. I look in the fridge but don't see anything I'd care to eat. There's some leftover Chinese carryout that may have been there for a month or more, a couple of bananas that have turned inexplicably black and some milk that's become home to a thriving colony of something green and nasty looking. I shudder and shut the door. Rob will dine out tonight.

I lock up my new lair and go down the back stairs to

the parking lot where the maroon baby awaits. I click the button on the key fob and she answers with a happy chirp and winks her lights at me.

As I settle myself in the cushy leather seat I start to think about how to make the baby safe. She does have an alarm system should anyone try to break in, but after experiencing the stake-out at my former office I realize my car is a point of vulnerability. Obviously the killer knows her and could lie in wait for me here in the apartment parking lot, possibly using a rifle to kill me from a distance or coming out of the shadows with a shotgun or pistol.

Shit, I hate this, but I'm going to have to change my procedures. The baby needs to be parked in some secure location. Maybe Flores will let me keep her in the sheriff's department vehicle pound, but that's several miles away so I'd have to hitch rides or take cabs. That would be a royal pain in the butt, but as Mom used to say, better a live Rob than a dead duck. Well, no she didn't exactly say that but the thought was there.

I decide to stop by Sally's for a burger and to start my new policy of keeping a low profile I park the baby on a dark side street a couple blocks away. As I enter the bar I'm glad to see it's nearly empty. The after-work crowd has probably gone home to engage in traditional family activities such as beating wives, kicking dogs and watching football on TV, so the place isn't jumping with hordes of free-spending barflies as Sally would probably prefer. A couple of salesman types are sitting at the table in the far corner and there's a sad-looking little man at one end of the bar with his ruby-like nose hovering over a glass of whisky.

I slide onto a barstool at the other end. Sally offers me a menu but I wave it away.

"I'll have the usual," I inform her.

She responds with a perky smile.

"Is that the usual Danish with cherry or pineapple gunk or the usual half-pound cheeseburger with fries?"

Hmm, she's in a smartass mood tonight. I make a point of looking at my watch to see if it's time for breakfast or dinner.

"That's right," I say after a pause.

"What, both?"

"Well, hold the Danish. Probably stale now anyway.

She grins and turns to shout my order back to the kitchen. Without asking she pops open a cold bottle of Modelo and sets it on a coaster in front of me. I take a long drink of the smooth Mexican beer.

"Well, you look a little better than you did this morning," Sally remarks, leaning her elbows on the bar and studying me like some mysterious abstract artwork. I nod and take another hit on the bottle.

"Rough night, huh?" she says at last.

"Honey, you wouldn't believe it."

"Try me."

I start at the beginning and bring her up to date on the break-in at my office, the failed raid at the Wilson house and the dead end nature of my case. She listens intently, breaking away only to refill the sad man's glass and collect the check from the sales characters as they leave.

My burger feast arrives and Sally goes to attend to some new customers. As I eat I listen to the piped in music. Someone affecting a twangy voice is extolling the benefits of cowgirls, pickup trucks and roadhouse beer. I imagine he wears a black hat and boots and wouldn't know one end of a horse from the other. His guitar picking skills are limited to about five chords and the gain on the recording machine's set too high.

Whatever happened to the concept of music as a thing of beauty? I remember the days when crooners had actual singing voices and musicians could coax pleasant sounds from their instruments. They're all gone now, Old Blue Eyes, Perry, Bing, Patti and all those other golden voices of the past, not to mention the marvelous big bands and jazz greats.

All that was already being swept away when I was a youngster. What's passed off as "music" today is mostly just irritating noises made by people with no talent or training, and somehow they make millions from mobs of devoted fans. It never ceases to mystify me, but it proves the truth of the old adage "There's no accounting for taste."

I finish the destruction of my burger and fries and Sally and I continue our conversation. I tell her about the move to my new home office and how I'd had the locks upgraded.

"So you think this guy's gonna come after you?" Sally's genuinely concerned.

"Well, after he staked out my office and stole my files, yeah I'd say I'm in his sights. He knows I'm on his trail. Plus he's gotta be really pissed by this morning's raid."

"Getting those locks installed was a good move," she says approvingly. "When you're at home you might think about stacking some empty cans on the floor just inside the door, just to be sure. If he should manage to get it open, at least he won't catch you sleeping."

I agree that's a good idea and tell her about my decision to keep the maroon baby out of sight. She ponders this for a moment.

"You know, I've got a garage here in the back that I don't use except to store some stuff. There's plenty of room to keep your car there if you want. It's got a security lock and it's hooked up to the bar's central alarm system."

That sounds like a good idea. My apartment's less than a mile away and I can use the exercise. I readily accept the offer.

"I assume you're carrying?" she inquires and I twitch open my jacket to reveal a glimpse of the Glock. "What about a vest?" she continues.

"No, I don't have one although I used to wear them when I was in the Bureau. Maybe I could borrow one from Flores," I muse.

"Good idea."

"Of course, vests don't do much against real firepower, like a high-powered rifle."

"Actually, what you need is a full armor vest," she informs me. "They've got Kevlar plus ceramic plates. The military and SWAT guys use them."

Goodness, she's got knowledge. I file it away.

"If the guy follows his previous pattern what I've got to worry about is a kidnapping attempt," I tell her. "I don't want to end up as one of his retirees, with a twenty-two caliber hole in my forehead."

She grimaces.

"I've got to be on my guard twenty-four seven," I point out. "I've gotta act like a cat in a room full of rocking chairs, trusting nothing and nobody."

"Good plan."

"Yeah."

The engine of our conversation runs down and we simply gaze at one another for a minute or two. I notice that Sally's eyes are the kind that seem larger than life, wide-open windows to her soul if the poets are correct. I motion for another beer and she turns to get it without saying anything.

Some more customers come in and Sally drifts away to serve them, leaving me in the company of the twang-voiced cowboy. I sip the cold beer and lapse into my contemplative mode.

I've run against another blank wall in my efforts to identify and stop the killer. Now the best plan might be to let him come to me, something I believe he's very much inclined to do.

I don't particularly like the thought of being bait like the cheese in a trap, but sometimes there's only one way to catch a rat. I'm reminded of something an old associate in the Bureau used to say when things were going all pear-shaped. "Sometimes you eat the bear and sometimes the bear eats you," he'd remark with a resigned shrug. Trouble is, to find out which you've gotta actually confront the bear.

I decide to suggest to Flores the idea of offering myself as a target. I hope he'll be able to muster some support, perhaps a couple of undercover deputies to watch my back. It could be the beginnings of a plan.

Meanwhile I'll keep poking at the evidence I've got. Even though my paper files are gone I still have the list of UNM students and my notes transcribed onto my computer backup. It's likely that the burglary at my office resulted from my inquiries into the death of Shelly Richards, so somewhere among those dozens of names must be a slender thread that will lead me to her killer.

I decide to change my approach. Before, I contacted people at random. Obviously one of those I reached was somehow connected with Retirement Man, most likely the person himself in the flesh. That gives me a list of suspects, the names of the males I'd already contacted. All the rest of the names on the list could be presumed not to be the perp, but some might be able to help me in my search.

I have another thought. If anyone might know something about Shelly Richard's personal life it would likely be another woman, not a man. I decide to continue to make calls but limiting my reach to females. Somewhere, I hope, there's someone who Shelly Richards told of her date on that fateful last day of her life.

I've got another idea. When talking with her former classmates, what if I mention the names of males on my earlier call list? Might that trigger some memories? I think it will.

Satisfied with my plan I consider ordering a third beer but after a glance at the drawn face in the bar's back mirror I decide to quit while I'm ahead. I'm due for some well-deserved sleep and I need to keep in top form. I move the baby to her new home in Sally's garage, give her a reassuring pat on the hood and walk the mile to my fortress of solitude.

Chapter Thirty-six

Jeremy Barth

In his Robert Singleton alias, Barth returns from Colorado in early afternoon the following day. He's left his Kia behind, driving the Singleton metallic blue Bronco instead of the brown van used to kidnap and murder Morton Drake. Barth prefers the vans for their ability to conceal his works in progress, but now that Jim Craig and Jake Wilson have been connected with vans he's decided to change his methods.

As with Craig and Wilson he's created a complete fake history for the Singleton legend, using the guise of an international business consultant. In this persona Barth affects the look of a traditional college professor, in keeping with Singleton's supposed Ph.D. in international marketing. The usual dress style runs to Hush Puppies, open-collared Oxford cloth shirts, wash slacks and tweed jackets with leather elbow patches. Barth had considered making his creation a pipe smoker, but decided that would be going too far.

As Singleton he wears distinctive tinted glasses and a dark brown toupee with touches of gray at the temples. He once tried using a fake moustache but found it inconvenient and uncomfortable. He does add bristly eyebrows to match the toupee, carefully cementing them into place with theatrical adhesive. Finally, applications of makeup add color to Singleton's cheeks and lips, in contrast to Barth's natural pale complexion.

Singleton speaks with a cultured New England accent, affecting a slight lisp. He has an easy manner of conversing during rare encounters with others, making many references to foreign cities and sometimes spicing his sentences with French, German and even Japanese words. Somewhat of a geek, he's a video gamer and card player. It was through his weekly poker games that Barth, as Singleton, drew close to Morton Drake to ultimately retire him.

Back in Albuquerque Barth checks into a motel under Singleton's name rather than going immediately to his house. As always he keeps as much distance as possible between himself and his legends. Tired from the thousand-mile round trip drive to Colorado he calls room service for coffee and a chef's salad. After eating he takes a nap, waiting for darkness to reconnoiter Rob Charlton's office and apartment.

Barth awakens sometime after 7 p.m. and begins to prepare for his evening reconnaissance. To keep the Bronco in the background he's used an untraceable Amex card to reserve a rental car, a plain Jane compact with an out-of-state license.

Barth begins by cruising Charlton's office at the barren and nearly deserted strip mall. He drives through the parking lot, observing a heavy chain and padlock on the broken door to Charlton's office. He concludes that probably means there are no plans to repair it, and if so the office is no longer a possible ambush site. He drives on, taking side streets to approach the detective's apartment building.

Barth pulls into the parking lot behind the building

without hesitating, wanting to look like a tenant or guest with the right to be there. He pulls into a guest parking space and shuts off the engine and lights. Using a compact pair of binoculars he scans the lot, looking for Charlton's maroon car. It's not in its assigned place and there's no sign of it elsewhere.

He smiles. If Charlton is away, he must eventually come home and will park in the assigned spot. It's the perfect place for a kill. He starts to think about how to set it up. With luck this could be done tonight.

He sees what he's looking for. At the far end of the lot is a patch of untrimmed bushes. He can park his car on a nearby side street, ready for a quick escape, then creep into the bushes with the sniper rifle. Perfect!

He opens the car door and gets out, glancing around to learn the details of the potential killing ground. There's a clear field of fire between the bushes and the area where Charlton will park and exit his car. It couldn't be better.

Barth has a way of vividly previewing his crimes in detail. Now his head fills with images. Even though he's standing in the middle of the parking lot, in his mind he's hidden back in the thicket with his rifle.

It's dark here in the bushes but the lot is illuminated with overhead sodium lights. They cast strange orange shadows. A car turns into the lot. It's Charlton's distinctive Ford. It moves slowly. His target is cautious, checking out the scene. In his vision Barth chuckles, invisible in his killing lair.

He raises the rifle, puts his eye to the scope. He sees the outline of the former FBI agent inside the car. He lowers the rifle and checks the settings on the scope. It's a 30-yard shot, an almost insignificant distance at which he can't possibly miss.

> *Carefully he releases the safety of the high-powered Sako rifle, preparing it to send its message of death.*
>
> *Charlton pulls into his parking space and Barth raises the rifle to his eye again, waiting for his prey to step out of the car. He decides to shoot as soon as Charlton stands up, before he starts to move. At this range a head shot will be as easy as shooting a catfish in a barrel. One squeeze of the trigger and Barth will be off, out the back of the thicket and into the waiting car. In a matter of seconds it will be over and his enemy will be dead.*
>
> *The door of the maroon Ford opens and Charlton steps out. Barth centers the crosshairs on his target's face. His finger caresses the trigger. As his target stands upright and prepares to shut the car door he squeezes slowly, slowly …and the rifle fires.*
>
> *Charlton's head explodes in a cloud of blood and brains. The echoes of the shot beat back from nearby buildings like the claps of an invisible audience. Barth feels a rush of pleasure and the swelling in his pants that always follows a killing.*

Suddenly Barth stiffens, his fantasy forgotten. In the dimly lit area at the far back corner of the lot he notices something he'd missed. It's a dark-colored car that's out of place, parked at an angle facing the center of the lot. He can see the tiny reflections of lights hidden behind the car's grill.

No! It's an unmarked patrol car. The lot's under surveillance.

Acting nonchalant Barth begins to stroll toward the

apartment door, then stops and pats his pockets as if he's forgotten something. He turns back, avoiding looking at the parked car as he returns to his own vehicle. Fortunately he'd come from the other end of the lot and can exit without the cop being able to make his license plate. He gets in, starts the engine and drives slowly away. Tomorrow he'll exchange the rental car for something different.

"Shit!" His plan has failed. Again Barth rages.

For long minutes he drives the back streets, his mind at work. He'll need a different plan. He drives, thinking, analyzing, and with a sudden flash of understanding his rage abates.

There's no way Charlton is going to return to the parking lot. They've set a trap. The unmarked car must be one of Flores' deputies, probably one of a pair, waiting to catch him. But being onto their game gives him a tremendous advantage.

Barth continues to drive for another half hour, thinking, plotting. At last he returns to the motel, his course clear in his mind. His enemy has attempted to turn himself from hunted to hunter. Now the play will be reversed again.

Barth the hunter returns to the motel and prepares for a good night's rest. Tomorrow will be a busy day.

Chapter Thirty-seven

Rob Charlton

I **spend a day getting organized** at my new home office and preparing for the next phase of my search for Retirement Man. My first task is to go over the list of former students I'd already contacted. There are about 70. I make a separate list of the men on the assumption that one of them could be my subject.

Flores and I agree that my calls must have tipped off the killer to my interest in him. My plan now is to continue to contact former students who might have known Shelly Richards. When someone recalls her I'll go over the list of men's names to help refresh their memory. It's a long shot, but about the only thread left to follow.

Meanwhile Flores calls to let me know he's gotten authority to help set the trap, operating on the assumption that the killer will make a move on me. He's already assigned two deputies to watch my apartment building at night. Others will be on call to assist on short notice should something develop. He says he'll have them give me a radio handset assigned a special band.

Luis also orders the department's IT group to place video cameras to cover the building's doors and the hallway outside my apartment. They're connected to the Internet by an encrypted WiFi link so I can tap into the video feeds on my computer or iPhone. It's like having several extra pairs of eyes.

Meanwhile, as the cheese in the trap I'll play it safe. When I'm not using her, the maroon baby will hide in Sally's garage. When I come and go from my new home office I'll use the service entrance where there's a loading dock. From there it's an easy walk around the corner and then about a mile by back streets to Sally's Place.

I sneak out for dinner at a nearby Chinese restaurant. As I return to the apartment building on foot I'm gratified to see one of the Sheriff's cars parked nearby. I use the radio to tell them I'm incoming and after catching the ten o'clock news I climb into bed and start to count my flock of sheep. Apparently I don't have many of the fluffy little buggers because after about a dozen I'm sound asleep.

The next morning I'm up early to start making calls to the Eastern time zone. I have phone numbers for about three quarters of the students on the list, thanks to the UNM alumni association. That gives me a total of about 300 names. It's a rather daunting but necessary task, so I buckle down and get to work.

I set up my iPhone next to the new computer and plug it into the charger cord. I dial the first number and hit the speaker button to leave my hands free. I get voicemail and leave the brief message I've drafted, asking the party to call me about an important matter. I mention Shelly Richards' name.

I hang up and dial another number. Same thing. I place three more calls before someone answers. It's a woman's voice, sounding wary.

"Hi, my name is Rob Charlton," I inform her. "I'm calling about one of your classmates in New Mexico."

"I already gave," she says. "The school's mentioned in my will."

I can tell she's about to hang up and that I'm going to have to change my opening lines or they'll all think I'm a university fund-raiser, trolling for donations.

"No, wait. That's not it. I'm a detective looking for leads in a crime."

There's silence then:

"What?"

"You had a fellow student named Shelly Richards. She died back in 1975. Now we think she was murdered. I'm looking for any information about her that could provide a lead to her killer. Do you remember Shelly?"

The woman takes a couple of deep breaths, thinking.

"Well, I kind of remember someone who died but I'd forgotten her name. I thought it was an accident?"

"That's how it appeared but now we have reason to think otherwise."

"Hmm, wish I could help. I didn't know her, just someone you'd see around, you know? Wouldn't recognize her if I passed her on the street."

"Yes, I understand. If you happen to think of anything, would you please give me a call?"

I recite my phone number and hang up. One down, 299 to go. I keep slaving away all morning, finally taking a break around noon. I look in the refrigerator where the black bananas are beginning to split open and ooze greasy sludge. I use a paper towel to pick them up and shove them down the garbage disposal. Yuck.

Instead of going out to eat I decide to call for pizza. While waiting I click on my computer to check the video feeds.

After about twenty minutes I watch as a car with a magnetic roof sign pulls up in front of the main entrance. The pizza guy. I track him through the front door and a few seconds later he's on the intercom. I buzz him in and soon gaze fondly at a freshly baked thick crust pizza, complete with onions, sausage, mushrooms, green pepper and anchovies.

I inhale the first slice standing at the kitchen counter then settle down at the table to eat the rest. I probably don't have to point out that it's another example of a healthy, well-balanced meal, one the USDA would happily endorse. Plenty of grain in the form of pizza dough, dairy as cheese, moderate servings of meat and fish, plus olive oil and three veg's, four if you count the oregano. It's as if the Food Pyramid itself has come to life in the form of a pizza.

What a wonderful world we live in.

After knocking off the pizza I decide to take a rest. This home office thing has some real advantages. I had a couch in one corner of my strip mall office but never felt comfortable sleeping, as it were, on the job, even though I often had nothing to do but surf the Internet or play video solitaire. Here in my own apartment it's my life to live as I wish. I kick off my shoes and crash on the bed, hands behind my head. I gaze at the ceiling for a while, running over the details of the case in my mind. After a while I drift off for a nice nap.

After my rest I get back on the phone, placing about thirty more calls during the afternoon. None of them yield any obvious smoking gun. In fact only one provides any real information at all.

It's a conversation with a mid-level corporate exec in Minnesota named Norma White. She clearly remembers Shelly Richards, recalling that they shared a course in graduate school at the time Richards died. White tells me they weren't close but often chatted before or after classes.

I probe for details, hoping she'll recall something to connect Richards with her killer. She doesn't remember any talk of boy friends or dates, but as I read the list of male students she stops me after a name.

"Barth, yes, Jeremy. I remember him," she tells me. "In fact, I think he was in the same class with us, and if I remember right, he and Shelly were seated together."

"Did they show any interest in each other?" I ask. "Could they have been dating?"

She laughs. "Oh, I don't think there was any kind of relationship. It was assigned seating. Jeremy and Shelly were as different as salt and pepper. I remember him as a shy boy, very self-conscious, kind of geeky. He was one of those people that can't look you in the eye, kind of a social wallflower if you know what I mean. He wasn't much of a dresser and never seemed to have much money."

"Any idea what became of Barth?"

She thinks for a moment.

"Actually, I remember reading something about him in the alumni magazine. He did pretty well as I recall. Ended up as an executive at a Wall Street investment bank, which kind of surprises me."

I ask a few more questions before going to the next call. Later, as I go over the fruits of my day's work I ponder White's words. Jeremy Barth, a bumbling kind of person, a geek, lacking in social graces. That could describe the mystery man at Bruno's. On the other hand, the presumed killer was well dressed and had a nice car. That part doesn't fit.

I check back to my older notes from the backup hard drive and discover that I first attempted to call Barth in New York, speaking with a woman named Carla, his former assistant. She told me he'd just retired a few weeks earlier and gave me a phone number here in New Mexico. I'd left a voice mail for him but he hadn't returned the call. That isn't remarkable, for in fact most of my messages had gone unanswered.

But I can't get away from the fact that there was a connection between Barth and Richards. No matter how slender, it was a thread that should be followed. And there's the fact that he's right here in New Mexico. On balance I decide Barth is worth some extra attention as my investigation continues.

It's time to quit for the day so I shut down my computer after checking the video feeds. It's a quick walk to Sally's bar. I can tell I'm getting back some of my old vim and vigor. Maybe there's something to this exercise thing. I decide to celebrate my improving physical condition by indulging in one of Sally's burgers and fries.

It's not quite five when I arrive at Sally's Place and the evening crowd is yet to arrive in force. She's busy at her endless glassware polishing project. I climb onto a stool and she comes over to inspect me. Apparently I pass muster because she doesn't make any hurtful comments about my haggard appearance or the danger of early onset dementia.

She hands me a cold one and we chat for a while. I tell her about my less than exciting day spent making cold calls to strangers. After a few minutes the after work crowd starts to trickle in and she gets busy taking orders and serving drinks.

I look at myself in the back bar mirror. Yep, I do look better. Those extra hours of sleep have paid off with interest. The Rob in the mirror looks, well, at least not any more old and broken down than his calendar age would suggest. There's even a hint of that old sparkle in his eyes and he's sitting up straight, not slumped over like a battered boxer. That's encouraging. Maybe there's hope for him after all. I raise my beer bottle in salute and he returns the gesture in perfect harmony. I wink and he winks back.

My burger arrives on a steaming platter surrounded with yummy fries and I tuck into my supper like a starving lumberjack. I'm about halfway through when my iPhone goes off with *The Untouchables* theme. I look at the caller ID and it's not familiar so I start to put it back in my pocket, but decide I'd better take it.

"Hello, this is Rob Charlton," I say, keeping my voice down.

"Mr. Charlton?" It's a girl, a teenager from the sound of her voice, and she sounds disturbed.

"Yes. Who is this?"

"It's Emily. My Dad's Luis Flores." There's a sound like a suppressed sob.

"Yes, Emily. I know your father. What's wrong?"

"He's gone! He took him away!" She begins to cry openly. I push back my unfinished dinner, hunching over the bar with the phone to my ear.

"Emily, please calm down. What's happened? Who took him away?"

In broken sentences interspersed with sobs she tells me that her father was taken from his apartment just a few minutes before by a gunman wearing a mask. The kidnapper somehow opened the door, catching Flores and his daughter by surprise in the middle of dinner. He threatened Emily with a gun and told Luis to put his hands on the table. The masked man slid over a pair of looped plastic wire ties, a commonly used form of handcuffs, ordering the deputy to put them on.

"He said he'd shoot me if Dad didn't cooperate," Emily tells me tearfully. "I was so scared…"

"Yes, I'm sure you were," I agree. "Why did you call me instead of the Sheriff's office or the police?"

She breaks into a new round of piteous sobs before responding.

"He told me not to call them, that he'd kill Dad if I did. He said to call you."

"What? The kidnapper told you to call me?"

"Yes. He even gave me your business card with the number. He said you were the only one that was to know."

Oh my freaking God, we've been pawned. I was sup–posed to be the bait and the killer has taken Flores instead. I stare at the mirror. The killer must have taken some of my business cards when he broke into my office. My stomach is churning.

"Emily, please stay calm. Are you safe now?"

"Y-yes, I guess so. He's gone."

I think for a moment.

"What did this man look like?" I ask her.

"Oh!" My question seems to take her by surprise. "I don't know. He was just a man. He was wearing a mask."

"Yes, but anything you can remember might help. Could you see his hair?"

She thinks for a moment.

"I don't think so. All I remember is the gun. He was pointing it right at me. I really didn't see anything else."

I'm getting nowhere so I give up this tack.

"Honey, I want you to call your Mom. Tell her what's happened but that it's important she doesn't call the police. Ask her to come to get you. When she gets there ask her to call me at this number."

"Okay."

"Your father's going to be all right."

I know in my heart I may be telling a lie but it's for a good cause.

"I'm going to find him," I assure her.

"Okay." Her sobs are diminishing.

"You can call me, but don't call the police. The man who took your father may be able to monitor their radio talk. Do you understand?"

"Y-yes. I'll call Mom now."

"Good girl. I'll be in touch."

I put down the phone and look up to see Sally staring across the bar with grave concern.

"What is it?"

"Flores. He's been kidnapped. That was his daughter."

"Oh my God! What can we do?"

I hear the determination in her voice. She wants to be part of this. My mind's whirling with possibilities.

"Listen, Sally, he's threatened the girl not to call the cops, only me. We have to keep this on the down low."

She nods.

"He's gonna use Flores to draw you out," she says in a flat, matter-of-fact tone. "He wants to kill you both."

The truth of her statement crashes down around me like a ton of bricks. I look at her for a moment, reading the concern in her eyes.

"Yeah," I muse. "I actually think you're right."

"What do you have to go on?" she asks.

I shrug dismissively.

"There's one possibility but it's not solid," I tell her. I'm thinking of Jeremy Barth, the recently retired investment banker. "It's really nothing but a gut feeling, some suggestive facts."

A customer halfway down the bar begins to tap his empty glass impatiently with a swizzle stick. Sally glances that way for a moment then walks over to the kitchen door.

"Bob, come here," she calls.

The cook comes out, wiping his hands on a towel.

"You've got to take over for a while," she advises him. "Something's come up. Shut down the kitchen. Say there's something wrong with the grill and give them rain checks for a free burger. Be sure to set the alarms when you lock up. Open up tomorrow at the usual time if I'm not back."

She hands over her bar cloth and gestures toward the customer. Bob grins and hurries to serve him a drink.

"Sally…" I begin.

"Don't start," she advises me, like a mother addressing an unruly child.

My goodness. I shut my mouth.

She takes off her barkeeper's apron and snatches a purse from under the bar. I see her slip something inside and know it's the Smith & Wesson. She starts to come out from behind the bar, then turns back and picks up her bat. It's a classic hardwood model that's had about ten inches cut off the business end, making an effective one-hand head buster.

She marches toward the door, curious customers staring for a moment before returning to their drinks. I hesitate for a moment before following. She's heading around the corner to the garage. In the back alley she stops to let me catch up.

"Sally, what the hell are you doing?"

She shifts the bat onto one shoulder and looks at me for a moment before answering.

"You're going to get a call," she says. "You know he'll do it. He'll draw you in, threaten to kill the deputy. You're too nice a guy not to fall for it and you'll need some backup. I may not be much, but I'm all you've got."

I stare at her determined face. Her eyes glitter in the dim glow of a distant streetlight. There's a feral look about her that I'd never noticed. This is a different side of Sally.

"You said you have a lead," she says. "It may be wrong but there's no time now. If you don't take the initiative he's gonna win."

What can you do when faced with an irresistible force of nature? I need to think about this, but she's right: there's no time. I nod and turn to open the garage door, I click the key fob and the maroon baby chirps and flashes her lights.

"Get in," I tell Sally.

My goodness, what are we doing?

Chapter Thirty-eight

Jeremy Barth

Barth in his Singleton disguise rides on a wave of triumph. He has Detective Flores locked in the trunk of his rental car, hands and feet bound with plastic wire ties, mouth silenced with a wide strip of duct tape.

They thought they'd trap me! Me!

Whooping insanely he laughs so hard that tears spring from his eyes. He pulls over to the side of the road to savor the manic joy.

He's once again on an unpaved track west of Albuquerque. The city shimmers in his rear view mirror like a glowing inland sea. Ahead, the last remnant of day fades in the west. He shuts down the engine and steps out of the car, stretching and breathing the cool, dry air of his beloved desert. A gentle breeze carries the scent of juniper. As they evaporate freshly-shed tears cool his cheeks.

He steps to the back of the car and uses the remote to pop the trunk lid, standing well back on the off chance Flores has managed to work himself free. He hasn't and Barth gazes fondly at the bound and helpless lawman.

"Well, Mr. Sheriff's Detective, how does it feel to find yourself in the trap you set for me?"

Flores struggles vainly against his bonds and Barth begins to laugh again, beginning as a chuckle that grows to open peals of laughter. After a moment the manic outburst runs its course and he begins to think.

What next? Should he take the prize to his own nearby house? No, he decides, that would be unwise. He's Robert Singleton now and must retain that cover, protecting his true identity at all cost.

There in the gathering dark he lays out a plan of action. First he must transfer the prisoner to Singleton's vehicle then turn in the rental car and drive to Colorado. He'll hide Flores under a tarp in the back of the Bronco and drive well within the speed limits to prevent any chance of interference by those highway predators in their state patrol cars.

Once Flores is imprisoned in the Singleton house he'll use him as a pawn to play as he wishes. Let Charlton try to find him there! Meanwhile, he'll tease the meddling private detective with hints to lead him into a trap of Barth's own making.

When both men are under his power they can die at his leisure, the latest in his series of retirements.

He slams the trunk lid down, gets back in the car and starts the engine. His course of action set he puts the car in gear, accelerates and makes a sliding 180 degree j-turn in the sandy road. Barth is careful not to attract attention but sometimes he can't resist exercising the skills learned at a high-speed evasive driving course taken in the guise of Jim Wilson. The maneuver sends up a cloud of dust as the car whirls around in a controlled slide. The tires spin to reverse direction, heading back to the city.

Approaching the motel where the Bronco awaits he parks the rental car in a dark and empty parking lot a few blocks away. Walking the short distance he goes to his room and carefully removes any trace of his presence there. Not only does he pack and take everything he'd brought with him, he wipes down any surfaces he may have touched and uses a powerful mini-vacuum, part of his usual travel kit, to pick up any hairs or fibers that may have been shed.

Barth has studied crime scene investigation and is always alert to the teaching of the French criminalist Edmond Locard who believed that in every contact a criminal leaves some trace that can identify him or her. Barth treats every place he goes as a potential crime scene, taking every precaution not to leave trace evidence, and in particular fingerprints. He's practiced this caution almost obsessively for many years and it's served him well. He's proud the authorities have found no prints that could tie him to Wilson or Craig.

Packing his tools he goes to the front desk to check out, explaining that an emergency has come up at home. He pays with one of Singleton's credit cards, knowing the account goes through several cutoffs to an offshore shell corporation that cannot be connected to Barth.

He starts up the Bronco and drives to the nearby rental car. It's the work of only a moment to move Flores into the back of the four-wheel-drive vehicle. He checks the deputy to make sure his bindings are secure. Assured the prisoner is unable to resist or attract attention he returns the rental car to the motel parking lot. Using some of his anti-trace tools he gives the door handle, steering wheel and gearshift lever a thorough rub down with a lint-free cloth. He runs over the driver's seat with a sticky roller to pick up any hairs or flakes of skin that may have been left there. After wiping them he slips the keys under the floor mat. He pulls out an untraceable throwaway cell phone and calls the car rental office to instruct them where to pick up their auto. As with the motel, payment has been made with one of Jim Singleton's credit cards.

Now he strolls back to the dark parking lot where the Bronco waits. Smiling with satisfaction he adjusts the tarp over the prisoner in the back, gets behind the wheel and starts to drive.

As he approaches northbound I-25 he begins to hum a tune from the past. It was soon after the death of Shelly Richards that Barth first heard the Queen song "Death On Two Legs". Its cruel imagery resonated with him and in those years he'd made it his personal anthem. Even today the heavy beat stirs happy thoughts in his breast.

As he merges into the stream of traffic heading north he whistles and thumps the rhythm on the steering wheel.

Chapter Thirty-nine

Rob Charlton

Sally jumps into the car and slams the door. She looks over at me.

"Okay, what do we do?"

I sit there thinking for a minute or two, staring out the garage door into the dark alley behind her bar.

"I learned about a man that could be a suspect," I tell her in a quiet voice. "His name is Jeremy Barth. He recently retired from a job on Wall Street and moved back to New Mexico. He's got a house here in Albuquerque."

"You think he's the one?"

I don't answer right away. She keeps looking at me expectantly. I drum my fingers on the steering wheel.

"Damned if I know," I admit. "It's a possibility, but there's nothing for sure."

I explain the connection between Barth and Shelly Richards, the woman who was murdered many years before. The fact they sat next to each other in a class is hardly evidence, I point out to Sally. She waves that off with a shrug.

"Yeah, so he's probably a fucking angel. Unless you've got something else, let's check him out."

I admit that Barth is the only name on my suspect list.

"Do you know where he lives?" she asks.

"Um, no. But I can find out."

I use the police band radio Flores issued me, asking the dispatcher to check the name of Jeremy Barth. In a few moments she comes back on the air with an address. I punch it into my GPS navigation system. It's not far away, about twenty minutes I guess. I start the engine and pull out of the garage. Sally jumps out and runs back to close the door and set the alarm. Then it's just the three of us — me, Sally and the maroon baby — off on what could be the biggest wild goose chase of my life.

We haven't driven more than a couple of miles when my cell phone goes off. It's Flores's ex, calling me as I'd suggested to her daughter. She's frantic and wants to call the cops despite the kidnapper's threat to kill the sheriff's detective if the authorities are brought in. I pull to the side of the road to listen, putting the phone on speaker.

I spend several minutes convincing her to keep things on the down low, at least for now. I tell her I'm working on a lead and will try to rescue Flores. At last she agrees, although not without leaking tears all over her phone and treating me to some first class bitchiness. I put away the phone and start to drive.

That brings back ugly memories of my own ex when she was on the warpath, breathing fiery fumes like a Valkyrie's steed. For about the zillionth time I think how wonderful it is to be in New Mexico with Greta in Boston.

When I hang up Sally brushes her forehead with the back of her hand in a histrionic gesture.

"Whew!" she exclaims. "No wonder Flores divorced her ass."

"I'm sure it's only because she's worried about him," I say in my best Rob the Reasonable tone. "She's probably under a lot of stress."

"Yeah."

Sally looks away without saying any more. I wonder

what she's thinking. Had she, too, had a failed marriage? I realize I don't know. Probably too personal a thing to ask your bartender, I guess, although I seem to remember complaining to her about Greta over several cold brews one night when my business was floundering and I was feeling down.

Like the song says, some rain is bound to fall into every life. Hell, most of the time even Greta wasn't too hard to take. It was just when she'd go off on me like a broadside from a Spanish galleon that it got to be too much to take.

In the end it was either Greta or my career, and I loved my work too much to give it up and become an insurance salesman or capital R Realtor® as Greta would have liked. She had a vision for me that was quite different from my own, that of a nine-to-five rat on the racetrack of life, arriving at our comfy little home for cocktails at six and dinner at seven, followed by the latest crap on TV. I could never live like that, not as long as there are bad guys that need catching, and there always are.

I realize Sally's looking at me.

"Hey," she says softly. "You went away there for a while."

I laugh, but it comes out a bit more like a strangling sound.

"Yeah, I was having flashbacks about my ex wife," I admit, shaking myself as if shivering.

Sally laughs too, and hers is clear and melodic.

"You told me about your ex," she says. "Greta, wasn't it?"

"Yeah, and let me tell you Greta wasn't Great." I laugh again and this time it comes out naturally. Even outside her bar, Sally has the knack of making people feel relaxed. I snuggle back in the soft leather of the maroon baby's upholstery and check the GPS map. We're nearly there.

I pull off the road about a hundred yards short of the driveway and we sit in the car for a minute, engine idling to keep the air conditioning going.

"I want you to stay here while I go check it out," I tell Sally.

"No way Jose," she responds, picking up her bat.

"My name isn't Jose," I remind her. "And you're a civilian."

"Yeah and so are you," she shoots back. "Next you'll tell me I'm a woman, right?"

"Um, well, yeah I was about to mention that," I admit, feeling a bit of a blush creep up my neck.

Sally gives me a sour look and says nothing. She opens the door and gets out. She leans into the car.

"Well, are you coming or not?"

I give up and turn off the engine. I get out and pop the trunk to get a few things from my detecting kit. We start to walk down the road, Sally striding purposefully with the bat on her shoulder. I watch her in wonder. I realize she's not like any woman I've ever met, and that I'm lucky to have her with me.

We pause at the foot of the driveway for several minutes, letting our eyes adjust to the dark. There's no sign of life. Keeping my voice down I suggest she wait there while I go up to the house. She responds by punching me on the arm, hard, so we walk up the driveway together.

We detour cautiously around the house, looking and listening for any sign there's anyone inside. We meander over to the detached garage in the back and I peek inside the tiny window on one side, shielding the light from my flashlight like Flores did at Jake Wilson's place. Except for some lawn mowers and other equipment it's empty.

We walk back toward the rear of the house and I pull out a little gadget we detective types like to use. It's a tiny microphone that sticks onto a window with an earplug that lets you hear what's going on inside a room, kind of like a doctor checking a patient's chest with a stethoscope. Since going into the private eye business I'd used it only twice, both times to spy on wandering husbands, which made me feel like a rat.

I place it on the rear window and listen for a long time. There's a faint whooshing sound from air passing through the ventilation system and at one point I hear something that sounds like a gas water heater lighting up.

There's nothing to suggest anyone's inside.

Sally is standing off to my left, her face a blur in the dark. I step close to keep my voice down.

"I don't think there's anyone here," I tell her.

"So, are we gonna go in?" she asks. There's an eager note in her voice.

"You've seen too many movies," I tell her. "Breaking and entering is a crime. We're not law enforcement officers and even if we were we don't have a court warrant."

She tries to stifle a giggle.

"Yeah, and I'm the Easter Bunny," she whispers back.

"Okay," I admit, "there may be a life at stake so I'm gonna make an exception to the rule. I don't want you to think I do this kind of thing all the time."

I reach into my pocket and pull out a little leather case containing a selection of bump keys and lock picks.

"I just happened to have these with me," I inform her. "In case I lock myself out of my apartment," I add, realizing too late just how lame these words sound.

"Uh huh," she says in a flat tone.

I can't see her smirk but I know it's there.

"I knew those movies had it right," she advises me. "You forget I used to be a police dispatcher. I know what you guys get away with. No warrant means we can't use anything we find as evidence in court, but we can sure use it to help Flores, if there's anything to be found."

We move around to the front of the house and approach the porch. There are a couple of big wooden chairs on one side and the door seems to be pretty secure. This is going to be a challenge. I try some of the bump keys with no luck. I reach into another pocket and pull out an electronic pick gun.

I can feel Sally's smirk behind me as I stick the snout of the battery powered gadget into the lock and start it up. It buzzes quietly for a moment then there's a little click and the door's unlocked. I turn the handle and open it a crack, waiting to see if an alarm goes off.

Nothing happens and I swing the door wider. Shit, there's a keypad right inside and it's blinking away, excitedly counting down to home security Armageddon.

"Just a minute," I tell Sally, pulling out another of my detecting thingies. It's an electronic gadget, a little LED readout pad that looks like a pager, but with two wires and alligator clips. I snap the leads onto the wires at the bottom of the keypad and push a button. Lights begin to flash and numbers swirl across the readout. In a few seconds they stop, displaying four digits. I punch them into the alarm keypad and it goes silent. I can almost feel its disappointment.

"*Voila,*" I whisper to Sally, channeling a bit of Bruno Bisset. Giving me high fives she steps into the hall and we prepare to cautiously explore the house, possibly the evil lair of a serial killer — or maybe just the happy home of an innocent man.

Chapter Forty

Luis Flores

Flores is lying on his side in the back of the Bronco with a tarp thrown over him. His hands and feet are bound with plastic wire ties, pulled too tight for comfort. A piece of duct tape covers his mouth, making it hard for him to breathe. He feels the vibration of the truck as his captor navigates city streets, stopping for lights, turning left then right.

The Bronco speeds up and the tires begin to whine, telling him they're driving on one of the Interstate highways. But which? I-40 goes east and west, I-25 north and south. He could be going in any direction.

In the driver's seat his captor is whistling in an off-tune, ranting away and pounding a heavy beat on the steering wheel, sending vibrations through the floor of the vehicle. Carefully Flores wriggles around, seeking some–thing, anything that he can use to work free of his bonds. The rear seat has been removed leaving a flat space in the back of the truck. Wriggling and twisting his neck back and forth he finally frees his head from the tarp, gaining a limited view of his surroundings. His feet are positioned toward the rear of the vehicle, his head immediately behind the driver's seat.

Beneath his hips he feels the mounting brackets for the missing rear seat, broad bands of cold steel. He turns on his back, moving slowly so as not to attract the driver's attention. Now he can touch the brackets with his hands. Is there something there that he can use to rub and sever the plastic ties on his hands? No, he finds nothing.

Sighing Flores lies still, thinking. Hidden inside his belt buckle is a tiny knife, but his hands are tied behind his back so that blade might as well be miles away. He tries twisting his wrists in hopes of working them loose but the plastic merely cuts painfully into his skin.

The Bronco surges ahead, bound away from Albuquerque. Through the side window Flores catches a glimpse of some familiar stars that tell him he's headed north, but that could lead practically anywhere.

He begins a careful analysis of his situation. His feet are immobilized with double zip ties around his ankles, pulled so tight that even the slightest movement hurts almost more than he can bear. The belt knife is completely beyond his reach, and the ballpoint pen in his shirt pocket is not only out of reach but would be useless.

But that's not all he's got. Flores rocks onto his left side and feels the pressure of the Zippo lighter in his pants pocket, a hard, chunky block of brushed stainless steel. Even though he gave up smoking a few weeks back, out of long habit he still carries the lighter that had been an integral part of his life for more than two decades, all the way back to his days as a Marine. He rocks back and forth on his side, feeling the lighter dig into his thigh.

He's thinking: *plastic melts*, and wondering if he can manage to free the lighter and use it to burn the plastic ties around his wrists. Remembering some magic acts he'd seen he knows that such things are possible—but he's no magician.

If only he can reach the lighter. Slowly he begins to

twist his arms around to the left side, hoping to reach into the pocket. The binds cut deeper into his flesh and his right arm is bent painfully across his back. He stops to let things settle down then moves his arms a little more. Each time pain flashes, but he learns that after each pause the agony subsides. Slowly, an inch at a time he twists his arms leftward, closer to the goal.

Half an hour passes and in in the end he knows this is not going to work. The wire ties have locked his wrists together in a painful knot and he's reached the limit of his ability to stretch his arms into an impossible position. His shoulders have nearly pulled out of their sockets and the plastic ties have cut deeply into his wrists. He can feel blood dribbling from the wounds.

Shit! For a long time he lies still, arms still twisted painfully to the side. If only he could get the lighter to fall out of the pocket, then it would be easy to pick it up. It seems so simple, and yet so impossible.

After some thought he realizes that if he can't reach the lighter directly, perhaps he can work it out of his pocket some other way. Slowly he hitches his body up so that the seat bracket is pressing on his thigh just below the bulge of the lighter in his pocket. He slides himself downward, thrusting against the lump in his pocket, letting the steel bracket push against the lighter. *Yes!* The lighter moves, slipping upward an inch or so before his pressure on the bracket slips.

Arching his body, he wriggles to line the lighter back up with the bracket then slides slowly back, wriggling his body from side to side in snake-like moves. Again the lighter moves, another inch. Again and again he slides up and back, slowly working the Zippo toward the top of the pocket. Sometimes it moves only a quarter inch, sometimes not at all, and sometimes it actually seems to slip backward. For nearly a half hour Flores struggles before at last the Zippo slips out of his pocket and falls to the floor of the Bronco.

Exhausted, he relaxes for a long moment. The Bronco is still moving fast on the highway, its tires singing with the sound of speed. His manic captor has stopped whistling and pounding on the steering wheel but somehow the silence is even more menacing. Flores feels like he's been caught up in a nightmare.

Slowly he rolls onto his back, fumbling for the lighter with his bound hands. Here it is; he's got it. He grasps the familiar cold, hard metal of the lighter in his hands. Cautiously he turns back onto his right side, clutching the lighter behind his back. This isn't going to be easy. His hands are immobilized, the plastic ties cutting into his flesh. Can he bring the flame of the lighter into position to melt the plastic binder?

It's not easy, and there's no room to separate the plastic band from his wrist. Flores realizes that to melt the plastic he must also burn his own flesh, and to do so without crying out and alerting his captor. He knows the man is armed and would as soon kill him as not.

Huddling beneath the tarp with only his face in the open he takes several slow, deep breaths. His fingers are numb from the constriction of the bindings, barely able to feel the cold steel of the lighter. Awkwardly he flips up the cover of the Zippo to reveal the wick and the little wheel that sparks the flint.

Did he remember to fill the lighter with fluid? He thinks so. Twisting the Zippo he manages to get one finger onto the wheel. He presses but fails to get a spark. Struggling to get a better grip he flicks again and there's a burst of heat. The flame is lit, burning intensely at more than a thousand degrees. Now comes the hard part.

Quickly he twists the lighter in his fingers, pressing it backward against his wrist, hoping to direct the flame to where the plastic band is tight against his flesh. The pain is immediate and Flores writhes in uncontrollable reaction. He can hear the hiss of searing skin.

The steel case of the lighter is quickly heating up, too hot to hold yet he knows this is his only chance at free–dom. Now his fingertips are blistering. The problem is that he can't see what he's doing. He could be burning away the flesh of his wrist inches away from the plastic bind.

My God, the pain! Every instinct tells him to pull the lighter away, to drop it to the floor, to stop the burning and end the excruciating pain. But he knows he can't let up.

Flores bites on his own lip, stifling the urge to scream. He tastes blood and feels the flame eating into his wrist. But now he catches the rewarding scent of melting plastic seeping from beneath the tarp. He strains to pull his wrists apart, stretching the burning band, stretching, stretching … and with a little snap it gives way.

At once he drops the hot lighter and smothers the flame by rolling over onto it.

For a long time Flores lies very still, fighting to hold down the screams that want to surge from his lungs. Slowly the pain subsides but still there's the faint odor of burning flesh and plastic beneath the tarp. Surely his captor will smell it and suspect what he's done. But the air conditioner is running, blowing cool air back from the dashboard. Time seems to crawl as the Bronco continues to flee toward the vast expanse of the north. The acrid smell of burned meat and plastic is replaced by fresh, cool air.

Now what? Slowly Flores pulls his hands apart and rolls from side to side to move his arms around in front of him. He peels the duct tape away from his mouth then reaches to his belt and brings out the little blade hidden in the buckle. He uses it to cut away the second plastic binder on his other wrist. His hands are numb and his arms ache like the devil. Slowly, lying on his side, he bends his knees to pull up his legs until he can reach between them to slice the ties from his ankles.

He's free, but still his only weapon is the little two-inch blade against his kidnapper's automatic pistol. To attempt to overcome him would be suicidal.

Flores decides to wait. Exhausted by his efforts he settles beneath the tarp and tries to get some rest, preparing for the right chance when it comes. The Bronco roars on, cutting the night wind like a blunt and angry knife.

Chapter Forty-one

Rob Charlton

Sally and I complete a survey of the main floor of the Barth house. Aside from a rather nice wine humidor built into one corner of the kitchen it's rather ordinary, filled with everyday furniture and nothing to suggest the owner is engaged in any criminal activity. But there's one unusual feature, a reinforced door on the hallway just past the kitchen. There's a second keypad on the wall next to the door, a little red LED quietly blinking a warning.

We study it. I think I can pick the lock, but it's even more secure than the one on the front door, more like the kind used in banks or lock-down facilities. I hand my flashlight to Sally, asking her to hold it for me. We don't want to attract attention by turning on the house lights.

The first task is to disable the keypad and my little electronic analyzer quickly yields the code. I punch it in and the red light turns to green. Now to the lock itself, which is going to be the far tougher challenge. I insert the snout of my little electronic pick gun and press the trigger.

The gadget whines and chatters but yields no result. After a few minutes I give up on it. I'm going to have to do this the old fashioned way, using slender steel picks. I select two and begin probing the invisible interior of the lock. I can feel the tumblers but the lock was designed to resist picking so it's a challenge. Long minutes pass before I feel the gentle movement of the first tumbler clicking open.

It takes nearly twenty minutes to open the lock, but finally it gives up its last secret to my probing. I turn the handle and the heavy door swings ponderously inward to reveal a set of downward-leading stairs. Lights come on automatically with the clunking sound of a relay, causing us to start.

We look at each other in wonder. Sally gives me an admiring look and hands me my flashlight.

"Into the dragon's lair," she breathes, picking up her bat from where she'd leaned it against the wall.

I chuckle at the thought of a fair maiden prepared to fight a dragon. But what would the reality be? Is this truly a monster's lair, or merely an innocent man's secure storage room? Well, we'll soon find out. Slowly I begin to walk down the stairs with Sally right behind.

We emerge into a lavishly appointed room, far different from the upstairs part of the house. Here there are deep plush oriental carpets, expensive looking paintings and designer furniture. A seating area with fine leather couches and easy chairs occupies one end. At the other is a heavy desk and executive swivel chair. Bookcases filled with rare volumes in leather bindings are ranked along one wall and there are three built-in filing cabinets near the desk. It's the ultimate man cave.

So far this looks like what one might expect a successful Wall Street investment banker to have—but why hide it behind a secure door and alarm system? I walk over to the desk and try its drawers, using my handkerchief to avoid leaving prints. Locked. So are the filing cabinets. Sally is checking the pictures, thinking there may be a wall safe behind one of them. There isn't.

I decide not to pick the locks on the desk and filing

cabinets until we've completed our survey of the downstairs. From the right corner of the lavish room a simple hallway leads back into the rear part of the lower level. I step down the passageway and come to a door on the left. It doesn't appear to be locked or alarmed and when I turn the handle it swings open to reveal a workshop-like room.

To my right, down one entire side of the room is a long bench with various tools and machines. To the left are a tall foreman's desk and what appears to be a massive gun safe.

I step further inside and something familiar catches my eye. It's a machine of some sort, sitting on a little workstation beyond the gun safe at the far left corner of the room. There's a computer screen and keyboard at one side.

I've seen this before, but where? I dredge my memory for a moment before it comes to me. Yes, I saw exactly such a device—at the jewelry shop where I'd taken the fake Rolex watch found on Donald Greenwald's body.

It's a computer controlled engraving machine.

I turn to Sally and point to the device.

"There's our evidence," I inform her. "This is our guy, no doubt about it."

Even if there had been any doubt it's soon dispelled. As we approach the engraving machine we spot a pair of watches on the table next to the keyboard. I pick one of them up with my handkerchief and turn it over. On the back are the engraved words "Happy Retirement, September 21, 1997."

Jeremy Barth is Retirement Man—but where is he, and where is Flores? Lord, please don't tell me this is another dead end.

We spend another hour or so searching the Barth house. I

tackle the desk and filing cabinets first, but find only business records from a long career. There is nothing to tie him to any of the fake identities, the crime victims, or anything else that might be incriminating.

At last we return to the workshop and I use my magic on the gun safe lock, opening it within less than a minute. We swing the double doors wide and see a veritable arsenal, long guns standing to the left and pistols in pigeon holes down the right side. There are two gaps in the ranks of long guns and one of the handgun slots is empty.

Across the bottom is a wide, deep drawer. I slide it open to reveal a row of narrow record binders, each with a name on the label. The first one on the left is labeled Donald Greenwald, the second Morton Drake, and the third Brent Fitzgerald. The names of the first two victims plus the man who escaped in Texas.

More than two dozen more names jump off the spines as my eye travels across the row of binders. At the end I see several that appear to be new. The first are Bruno Bisset, Willard Humphrey, Dr. Brian Stuart, Marsha Greenwald and Luis Flores. The last name, written in bolder letters, is my own.

I recognize this as the fruit of my stolen case files. The bastard was prepared to kill everyone I'd talked to, anyone who might provide a link to him and his murderous program of revenge.

And where are those files? Surely they must be here. There are three smaller drawers at the bottom of the gun safe and when I open them I find not only my hard copy files but also my laptop.

We've sewed up the case as far as Barth's guilt—but he's still at large and has a hostage. The life of Luis Flores is hanging in the balance and I've got nothing to go on. Nothing.

Chapter Forty-two

Rob Charlton

We spend another hour going through the contents of the gun safe. It paints an ugly picture of a man whose twisted brain has turned him into a monster Each of the flat file boxes contains details about one of his selected victims, information that must have been developed over a long period of time and at great expense. Barth has invested heavily in his program of personal retribution. I fondle Donald Greenwald's Rolex and consider taking it to return to my client, but replace it in the file to be entered into evidence later.

In one of the bottom drawers we find more evidence in the form of trophies taken from early victims. Clearly Barth was an active psychopath even from childhood. There are clippings of news stories about the death of his parents and a gloating written account of how he sabotaged their car to cause a fatal accident. There's also a clipping of the news story I found about the death of Shelly Richards, and so help me there's even a pair of her pearl earrings and a Polaroid of her body sprawled at the foot of a stairway. There are other examples, including negatives and five-by-seven black and white prints of flash photos showing the body of a young boy lying in the desert, naked and covered in blood and gore. One leg had been amputated, fingers were missing and his abdomen had been sliced open. Gasping, Sally turns away.

At last we stop, exhausted by a long day and drained by the revelations of horror. It's past midnight now. We go upstairs and find bottles of water in Barth's refrigerator. We walk out to the porch and sink into the large, wooden chairs. For a long time we sit in a state of bemused shock, staring into the dark and sipping from the plastic bottles.

After a while Sally stirs in her chair and turns toward me.

"Is that it?" she asks, frowning. "Isn't there anything we can do?"

I know she's talking about Flores. Based on what we'd seen, the likelihood the deputy will survive in the hands of Barth seems slim. Slumped in my chair, defeated, I say nothing. But there are those special times when the deepest night turns to the brightest dawn. Just as I fumble for an answer my phone goes off in my pocket, on vibration mode. Already tense, I jump as if I'd been shot. I'll never get used to the damned thing, startling me like that. It might as well be a rattlesnake in my pocket for all my hyperactive instincts know.

I swear and jump up to fish it out of my pocket. I check the caller ID but it's an unfamiliar number. I press the talk button and put it on speaker.

"This is Rob Charlton. Who is this please?"

There's a pause, then:

"Rob, it's Luis. I was kidnapped. I think it must have been our guy."

"Luis! My God! Of course you were. We've been worried sick. Are you all right?"

In the face of my torrent of statements there's another pause as he considers how to respond, then: "Yeah, I guess I am. I'm at the ER in Las Vegas, New Mexico. I managed to escape when the kidnapper stopped to take a leak at a rest area on I-25. After he gave up looking for me and left, a nice couple picked me up and dropped me here."

"Are you injured?"

"Oh, nothing that won't heal. I used my lighter to melt through a plastic handcuff and I burned myself pretty badly. The docs have me doped up with some pain meds and I won't be able to use my hands very well for a few days."

"Luis, this is great news," Sally chirps happily.

Again there's a pause, then Flores asks, "Hello? Who's that?"

"Oh, I'm sorry. This is Sally Birch. You know, Sally's Place? I've been trying to help Rob find you."

"Oh, great. Thanks."

"Have you told your wife?" I inquire.

"Sure, I just got off the phone with her. She was half frantic. Said she'd talked to you and that you wouldn't let her call in the police."

"Did she tell you what your daughter was told about that?"

"Yeah, that he'd kill me if they did. To tell you and no one else. She had a hard time accepting that, but I'm glad you talked her out of going to the cops. No telling what that man's capable of."

"You have no idea," I inform him. "Sally and I are at his house now, and we've seen his files. It's Jeremy Barth and he's the worst kind of psychopath. I have no doubt he would have killed you in a second if it suited him. The reason he wanted you alive was to draw me in, then kill us both."

"Well, it didn't work, did it?" There's a defiant note in Flores' voice, then his mood drops. "But he got away, damn it. I couldn't have stopped the murdering son of a bitch. I was in pretty bad shape and he had an automatic that looked bigger than life. It was all I could do to get out of the vehicle and hide without him seeing me."

I think for a minute and Sally chimes in.

"Luis, listen. Stay there. We're coming to get you. Should be about an hour and a half."

Jesus, the woman is thinking faster than I am, and making decisions like a Marine gunny. I like it.

"Good idea," I agree. "We'll be there as quick as we can."

"Okay. I told my wife not to come. Remember it's Las Vegas, New Mexico, just a little one-horse town. Don't go to the Sin City one because I won't be there."

We all laugh and I click off the phone. We go inside to tidy up, removing traces of our illegal search. When the time comes a warrant will be issued and all we've discovered will be entered into evidence.

As we prepare to lock up the gun safe Sally stops me and points at the array of weapons, cocking her head. What the hell, it couldn't hurt to have more firepower. There's plenty of evidence without this armory. She picks out a heavy Colt automatic pistol to supplement her little .38 and grabs a tactical shotgun and a box of shells.

I pick out an AR-15 semi-automatic rifle and a couple of extra 30-round magazines. I used to carry one of those in my car when I was with the Bureau. It's a sweet little gun with lots of stopping power.

I lock up the house and in a few minutes we're heading for the Interstate, loaded for bear. Now that Luis is safe I'm no longer concerned by the fact that we have no idea where Barth has gone, for in my mind we'll find the bastard. He's made too many mistakes and we know who he is. He's lost his base and is on the run now. Somehow, some way I know we'll find his trail.

The maroon baby is in her element on the open road. I have to hold her back as she surges ahead into the night. At this hour I know the highway is free of patrol officers, all safe in their beds or waiting to respond to emergency calls, so I keep her at ninety, fifteen over the speed limit.

The miles roll quickly by and we soon pass the exits for Santa Fe and sweep around the southern edge of the Sangre de Cristo range and into the open plains.

It's about 3 a.m. when we pull into the parking lot in front of the little regional hospital. The ER looks as quiet as a morgue, unlike big city hospitals that are usually jumping at the witching hour, what with gunshot and knife wounds and the consequences of drunken drivers meeting immovable objects. There's something to be said about small town life.

There's nobody at the reception desk and we walk through the waiting area and push open the swinging doors into the ER proper. Flores is sitting in a wheelchair just inside. He's got a line in his right arm attached to a drip bag and looks like hell but he perks up at the sight of us.

"Hello, my friends," he calls out, raising his bandaged left arm in greeting. We cluster around him like a pair of mother hens. Sally picks up a towel and wipes sweat from his forehead. There are smiles all around.

"I was a little dehydrated so they've got me on a saline drip," Flores explains, nodding toward the little bag. "But I'm okay. They're ready to release me."

"What about a police report?" I ask him. Flores shakes his head.

"I didn't want to get them into it," he murmurs, looking around. "Too many complications."

"Good move," I tell him. "So you gave them some story about how you burned yourself?"

"Yeah, I told them I was playing with matches." He laughs and we join in. "Actually I said it was an accident with a camping stove. I'll tell you the whole story, but first let's get out of here. Hospitals make me nervous."

In a few minutes a nurse appears, unhooks the drip and removes the port from his arm. She hands the deputy a clipboard with a form to sign and in a moment we're free to go. Flores wobbles a little as he first stands up from the wheelchair but soon steadies as we walk out into the parking lot. We climb into the maroon baby and go in search of an all-night cafe. We find it at a truck stop near the north side interstate exit and settle into a corner booth. Our waitress appears immediately. She's built like one of those prehistoric Earth Goddess statuettes, all thighs and boobs, but she has a nice smile.

"You guys look like you need this," she says, setting a carafe of coffee on the table. She plops big menus in front of us and goes to fetch cups and saucers.

I look at my watch. It's after four now, not too early for breakfast. I open the menu and search for my favorite items. Still looking a little pale, Flores awkwardly picks up his menu with his good hand and after a moment Sally does the same. In the end we place identical orders: biscuits and gravy, two eggs over easy, bacon, hash browns and orange juice. Rob's favorite breakfast.

As we wait for our food Flores fills us in on the details of his kidnapping.

"The bastard broke into my apartment and pointed a gun at my daughter," he relates. "My piece was in the lock box by the door, something I've done for years as a matter of habit." He pauses. "I always thought my home was safe, not a place where you need a gun. Guess I'm gonna rethink that after what happened last night."

"When I'm home my .38 is right by my side," Sally chimes in. "There's too many sex-crazed men around for a woman to take any chances." She tosses her head, flipping her ponytail over her right shoulder.

"Yeah, my Glock stays with me, too," I add. "And I used to keep a shotgun in the bedroom. Actually, I may start doing that again. Of course, you had a child in the house so I understand the problem."

"Shit, Emily's practically grown now and I've had her out to the range plenty of times," Flores tells us. "She's a better shot than most of my deputies so I don't have to worry about gun safety. But damn it, we were sitting at the table eating dinner when the guy burst in. Must have picked the lock. It wouldn't have mattered about my weapon because he had the drop on us. Well, on her actually. I had to go along with him like a sheep to slaughter."

We sit in silence for a moment, sipping our coffee. The waitress appears with a large tray and sets out our platters and glasses of juice. We dig in like a pack of hungry wolves.

When the feeding frenzy is over I tell Flores about our visit to Barth's house and what we found there. When I finish Flores sits back in his seat.

"He was driving a metallic blue Bronco with New Mexico plates," he tells us. "I got the number, of course, and I checked it with dispatch while I was waiting for you. There's no Bronco in Barth's name, so we can assume it's listed under one of his fake identities. Or possibly stolen. The plate itself is registered to a Ford Fiesta owned by a 77-year-old woman who lives in Albuquerque. Obviously taken from her car."

"So it's another dead end?" Sally murmurs, more a statement than a question. But something has stirred in my memory. I take a moment to think it through.

"Luis, remember when I suggested that you compare the driver's license pictures of Jake Wilson and Jim Craig? You were able to tell they were the same guy, despite different wigs and glasses and a little stage makeup."

"Yeah?"

"Well, what if we could do a wide search, compare those two images we already have with entire DMV databases? Now that we've identified Barth we can add his picture, too. That gives us three sets of reference points. There's some pretty fantastic facial recognition software out there. I know a guy in the Bureau that's been working on that for years. He helped me out a few times, and he owes me a few favors, too."

Flores is doubtful.

"Well, I can see how it worked when we actually had two names to compare. But there are millions of DMV pictures. Do you really think it could pick out one guy? Or, come to think of it maybe more than one since we don't know how many legends our perp has."

"For one thing we wouldn't have to search the entire country. Craig was in Oklahoma, and both Wilson and Barth himself were here in New Mexico. The second murder took place in Colorado, and that's the direction he was headed tonight. I think we'll find our man there."

"It's sure worth trying," Sally remarks.

"Okay, sure, of course," Flores agrees. "How would we do this?"

I look at my watch.

"It's nearly seven in Virginia. My guy's an early riser, and he has a workstation and a T3 line at his house. We might be able to get to the bottom of this before we leave here."

I reach for my phone. Sally gestures to the waitress to bring us a fresh pot of coffee. We're on the trail again.

Chapter Forty-two

Rob Charlton

I go to the address book on my iPhone and look up the home number for Josh Benton, an FBI special agent and electronic forensics specialist. He's an old friend from my days in the Bureau, when Josh and I worked together on several of my cases. He's an expert on data mining and an all-around wizard with computers.

His facial recognition software is second to none, except maybe for the Mossad's. Using Boolean logic and deep computing power, it can provide matches even for heavily altered faces by comparing dozens of data points. Except through radical surgery, things like the shape of the nose, the position of the eyes, the curves of the cheek bones and the angle and shape of the ears cannot be completely disguised.

I set the phone on speaker and dial. Josh picks up on the third ring. "Josh, it's Rob Charlton."

"Rob! I heard they retired your ass. How's it going?"

I take a moment to explain my new career, ask about Josh's wife and kids, then get down to the nitty gritty.

"I'm tracking a serial killer in cooperation with the Bernalillo County Sheriff's Department," I tell him. "Their chief detective is sitting here right now. Say hello to Lieutenant Luis Flores."

Flores gives Benton a brief description of our working relationship and a capsule description of Barth's modus operandi, particularly his use of disguises and false identities.

"We're wondering if you could give us a little help, off the record," I pick up the thread. "We think it's one man working under different aliases. We were able to connect two of his false identities from DMV pictures. Now we know who he is, so there are three sets of images that might be of the same man, including two in disguises. What we're wondering is whether you can use that information to locate another legend, or perhaps more than one."

Benton thinks for a moment before answering.

"Rob, I can try. You should know that it's not 100 percent, and there are well over a hundred million mug shots in the databases. You may get a false positive, maybe a lot of them."

"I understand. We suspect the guy is going to be in this region, probably Colorado, so you can narrow the search."

"Okay, let me pour a cup of coffee and get to my computer. Stay on the line."

We hear the rattle of cup and spoon, a door opening and closing, then the squeak of a chair as Benton sits down.

"All right, I'm firing up. You said there were two false IDs. Let's start with one of those and see if we can find the other. That will give us a good baseline."

"Great," I agree. "Let's start with a Jim Craig of Oklahoma City."

"Okay, I'm accessing the Oklahoma DMV records." He pauses for a moment. "It's giving me three James Craigs but only one in Oke City. I'll email you his mug shot to identify."

I give him my email address and a moment later my phone pings to announce a message has been received. Keeping the phone active I click over to open the email and a picture appears. I hold it up for Flores to see and he nods.

"That's the guy. Now using that as a base, search for similars in the New Mexico database."

"All right, it's running. This is going to take a few minutes."

As we wait Josh and I talk about some of the good old days when I was still with the Bureau. I tell him about my year as a beach bum in the Caribbean and my frustrations at trying to start a new career. He commiserates, noting that he's only a few years from retirement himself. He's obviously a lot smarter than I because he's already started a small consulting business and will make a smooth transition into offering electronic forensic services to people like me, police departments and the Bureau itself. Shit, why didn't I think of something like that.

In a moment we hear a ping from Benton's computer announcing the end of the search.

"Okey dokey, let's see what we've got here," he says. We hear the clicking of keyboard keys.

"Now just to let you know, the way this thing works is that it locates similars and ranks them by probability. From my experience I consider any match below 90 percent certainty to be very questionable. I've got about thirty names here that are 90 percent or above."

I glance at Flores and he's looking glum. Sally sighs and sinks back in her seat.

"But don't let that bother you," Benton continues, "because I've got only a couple that are ranked near the top and thus most likely to be correct. There's one starred at 99 percent and another at 98. Shall I give you those names?"

"Sure. Let's have the top one first."

"The 99 percenter is someone named Jeremy Barth."

"Yes!" Flores slaps the table with his good hand and Sally leans forward again, eyes sparkling with excitement.

"Josh, you've hit our number one suspect. Now what's the second name?"

"It's someone named Jake Wilson. Both men live in Albuquerque."

"You've got it." Flores and Sally are squirming around in their seats and even jaded old Rob is getting a rush from this. We're closing in on our killer.

"All right, Josh, you've correctly identified all the known parties. Now the hard part. Using the data points from those three subjects, actually only one man, search the Colorado DMV database to see if there's another match up there. This guy will be an unsub." I use the Bureau jargon for an unknown subject.

We hear more keyboard noises followed by a long wait. After a moment we hear the ping and his chair squeaks. I can almost see him leaning forward to read the results of the search.

"Well, I have several high-probability matches. Since you don't know the name of this one, it may be hard to know for sure which, if any, is the true match."

"How many are there?"

"I've got six that are 97 percent or above."

"Okay, let's start with the top match again. What's the name?"

"It's a Robert Singleton. Lives near Denver. Ninety-nine percent certainty."

"Can you cross check to see what vehicles are registered in his name? We have a possible ID on a vehicle.

"Sure, take just a moment." There are more keyboard sounds and Benton comes back.

"Singleton has a brown van."

Flores and I look at each other and he shakes his head.

"That doesn't help. Try the next name."

"Wait, I'm seeing a second vehicle under Singleton. It's a Bronco."

Oh, yes! Flores gives me a look of triumph and Sally reaches over to give me high fives.

"One last question, Josh. Tell me the Bronco is metallic blue."

"Why, as a matter of fact it is."

"Then we've almost certainly got our man. Thanks ever so much. Please email me the details on Singleton, picture, address, anything you've got."

"Sure, it'll be there in a minute. And you're welcome. Always happy to help a friend."

We end the phone call and I pour myself another cup of coffee. In a moment my phone dings and I open the email to find the mug shot and contact information for Barth's latest incarnation. Robert Singleton, living near Evergreen, Colorado just west of Denver. Owner of a metallic blue Bronco and a face that matches Barth's to within 99 percent certainty. Our quarry.

The waitress comes by to see if we need anything else and I inquire about their selection of fresh pies. She informs me that they have some Dutch apple, cherry, banana cream and her favorite, chocolate cream. I order the apple with a scoop of vanilla. The waitress looks at Flores and Sally and they stare at me as if I just dropped in from Mars.

"Jesus, Rob," Sally exclaims, "you just ate a huge breakfast and now you're having dessert at six a.m.?"

She gives me the kind of disapproving look I get when I ask her for those Danish with pineapple goo on top. If she doesn't like people to eat those things, how come she always has them on hand? There are some things that I'll just never understand.

"Bring two extra forks," I tell the waitress and she grins and hurries off.

"Well, maybe just a taste…" Sally looks embarrassed and Flores breaks out laughing.

We finish off the pie and ice cream—even Flores takes a bite—and pay our bill, giving the Earth Goddess a handsome tip. As we step outside the sun's rising over the plains, casting long, warm shadows. We stand for a moment inhaling cool, clean air and absorbing the good feelings of a fine early morning, that special time when life starts all over with a fresh new day.

Flores looks at the maroon baby, then at me.

"I figure it's a little over 350 miles to Evergreen, and it's interstate all the way," he informs us. "We can be knocking on his door before noon."

I think about this. There comes a time when the rational thing to do is call in the authorities and let them take it from there. But, damn it, this is our case and I can tell Flores wants to see it through to the end. Even Sally is hopping to go. And, hell, we've got almost as much high-grade weaponry as a modern SWAT team, what with our usual sidearms and the items we took from Barth's house.

"Um, should it come to that, are you up to a firefight?" I ask Flores, looking at his bandaged left wrist and right hand.

"Shit, I don't have my piece," he mutters, looking downcast.

"Well, we have a few extra items," I admit. "We liberated some stuff from Barth's house. Between us we have four pistols, including Sally's .38 and a big .45, plus my Glock and a little ankle gun. We've also got a tactical shotgun and an AR-15. And, oh yes, don't forget Sally's bat.

"Holy shit! We're armed for a minor war." Flores is obviously raring to go.

We drive to an isolated area at the rear of the truck stop and I open the trunk where we'd stashed the long guns and the .45. Flores tries the big pistol but his bandages make it awkward to handle.

The AR-15 is a different story. Despite his injured hands he can hold the weapon easily. He picks up a magazine and slaps it into the receiver with a snap.

"These always remind me of the M-4s we used in the Marines," he remarks. "This is my kinda rifle." He turns to look at me. "Well, what're we waiting for?"

"Yeah," Sally chimes in. "Let's go."

Again I mull over our options.

"Well, all right, I can see running a reconnaissance. If we sense real danger we'll call in the cavalry. But Sally, this time I want you to stay back."

Flores agrees and her disappointment shows.

"But don't think of it that way, think of yourself as our backup," I add. "Who knows, you may see some action yet."

She grins and turns to open the door and climb into the back seat. Without a word Flores goes around to the passenger side and I get behind the wheel. We pull over to the pumps to top up the gas tank and in a few minutes we're heading north, ready to pay a visit to Mr. Robert Singleton, a.k.a. Jeremy Barth, M.B.A., C.P.A., former investment banker, psychopath and ruthless mass murderer. It's a beautiful day for payback.

Chapter Forty-three

Jeremy Barth

Still raging at the loss of his hostage Barth arrives at his Singleton house just before dawn. He puts the Bronco in the garage and pulls out his Kia for the return trip to New Mexico, where he'll resume his true identity. He goes inside the house to freshen up before starting the trip back, another six hours of driving on top of a long night.

At least he'd had the foresight to switch license plates on the Bronco, so the Singleton identity is still good. He'd learned that lesson from the realization that it was the plates on the Jake Wilson van that led Charlton to the Wilson house. Of course he's carefully shielded his own home from any suspicion so he still has two safe refuges counting the one here in Colorado. Nevertheless, his enemies are obviously extremely dangerous. He realizes he must put his retirement plans on hold and wait for things to settle down.

Relaxed by that thought he decides to take a brief nap before starting back. Taking off his shoes and jacket he lies down on the leather couch and soon falls asleep.

When he awakens he finds that more than four hours have passed and it's after ten o'clock. Slightly groggy he heats water to make a cup of instant coffee, adding two spoonsful of the powder and putting it in an insulated travel mug. Always vigilant he takes another look around to be sure he's left no fingerprints or other evidence. He's already removed his shotgun and rifle from a hidden compartment under the floor of the Bronco and locked them in the trunk of the Kia. He's carrying the automatic pistol in a paddle holster inside his belt. He locks the house, gets in the car and drives away down the winding road that leads from the remote location in the forest to a main road a few miles away.

As he approaches the intersection he notices a big car slowing down and signaling to turn in off the highway. Something strikes him as familiar about the maroon colored Ford but he shakes off the feeling. Sometimes his old enemy Paranoia sneaks up on him and he fights a constant battle to keep it at bay. As he passes the car he notices the silhouettes of three passengers, but the smoked glass prevents him from seeing any details. Probably somebody going to one of the other houses scattered around the forest.

Thanks to his nap and the double-hit of caffeine he makes the trip back to Albuquerque non-stop, arriving at his house around 5 p.m. He locks the car away in the garage and goes into the house, relieved to be back in his private sanctum.

He realizes he's starving, not having stopped for breakfast or lunch. He busies himself in the kitchen, preparing a three-egg omelet with cheddar, mushrooms, onions and green peppers seasoned with fresh herbs. As it cooks on the gas burner set to low he opens a bottle of red wine and decants it to air. He takes a crystal wine glass down from a cabinet and wipes it carefully with a cloth, ready to receive the blood offering of the vine. As a side dish he makes a simple romaine salad dressed with balsamic vinegar and olive oil with a blend of sea salt, pepper, marjoram and thyme. The omelet turns out perfectly, golden brown with a rim of delicately melted cheese.

As he eats his mind travels over the possibilities of his future. Yes, he must lay low for a while. Charlton will become discouraged and Marsha Greenwald will cut off his retainer. Barth knows about that from the stolen case file and someday he'll fix the bitch. For his part, Flores will be drawn into other cases and Barth will slip into the forgotten backlog of unsolved crimes.

He has all the time in the world. He can enjoy fine meals like this one, continue to work on his plans and strike later when the pressure is off. His only regret is that with the passing of time some of his retirement candidates may die of natural causes. That would truly be a shame.

He puts the dishes in the sink and carries the wine glass, still half full, out to the front porch. He sinks into his favorite chair and sets the glass and bottle on the side table. The sun is bright in a cloudless sky. He raises the glass to the sun as if in salute. The wine turns golden rays to blood. Barth smiles.

A few minutes later he tips up the glass to finish the wine and returns to the house. He unlocks the door to his downstairs lair. Here he feels even more comfortable, basking in the security of his secret life. He sits down at the executive desk in the big room and unlocks the center drawer where he keeps pens and pencils. A strange feeling comes over him as he looks into the drawer. He would have sworn the pens were all at the left side of the drawer—Barth is very particular about things like that—but now two of them are several inches in toward the middle, next to a pad of sticky notes. Is something wrong? No! Paranoia, his old Nemesis, is creeping into his brain. He must have accidentally brushed the pens the last time he opened the drawer.

He works at the desk for a few minutes, making some notes on a legal pad. Always a businessman at heart Barth has documented each event in his career of crime and now he outlines his experience with Flores, the euphoria of success followed by the disaster of failure. He notes how one of the plastic ties was burned through. That had puzzled him for a long time, but as he thought about it during his long drives to Colorado and back he concluded the deputy must have used a cigarette lighter to somehow free himself. Clever bastard. Barth makes a note to himself: Failure to thoroughly search captive. He won't make that mistake again.

Now Barth rises and goes into his workshop, preparing to file away his notes. He opens the gun safe and is about to pull open one of the drawers when his eyes are drawn upward to the array of weapons. For a moment his mind freezes. *What the hell!* There's definitely something wrong. This is not the work of Paranoia. The empty slots where missing weapons had rested virtually shout at him. He falls back in his chair, stunned. For a long moment he can only stare, mouth agape, eyes wide.

With effort he calms himself and takes a closer look. The AR-15 is gone. So is a shotgun. And over here, in the pigeonhole where the Colt model 1911 .45 automatic lived, there's only an empty space. Boxes of ammo and loaded magazines for the weapons are also gone.

His mind races as he tries to understand. Did he take those guns himself in addition to the others? No, he can't imagine he wouldn't remember that.

Has he gone completely crazy at last? He's long feared it would happen, fought against it at every stage in his life. But no, this is something concrete, real, beyond questioning. There's no sign of psychotic paranoia here, just the disconcerting fact of the missing weapons. To be doubly certain he runs his hand over the empty spaces.

Then the answer must be the unthinkable—someone has penetrated his private lair. If they've taken the guns, they must also know his secrets.

Charlton! It has to be him. But how? And why was the house locked up, made to look completely normal? Again Paranoia whispers inside his head: *A trap! They've set a trap for you. For me. For Jeremy. For us*. The little voice bounces around inside his skull like a ping pong ball.

Fear races through his body like a wildfire. He begins to shake uncontrollably. Sweat bursts out on his back and chest, immediately soaking his shirt. He begins to gibber, mouthing what psychiatrists call word salad, meaningless phrases and odd, unrelated words. Paranoia is struggling to take full control of him.

Barth staggers to his feet and plunges back into the main room with its leather furniture and plush carpets, expecting to see policemen pointing guns at him. He throws himself down on the couch and draws his knees up in a fetal position, still trembling. Inside, a rational part of his brain is trying to speak over the voice of Paranoia, saying: *This can't be happening. No! It cannot be.*

Slowly the tremors subside. He stands up, unsteady on his feet, and goes to the trio of built-in filing cabinets. He presses on a hidden catch and one of the cabinets pulls smoothly out from the wall and swings to one side. Behind it is a secret space containing Barth's last trump card. Inside is a large suitcase plus a briefcase containing his one remaining secret identity, the person he had prepared to become if ever he was found out.

He opens the briefcase and removes a wallet, checking that the cash and credit cards are still there. He puts it in his pocket along with a passport in another name, bearing a picture of someone who looks a lot like Barth but with different hair and glasses. Also in the case are those very things, a fine human-hair wig and glasses. Barth quickly puts them on and becomes that other person, an Argentinian citizen.

He still has his millions and long ago he'd purchased a remote ranch in the Pampas. There he'll take up his new life as Don Grigor Alvarez, the long absent patron of his gaucho tenants and their families.

Quickly he snaps the case shut, grabs both the briefcase and the suitcase and heads for the stairs. In a moment he's in the Kia, driving out of the garage and away without even stopping to close the door. The sun is sinking to the west now, casting long shadows.

As Barth leaves his old life behind forever a kind of peace settles over him. Now he has time to think. He must cover his trail. It's no time to rush to the airport and buy a one-way ticket to Buenos Aires. Not when his enemies may be close behind. The Singleton identity is still secure, so his best move could be to head there and lay low for a week or two. It will give him time to decompress, plan, make arrangements.

And then a terrible image crashes into his consciousness. Like a video playing in his head he sees that dark sedan slowing to turn from the main highway toward the Singleton house. It had tickled his memory at the time and now the truth comes home like a hammer blow.

Charlton's car. That damned Crown Vic of his. It was him, and probably with Flores too.

Somehow they know it all.

Barth feels a pressure in his chest and his eyes blur. He pulls off to the side of the road. He's having trouble breathing, as if something is clamping down on his body. He wonders, is he having a heart attack? No, he realizes, it's only the result of severe stress. A panic attack. He's had them before and knows what to do. Initiating some meditation techniques to trigger the relaxation response he takes long, slow breaths and gradually the panic subsides.

Now the decision comes unbidden from his mind. He will not run, but stand. He knows the truth now, that his enemies know most of his secrets. Surely they'll try to trap him. They could be on the way to his house right now, expecting to catch him unaware. But he's a step ahead of them. He'll turn their trap around on them and close this down for good. His secrets will be safe once more, buried with their bodies in the ancient desert sands.

He starts driving again, turning back toward his house by a circuitous route. When they come, as he knows they will, he'll be waiting. Smiling in anticipation of his revenge Barth begins to hum the rhythmic beat of "Death on Two Legs," his old personal anthem from a Queen song of an age long gone.

David L. Brown

Chapter Forty-four

Rob Charlton

We stop when my GPS says we're about a half mile from the Singleton house. I pull the car out of sight into a little lane and we get out. I remind my companions that we're here to reconnoiter, not launch an attack.

I have some little hand-held radios with earplugs in my kit so I issue one to each of us and we synchronize on a channel. Sally agrees to stay back to act as our rear guard, armed with her .38 and the big .45, plus of course her cut-down Louisville Slugger. It will be her job to watch for anyone approaching up the dirt road, which the GPS tells us ends at our objective.

The house sits on a moderately steep slope, facing east. Flores offers to take the high side and get into position above the house to the southwest. I'll circle below and approach from the east and north. I give Flores my spare set of binoculars and we set off.

About twenty minutes later I hear Flores voice in my earpiece, reporting he's already in position.

"I've got a good high-angle view from about two hundred yards uphill to the southwest. I can see both the house and a detached garage. It's kind of similar to the layout at the Wilson house. There's no sign of anybody."

"Okay, hold there. I'm catching some rough going

down here, lots of loose rocks and brush. I'll let you know when I have the house in sight."

I'm wishing I had my hiking boots instead of street shoes, which are apparently made to slip and slide instead of gripping. I've brought the tactical shotgun with me as well as the Glock in its shoulder holster, and carrying the long gun makes awkward going with only one arm free. Another fifteen minutes goes by before I manage to clamber up the hillside and catch sight of the house.

I work my way up the slope to a spot slightly above and to the north. Now Flores and I have it covered from all sides. I check in with him and Sally, then settle in behind a fallen log and begin scanning with my binos. It looks quiet.

We watch for about forty-five minutes before starting to move in. Flores seems to accept my leadership, and it's a role that comes naturally to me after years in the Bureau. I tell him to work his way closer while I stay in place and watch.

When he's about a hundred yards out he takes cover and it's my turn to move. In a few minutes we've moved within about fifty yards to either side of the house. Flores is hidden in some bushes and I'm peering around the trunk of a big pine tree. Still no sign of life.

"Whatcha think?" Flores inquires over the radio.

"We need to get in there," I advise him. "Stay there to cover me. I'm going to sneak up on the north end of the house and try to get my snooper on the window."

"Sounds like a plan."

Keeping an eye on the two windows facing the north I step out from behind the tree and begin to crab walk across the slope. The windows have drawn shades and I'm alert to any motion that could signal someone is watching. My approach is uneventful and soon I'm listening to the sound of silence. Except for the occasional creak of a rafter and wind rattling windows and doors there's no telling sound of any kind coming from inside the house.

"Luis, there's nobody home. I think it's safe to come on down."

We meet in front of the house and circle around. The garage is locked, but like the others I've seen there's a small window on one side. A glance shows us there are two vehicles inside, a brown van and the Bronco.

"This is strange," Flores ponders. "Both his vehicles are here, but he's not."

"It's not so strange," I inform him. "Remember, "he" doesn't even exist. I bet Barth had left his personal car here and now he's exchanged the Bronco for it and left."

"Flown the coop, eh?"

"Let's take a look inside."

We walk back to the front door and I work my magic with a bump key. In a few minutes we're inside. As was the case with the Wilson house, this one shows no signs of a permanent resident. There's a teakettle on the stove, and when I touch it it's warm.

"Feel this, Luis. He was here, and not long ago."

He places his good hand on the kettle and nods in agreement.

"He had to have left before we got here or Sally would have seen him going out. We probably just missed him." Flores looks downcast. This would have been a perfect trap and our quarry has escaped.

After looking around some more we walk back to the car to decide on our next step.

None of us have had any sleep and it's nearly noon. We decide to find a restaurant for some lunch then check into a motel for shuteye. Before long we're sacked out in separate rooms at a Red Roof Inn. I sleep hard for a few hours, but then a dream steals into my slumber and starts to unfold.

-

I'm back at Barth's house, in the downstairs lounge. There are dead bodies all around me, some sitting on the leather couch and chairs, others scattered around the room. I see smears of blood on the furniture, the Persian rugs and even on the walls, splatters and gobbets of it everywhere.

Barth is here, too, alive, standing in the middle of the room. He holds up a watch and laughs. He reaches in his pockets and pulls out more watches, and yet more until there are dozens of them spilling out of his hands and scattering across the bloody carpet. Gold, platinum, stain–less steel, all kinds of watches. The retirement watches of men, women and even children. His maniacal laughter echoes around the room.

I look closer and recognize one of the bodies is Flores. His throat's been cut and the wound gapes like a terrible second mouth. Next to him is a woman slumped to one side and when I turn her head I see Marsha Greenwald. In one corner Bruno Bisset is curled up in a fetal position, clutching a bloody loaf of bread to his chest.

Other faces emerge from the fog of nightmare: Sally Birch, holding her bat. Dr. Stuart. Prof–essor Humphrey. All dead. There are others I don't recognize but three of them I somehow know are Shelly Richards and Barth's parents. The body of a dismembered teenage boy is spread out on the floor, the same one last seen in black-and-white prints.

There's someone sitting in the executive chair, but it's turned away from me. I swivel it around. It's a man whose face I'd seen many times before, but only in mirrors. The late Rob Charlton stares into eternity, a bullet hole like a third eye in his forehead.

I wake up as if someone had dumped a bucket of ice water on me. Hyperventilating, I've broken out in a sweat and my heart is racing. It takes me several minutes to slow my pulse. I climb out of the bed and walk over to the window, pushing aside the curtain to look outside. It's a perfect sunny late afternoon, with a view of snowy peaks to the west.

I open the mini bar and grab some scotch whisky. I twist the top and drink it straight out of the little bottle, dribbling some down my chin. I wipe it with the back of my hand, toss the empty bottle in the trash and sit down in the easy chair by the motel room desk. I dial Flores' room. It rings eight times before he answers, and it's with a sleepy voice.

"Luis, he's going back to his house. The Barth house."

"Aw, man, I just got to sleep..."

"He's on his way there now but we could lose him if we don't get there before he books."

"How do you know? Betcha he's already running."

"No, it makes sense. He doesn't know we've made him, or Singleton either. He didn't leave here because he thought we'd find him. He just came to drop off the Bronco and get his own car. He thinks he's in the clear. But he's sure to see signs that Sally and I were in his house, and when he does..."

"Yeah, that makes sense." Flores is alert now. "So we should get there before he figures it out."

"I think so. I know I can't sleep any more. You and Sally can catch some winks in the car. We gotta go now."

"I can call ahead and dispatch some deputies, put the house under surveillance."

I think about that for a moment before responding.

"I've seen how your guys work and let me put it this way, none of them are the Invisible Man. One glimpse and he could be gone. You know how devious he is."

"Yeah, well, they're not that bad. I can send a couple of guys just to watch from a distance, very low key. I'll wait to send them after it gets dark."

"We have enough against Barth to make an arrest if he's there," I suggest. "We don't want to tip him off. Plus, I really want us to be the ones to nail the rat."

"Okay, we've got a plan. We pin him down and come in ourselves around midnight to make the arrest." Flores sighs. "But who's gonna tell Sally? She looked really beat."

"I'll call her right now." I hang up and dial her room.

"Rise and shine Sally," I tell her, practicing my happy tone of voice.

She groans.

"For Christ's sake Rob, what time is it?"

"Nearly five."

"Five! I've had less than three hours of sleep!"

"Yeah, well, join the insomniacs club. I'll drive so you and Sleepy Head Flores can snooze all the way back to Albuquerque if you want. I'm pretty sure Barth has gone back to his house. We need to get down there ASAP, before he figures out we were there."

That wakes her up.

"I'll be dressed in five," she declares and hangs up. In a few minutes we meet Flores in the lobby and it's back on the road. Despite their claims of exhaustion, neither of my companions try to sleep any more. The thrill of the chase is stirring our hormones and we're hot on the trail.

"So, what makes you so sure Barth's returning to his house?" Sally asks me.

"Just logical deduction," I reply.

We're joining the rush hour traffic around Denver and

down southbound I-25. I decide not to tell them about my nightmare. I don't even want to think about it, but I know I'll revisit that horrible scene many times at dark and lonely moments of my life.

A little shudder runs up my back and I press into the leather seat to make it stop.

Chapter Forty-five

Jeremy Barth

Barth hides his car in a deserted area about a half-mile from his house. For nearly an hour he stays in the car, waiting for the cover of night. At last twilight fades and he begins his preparations. In the trunk of his car are emergency items and weapons. He decides to use the Sako sniper rifle in addition to the Beretta pistol. He adds a KaBar combat knife, strapping its sheath to his left hip. He puts on an insulated jacket and fills the pockets with several energy bars, bottles of water and extra ammunition. He hangs a pair of mil spec night vision goggles around his neck.

Barth's excited, experiencing what has been called "the hunter's rush." Paranoia has been pushed back into the twisted recesses of his brain. He's in a manic phase now, with its unrealistic feelings of invincibility.

His enemies will expect to catch him off guard, but he is the hunter now, they the prey.

He slips into the brush of the wild desert landscape that surrounds his remote house, moving slowly to avoid making a sound. He circles around to come at it from the east, approaching the road while keeping in cover.

Suddenly he stops. There's the sound of a motor. He watches as a patrol car slows to a stop just fifty yards away, around a curve from the driveway to his house. The officer pulls the vehicle off the road and shuts off the lights.

So, they think they've got him under surveillance, but it's the other way around. Barth thinks about his options. He knows that his true enemies are Charlton and Flores. He instinctively knows their egos will insist they make the arrest. He knows they were in Colorado, so they may not come until later. The deputy is there to make sure he doesn't get away before they come. He decides to wait and watch.

Two hours pass and Barth decides it's time to act. He rises from his hiding place and begins to move slowly toward the car, keeping to the right rear quarter of the vehicle in the driver's blind spot. For long minutes he draws closer, finally approaching to within a few feet of the car. He can see the head and shoulders of the deputy silhouetted against the distant city glow. The watcher is smoking a cigarette and smoke is wafting out the side window, telling Barth the window is open. He smiles and moves again, this time around the rear of the car, keeping low. In a minute he's crouched just behind the open window.

The deputy is still smoking. The low sound of routine radio traffic comes from inside the car. Barth rises to his feet, standing right against the car and just behind the deputy's shoulder.

"Officer!" he says in a loud voice. "Can you help me?"

Startled, the deputy drops his cigarette and begins to turn his head toward the sudden apparition. Barth strikes, reaching with his right hand to grab the officer by the hair and pull his head up. With a backhanded motion of his left hand he sweeps the razor sharp knife across his victim's throat, like a butcher slaughtering a pig. There's a gushing, gurgling sound and an acrid, coppery odor fills the air. The deputy slumps sideways in his seat and Barth melts back into the night.

He knows if there's one cop watching, there's another. During his long observation Barth has heard the deputy make only irregular radio checks, the last one only minutes before. He moves away toward the other end of the road, knowing his next victim will be there and unaware.

With the other surveillance cop eliminated it will be time to set up an ambush for Charlton and Flores. As Don Grigor Alvarez he'll sleep soundly at his Pampas ranch in the happy knowledge that his most dangerous enemies have been retired.

Chapter Forty-six

Rob Charlton

I make good time on the highway, pushing the maroon baby through the night. Just after ten o'clock we pass Santa Fe and spot the glow of Albuquerque ahead. About forty minutes later we're approaching the Barth house. We pass a sheriff's car, barely visible, pulled into the brush at the side of the road. Flores murmurs approvingly.

"If Barth is home, we've got him trapped like a rat," he announces. "He wouldn't have gotten past these guys."

I turn off my headlights for the last quarter mile and pull over near the driveway. We get out of the car and plan our approach. I've got one set of high-tech body armor, a Kevlar and ceramic plate vest Flores loaned me when we set up our failed trap with me as bait. I insist he wear it, and he agrees on the condition he's first in line at the door. Sally agrees to hold her position as backup.

We synch our watches and Flores and I slip into the yard, him going up the left side of the driveway and me hanging off to the far right along the edge of a shallow arroyo. I've got my Glock in my hand and Flores has the AR-15 at port arms, ready to fire.

We're nearly to the house when a shot erupts from the brush off to the left. In the dim starlight I see Flores fall to the ground and hear him groan so I know he's hurt. I take a few quick running steps and throw myself onto the ground behind a rock.

Oh crap! Barth's even more dangerous than we thought. We've made a grave error, not calling in a SWAT team at the first hint Barth might be at his house. Now Flores may be dead and I'm pinned down. At least the backup officers will have heard the shot and should be coming any minute. For now, I lay low and wait for them to appear. Meanwhile, I get out my binoculars. First I look to find Flores. He's down but moving, crawling toward the porch. I'm relieved to see him make it to the corner of the house and slip into cover.

"Hey, Luis," I call out to him. "Are you okay?"

"Thanks to the vest," Flores calls back. He sounds breathless. "Hurts like hell though."

I begin to use the binos to search for our attacker's position. Meanwhile, we're both pinned down, waiting for the Cavalry to show up. In fact, they should be here by now…

Chapter Forty-seven

Sally Birch

Sally's sitting on the front fender of Charlton's car with the big .45 pistol on her lap when the sound of the shot echoes across the yard. She can't see what's going on, but to her relief she hears Charlton call out and Flores' answer. She jumps down from her seat, picks up her bat and stoops behind the cover of the car.

She's agreed to stay back and wait for the backup cops in case of trouble, but after several minutes there's no sign of them. She looks up and down the road. Nothing.

Could they have failed to hear the sound of the shot? Are they waiting for more backup? From her years as a police dispatcher Sally knows that officers are trained to respond to the sound of gunshots. They should at least have moved up to her position by now. There's something wrong.

She wishes they'd remembered to take the handheld radios this time. Too damned confident, she thinks. We were so sure Barth would either be trapped in his house or already far away. We never considered he might have set an ambush for us.

Those damned guns! Worst idea I ever had. He must have noticed they were missing, and that told him everything he needed to know.

Standing up she begins to run back to where they'd seen the squad car parked off the side of the road. It's about a quarter mile and it takes her about three minutes. Puffing she runs up to the car. One glance inside and she turns away in horror. Even in the dim glow of the city lights she sees the man is dead. A great gout of dark blood is spilled down his shirt, his eyes are rolled up and staring.

In an instant she realizes the other deputy must also be dead, and with Flores and Charlton pinned down by the gunman she's the only one free to act.

Bracing herself she reaches past the dead deputy and lifts the radio mike from its bracket, drawing it to her lips on its coiled cord. She pushes the transmit button and her knowledge as a dispatcher comes flooding back from over the years.

"Ten-seventeen, repeat, ten-seventeen," she says, using the police code for urgent. "Officer down, Subject with gun."

A dispatcher comes on the air asking for the location. Sally gives him the address, asking for backup and an ambulance.

"What's your badge number?" the dispatcher asks.

"None. I'm a civilian. I'm using the radio of a dead officer."

"Ten-four. Ma'am, I'm sending backup now. Expect arrival twelve to fifteen minutes."

"Ten-four," Sally responds and drops the mike.

As much as a quarter hour! And with Barth out there somewhere in the night, armed and hunting. Moving away from the car and the butchered corpse she walks warily back toward Charlton's car, the .45 cocked in her right hand and the truncated bat swinging in her left.

Jesus, she thinks, it's like a scene from an old Western movie...and I'm in the role usually played by John Wayne or Clint Eastwood.

At the thought of Eastwood she murmurs under her breath, "Go ahead, make my day," the famous line from Dirty Harry. That makes her feel better, somehow. She grips the .45 with greater confidence.

Arriving back at Charlton's car she ducks into cover next to the front fender and listens. Flores and Charlton are apparently holding their positions, out of view of the gunman. The killer, then, must be the one to make a move.

She knows from the sound of the shot that Barth is somewhere in the brush to the left of the house. To get a shot at her friends he would either have to circle around the back side of the lot, or work his way up to the road and come this way from ahead of her position. Sally guesses Barth doesn't know she's here, so that's a plus for her side. Maybe she can set up an ambush of her own.

Carefully, keeping low to the ground, she moves a few yards past the driveway and takes cover beside the road in a clump of junipers. In the dim starlight she can get a view of the road looking both ways, as well as part of the yard. She guesses Flores has moved around to the back of the house to cover an approach from that direction. Charlton must be among the rocks to the right side of the lot, and from there he can cover the front. Now she's in position to protect the entrance from the road.

Several minutes pass with nothing but the distant sound of traffic and the wind gusting in the trees and brush. She strains to hear the sound of sirens. Not yet. Sally kneels down like a hunter in a blind, waiting for unwary game to appear.

She thinks she hears a branch crack, somewhere ahead of her along the roadside. In a moment there's the muffled sound of a shoe striking a pebble. Barth is coming her way, and he's already close. Sally's heart begins to race as an adrenalin rush prepares her for a confrontation.

Then there's a noise from the other direction, just beyond the parked car. Does Barth have an accomplice? No, she decides it must be Charlton, working his way toward her position. It would make sense, but what will he do when he finds she's not there by the car? He doesn't know the deputies are dead, so he may expect them to be waiting there for him. Meanwhile, Barth is approaching from the other direction.

Sally rises to her feet, clutching the pistol at the ready and with her bat in her left hand. She'd never fired a gun in anger, but that bat is another story. Over the years she used it more than once to stop barroom fights, sometimes breaking a bone or two and once giving a serious concussion to an insane gorilla of a man who was strangling one of her regulars over some presumed insult.

Her breath sounds so loud in her ears that she hardly dares to breathe. Her senses are on high alert. Again she hears a sound, this time very near. Barth must be almost within reach of the junipers where she's hiding.

Then in the dim glow of the distant city lights she sees a shadow move. Someone—Barth?—is creeping along the side of the road, keeping close to the underbrush. He's going to pass right by her!

Sally makes a decision. She tucks the .45 under her belt and hefts the bat in both hands. When he steps past her she'll jump up and strike him from behind. One good blow to the back of his head should finish it. Better to capture him alive than attempt to kill him with the pistol.

The shadow moves closer, slowly, cautiously. Now she sees a dim image of the man's face not ten feet away, huge eyes like some horrible insect. She realizes he's wearing night vision goggles. Oh, please, don't let him look this way. Suddenly the confidence of presumed invisibility under the cloak of darkness is shattered. With those goggles he can see her as if in daylight, merely by glancing her way.

She sinks back down into a crouch, holding her breath. The shadow moves again, one careful step nearer. Through the juniper branches she glimpses the goggles moving, peering left then right. Her heart flutters like a butterfly.

David L. Brown

Chapter Forty-seven

Rob Charlton

I'm not used to wriggling on my belly like they used to make us do at Quantico, but I manage to work my way from the rocks to take cover behind some bushes. Those deputies must be on their way and Sally is alone by the road. I decide to meet them by my car. If he watches his back Flores will be okay keeping close to the house.

I stumble a bit in the dark as I work my way toward the road, keeping deep in the brush. Barth must have spotted the missing guns and he knew we'd be coming. It was a mistake to take them. Well, he's still trapped and hasn't killed any of us yet so we're gonna get him.

I reach the car and crouch behind it, looking for Sally. She's not there. *Shit.* I told her to stay in place. I stand up beside the car and peer up and down the road, but it's too dark to see anything. Where the hell are the deputies? Where's Sally.

There's a sudden flurry of activity just a few yards down the road. I hear a shout and a sound like something hard hitting flesh. There's a clattering sound then a man's voice, cursing loudly and apparently in pain. There's the sound of footsteps running away down the road, followed by several loud gunshots and cursing from another voice. Sally's!

The gunshots are coming from nearby and aimed the other way. By the stroboscopic flash of the shots I see a figure running away. Silhouetted by the flashes I see Sally, standing with her back to me. She's the shooter! And Barth must be the target. She takes two more shots then he's out of view.

I step in front of the car and call out to her softly. My night vision is degraded by the flashes and hers must be too. In a moment she stumbles up to me. She throws her arms around my waist, one hand holding her bat and the other pressing the hot barrel of the .45 into my back.

"I let him get away, Rob," she moans. "The dirty bastard killed the deputies. Butchered the one we passed and I'm sure the second one too."

I gently pry her arms from me and she leans back against the side of the car. I grasp the pistol and she hangs on for a moment, then relaxes her grip and lets me take it. I'd counted eight shots, so I know the weapon's empty. I lay it on the hood of the car.

I murmur her name and run my hand through her hair in a calming motion. She sets the sawed-off bat down next to the gun and begins to cry.

"God damn it Rob, I had him right there and he got away. I chickened out when I had a chance. I should have shot him right then, like a rabid dog."

"No, no," I assure her. "I don't know what you did, but you sure won that round."

"You think?" She rubs tears out of her eyes.

"Well, you're safe and he ran away."

"Yeah, I guess."

"So, what exactly happened?"

She wipes her eyes again and straightens up, taking a minute to think.

"When the deputies failed to show up I ran down to that car we saw at the side of the road. The deputy was dead, throat cut. I used his radio to call for backup—they should be here in a few minutes—then came back here. I thought Barth might come around this way so I hid in some bushes. I heard him coming and he was wearing goggles. Then I heard you come up to the car, and I could tell that he did too."

She pauses and takes a deep breath. Her face is turned away from me and I know she's got a thousand yard stare in her eyes.

"He was right in front of me. I saw him stop and raise his rifle, aiming it this way. I knew he'd seen you and was getting ready to shoot."

Jesus!

"So you attacked him?"

"Yeah. I used my bat to strike his left arm above the elbow. Must have broken it. He dropped the rifle and started to run away so I pulled out the .45 and started shooting. You saw the rest."

"Christ, Sally, you must have scared the crap out of him."

She turns her head toward me.

"Rob, I scared the crap out of myself," she says in a low voice. "Totally."

She starts to shake and I can tell she's still hyped on adrenalin, working its way through her body as the fight-or-flight response fades. I take her in my arms and hold her tight.

We hear the sound of sirens approaching and in a moment three Sheriff's cars come screaming up the road, lights flashing frenetic blue, white and red. They slide to a stop, one blocking my car from each end and the third blocking the driveway. They light up the area like a baseball diamond ready for a night game. Men scramble out, guns at the ready. Sally and I turn toward them, empty hands held out.

"Lieutenant Flores is behind the house," I tell the first man to step up close. "He's been shot, but was wearing armor. I think he's all right but someone should get to him. The shooter was here a moment ago. He ran off that way." I point down the road. "We think he's got a broken arm and he dropped his rifle."

"So who're you people?"

I take a deep breath and begin an abbreviated account of what had happened. As I describe how Sally took on the killer the deputy looks at her with something like awe.

"They said a civilian called this in. That you?" he asks.

She nods.

"I found the deputy up the road and used his radio," she tells him. "His throat had been cut."

"Oh, God! And the other deputy?"

"No sign of him so we figure he must be dead, too."

Two more squad cars and an ambulance arrive and a sergeant takes over the crime scene. Flores appears, kind of stumbling like an old man in a bent-over posture. He gives us a weak wave.

"Got me square in the chest," he wheezes. "Knocked me down like a rag doll." He has to stop to breathe. "Didn't penetrate." He breathes again. "Gonna have a bruise the size of Texas."

Two paramedics lead him to a gurney, sit him down and begin to take his vitals. Other deputies are reporting back from the surveillance cars. As we'd guessed, both officers are dead.

Two more ambulances arrive and after conferring briefly with the sergeant they go to collect the remains of the slain officers. The paramedics are still hovering over Flores but he seems to be regaining strength. Sally and I walk over to where he's now lying on the gurney. They've got a saline drip in his arm for the second time in 24 hours. They've taken off the armored vest and his shirt and we see a large red area where the bullet pounded the vest against his chest.

"So, are you okay?" I inquire.

Flores looks up mournfully.

"They tell me I am. Still hurts like hell."

"No broken ribs?" I ask one of the medics.

He shakes his head. "It looks like it's just bad bruising. We're taking him to the ER in a moment," he informs us. "Just for insurance. He looks fine and they'll probably send him home."

Flores raises his right arm and I gently grasp his bandaged hand. Sally moves around to the other side and takes his left one. He looks up at her with one raised eyebrow.

"Did what I heard happened, er, happen?" He asks her.

"I don't know. What did you hear?"

Flores smiles. "Well, let's see, that you arm wrestled Barth and broke his arm, took away his rifle and emptied a clip of .45 ACP at his fleeing ass."

Sally laughs.

"Yeah, that's kinda what happened," she admits. "Only I used my bat to break his arm."

Flores looks at her with a serious expression on his face.

"Are you okay?" he asks.

Sally's smile fades too. She hesitates a moment before answering.

"Yeah, I think I am. Thing that pisses me off is that I let him get away."

The paramedics tell us it's time for us to step back. They secure Flores, lift the gurney and slide it into the waiting ambulance. In a moment they climb aboard, slam the doors and the vehicle drives away,

All the deputies have disappeared leaving Sally and

me alone at the side of the road. Some are helping at the two murder scenes, others are searching the grounds for evidence and yet others have gone in search of Barth. His car isn't in the garage so they figure he'd parked it somewhere nearby and may have escaped. They've set up a perimeter and have an APB out for his brown Kia.

Sally and I look at each other.

"Jesus, Rob, what a day," she sighs.

There are no words so I merely nod in agreement.

"There's no way he'll escape now," I tell her. "He's running like a rabbit."

We walk over to my car and Sally hops up on the hood and lays back. I lean against the fender and look around. For the first time in many years I wish I had a cigarette. The scene is like something from a movie set, glaring lights under a black sky. There are distant sounds of engines, men shouting to one another, the wind beginning to rise as the day slips over the midnight hour into another. Sally sighs again and stretches like a lazy cat.

And suddenly everything comes apart.

An apparition emerges from the bushes on the far side of the road. Barth, his left arm dangling uselessly, the other holding an automatic pistol. His face is scratched and bleeding, his clothes torn from the bushes he's crawled through. He's wearing a wig, but it's half fallen off his head, almost dangling from his left ear.

But all of that scarcely registers with me. My attention is drawn to his eyes, those of a mad predator. Almost glowing with hate in the brilliant lights of the sheriff's cars, red as cherries, they seem larger than life. Keeping the gun pointed between us he stalks forward. His intention is clear. He's going to kill us.

I start to lift myself away from the car and begin to raise my right hand toward the Glock in my shoulder holster. The muzzle of his pistol swings in my direction and he gives a little shake of his head, warning me not to move. I pause and he stops in the middle of the road about fifteen feet away, keeping the gun aimed at my chest. A smile breaks out on his face like a bad moon. He speaks and his voice is unnaturally calm.

"Do you like movies?" he asks, an odd and obviously rhetorical question, something only a madman could say in present circumstances. Perhaps he's responding to the movie set ambience created by the patrol car lights.

Dumbfounded, I simply stare and he continues.

"I do, and my favorite line is the one from *Goldfinger*. Bond asks if he expects him to talk and Goldfinger says 'No, Mr. Bond, I expect you to die'."

His smile breaks into a kind of manic laugh but the eyes are still focused, the gun steady and pointed at my chest.

"And now, Mr. Charlton, it's your time to die."

I can see his finger begin to move on the trigger. It's too late to reach my gun. There's nothing I can do. Time slows down. I close my eyes and that thing they talk about begins to run through my head. It's my life, rushing past like a spring flood.

There's a whoosh of air and a loud *smack*! Time begins to run again. My eyes snap open and I see Barth falling over backward, the pistol dropping from his hand. I draw my Glock and jump forward but he hits the ground and lies as still as a log.

I turn around and Sally is standing in front of the car with a triumphant look on her face. She's not exactly smiling but a glow of self-satisfaction seems to emanate from her.

I look back at Barth, then at her again.

"Sally," I inquire in the mildest tone I can muster, "can you tell me what just happened?"

"He was going to shoot you..." she says.

"Yes, I know…"

"…and my bat was right beside me. I can throw pretty well and the heavy end took him right in the forehead. It may have killed him but I don't really care."

Unable to think of anything to say I simply stare at her. I must be in shock. I walk over and kick the pistol away from Barth, then nudge him with one toe. There's no response.

He lies on his back in the middle of the road with his feet together, arms at his side, sightless eyes staring at the sky. There's something familiar about this scene and my mind flashes to a picture I saw in Barth's basement files: Donald Greenwald's body, lying in the desert like a corpse laid out for a wake.

Whether alive or not, Jeremy Barth has been retired.

"Damned good piece of work, Sally," I tell her. And indeed it was.

Epilogue

Rob Charlton

It was at Sally's insistence that we celebrate the conclusion of the case at her bar and grill, which she's closed for the purpose. So here we all are, gathered at Sally's Place as the real heroine of the story serves drinks from behind her bar.

There's Marsha Greenwald, Bruno Bisset, Dr. Stuart and his wife, and even Professor Humphrey and the secretary from the architecture school. Flores is here, of course, with his daughter Emily and even his ex-wife, who looks surprisingly possessive of the lieutenant. Several of Flores' deputies are clustered at one end of the room swapping tales with Harry George the Albuquerque police officer.

Bruno's prepared some special hors d'oeuvres, elegant little things with French names. He's brought his maid to pass trays around the room. I examine the dainty morsels with suspicion but none seem to include snails or any other weird stuff. I nibble a few, but Bob's in the kitchen and there's a cheeseburger on the grill for me. I'll take my healthy lifestyle over so-called *cuisine* any day. I've got a cold brewski in my hand and God's in his heaven.

Mrs. Greenwald is in her element, too, beaming and filled with compliments for me and, yes, even Flores. The day after Barth was captured she'd called Luis for one last time to apologize and congratulate him. She's announced plans to establish a memorial scholarship at UNM in her husband's name and to put Emily at the top of the list as the first recipient.

As for me, I'm the new golden boy of New Mexico investigators. Not only did Marsha reward me with a handsome bonus, she's spread the word among the movers and shakers of the city that I am "The Man" when it comes to crime solving. I've already got contracts and nice retainers from two leading law firms and just finished moving into my new office in a high-rise building near the courthouse in Old Town. I've even hired a real flesh-and-blood receptionist to keep away the hoi polloi and other undesirables, and am interviewing candidates for an assistant. I've become Albuquerque's first executive investigator.

Barth's emerged from his Sally-induced coma and has been charged with multiple murders. His own files offer enough evidence to put him away for a million years. It's too bad there's no death penalty in New Mexico, but someone's already suggested that after he gets his multiple life sentences here he might be sent up to Colorado to stand trial for the murder of Morton Drake. Colorado still sends its worst felons to hell instead of keeping them healthy and well fed for the rest of their lives.

My burger and fries are ready and I belly up to the bar to eat. Sally watches proudly as I take a bite. Grease runs down my chin and she hands me a napkin.

"Well, Rob, I've got a feeling things are gonna be kinda boring from now on," she remarks with a wry grin. "It's back to polishing glasses for me and spying on husbands for you."

"Oh, no," I exclaim, almost choking on a mouthful of food. I stop to chew for a moment before continuing. "I have a new set of guidelines for clients, and my number one rule is no divorce cases, no kittens in trees, and everything paid in advance with hefty retainers."

Sally laughs.

"Well, don't let it go to your head big boy." She pulls another cold Modelo out of the cooler and pops the cap.

"I don't usually drink on the job, but this is an exception," she informs me, tilting the bottle in my direction. I pick up my own and we click the brown bottles in a toast to our accomplishments.

The End

David L. Brown

Acknowledgements

My sincere thanks to those who read and commented on this novel as it emerged from my imagination, and in particular Alexandra Dell'Amore; Barbara Deputy; Robert Luebbers; and Cherie Major.

In its manuscript form, *Retirement Man* won first prize in the mystery/suspense/thriller/adventure novel category in an international competition sponsored by SouthWest Writers, based in Albuquerque, NM. The category was judged by Thomas Colgan, executive editor of Penguin Books, to whom I also offer my thanks.

www.ingramcontent.com/pod-product-compliance
Lightning Source LLC
Chambersburg PA
CBHW062111170626
46813CB00002B/403
9780996608534